Voyage to Infinity
Book One

The Spiritual Inception

Chris J Berry

authorHOUSE®

AuthorHouse™ UK Ltd.
500 Avebury Boulevard
Central Milton Keynes, MK9 2BE
www.authorhouse.co.uk
Phone: 08001974150

First published by AuthorHouse   6/3/2011

ISBN: 978-1-4567-7900-9 (sc)
ISBN: 978-1-4567-7901-6 (dj)
ISBN: 978-1-4567-7902-3 (e)

Front cover design
by
Sandy Clark
and
Chris J Berry

Contents

Introduction

THIS FIRST BOOK, IN THE 'Voyage to Infinity series, leads the reader further into the spiritual dimension. The Cyannian Trilogy, related the story of a cycle of events on a single physical plane. The Voyage to Infinity expands that idea; witnessing the birth of a spirit, and then following it on its journey across several material planes.

For the young soul and its two proven spiritual guides, the implications of this mission are two-fold. As mentors, the spiritual guides' assignment is to chaperone and counsel the young spirit during its search for the truth. If, or when the young soul achieves perfection, the reward for its guides will be the freedom of the Infinite One's Eternal Kingdom. For the young spirit, and its eventual companion, the successful completion of their voyage offers them the mentorship of a new-born soul, leading to a similar opportunity.

In the introductions of these books I seek to offer ideas, I hope, will raise the curiosity of my readers to explore the reasons for our own purpose here. As with all my books, I make no plans. I simply allow those beyond to use me as their pen; sitting at my computer, typing out their message as the information comes. However, to the sceptic, what is written will appear to express what I believe is taking place around us.

Over the years, I have learned to accept the spiritual world on faith; finding the proof that it exists, manifest from that faith. One of the most over-powering facts I constantly refer to, and which influenced my belief, arose from contemplating the definition of the word 'inevitability'. In the context of the physical existence, it implies how we will all make our transition from this life, and enter the spiritual dimension whether we like it or not—it is a fact that none of us can dispute.

The spiritual inception, portrayed in the opening chapter of this book, describes my understanding of how my sources imply a spirit might be created by an Infinite Being, and then set off on its journey. Whether viewed as fact or fiction, it symbolises the idea for me that we here, have also embarked on a similar journey to learn essential truths.

To illustrate the relationship between the physical and spiritual dimensions, I have placed text between three asterisks. These transcripts relate the relevance of the observations made by the mentors in the spiritual world. Used in the third book of my trilogy, Avataria, the idea seeks to describe how the physical planes are the arenas where the wills of these young souls are contested. Journeying through each material plane in the series, the reader learns how this threat from the dark influence focuses on these worlds; the deeds of the young souls there, governing the final outcome of their ultimate, spiritual achievement.

Another mystery, that has teased humanity's curiosity for centuries, is the lack of alien contact. It prompts me to deliberate on the question; are we unique? My sources tell me not; so why, then, have we not been approached? Answering that question, in sight of our present level of technology, clearly reveals our limitations in achieving viable methods of contact. But when viewed from the spiritual aspect, it would make more sense if advanced planetary civilisations were governed by a Divine protocol; preventing superior ones from interfering with others progressing at more infant levels of existence. I discuss this idea, to some extent, in my autobiography 'Sixty Psychic Years'.

My mother, a practicing spiritual medium of long standing, put forward an intriguing scenario she had learned from her sources. It implied that any physical, alien civilisation, possessing the freedom of the universe, were inhabitants of a higher physical plane; incarnated, proven souls in the service of the supreme Entity. To accept this as an answer to the protocol question, pivots upon an individual's ability to believe in what lies beyond the physical life.

My gut feeling comes down in favour of the Divine protocol theory. The prospect of cruel, greedy, immoral civilisations, existing with the ability to extend their life-styles beyond the barriers of their worlds, places a huge question over the moral success of any developing world. The belief in a supreme entity governing the universe may be viewed as fantasy within a civilisation. But my experiences in life have convinced me of His presence, and that a world's atmosphere is the barrier He places around it, and which can only be breached by a morally, united people... CJB.

Preface

Book one, The Spiritual Inception, opens in a divine part of the universe. In a place known as the Hallowed Sanctum, two proven spirits, Sarah and John, await the birth of a young soul. Having partnered each other on their voyage to infinity across several physical planes in the universe, they have achieved perfection. What stands between them and entering the Infinite One's Eternal Land, is the task of mentoring this young spirit on its own voyage to infinity.

The success of this assignment offers them the opportunity to enter a world of unimaginable joy and happiness together. The awesome scene that confronts them, while they wait, fills them with wonder; witnesses to the Infinite One creating a spirit in his own image. They reflect back over their own voyage to infinity, and the confrontations they had with the Evil One's legions. They know their young spirit will face those same challenges, and it will fall to them to guide and counsel it on each occasion when that young soul returns from its current incarnation.

As the first chapter ends, the scene is set on a world called Orburn. Similar to Earth, it is another world that provides the young souls with the means to learn the Infinite One's truth of life. The young spirit is drawn into this world by the human process: it is not long before the first tragedy touches the lives of its parent hosts. As an infant, it is unaware of that event, but as the incarnated young spirit grows, the dark influences begin their bid to take control of its will: the eternal conflict begins, and the challenges in life start to take their toll...CJB.

**Dedicated to
Sandy Clark for her
unstinting support and
ingenuity in generating
the graphics for
my books**

Acknowledgements

*

With grateful thanks to
Anne and Pam, as
Character models
For the front cover.

*

Book two of the series

*

The Voyage to Infinity

*

A Rendezvous with Evil

*

Follows.

The Spiritual Inception
*

**Book one
in the series
A VOYAGE TO INFINITY**
*

by
Chris J Berry

CHAPTER ONE

THE INCEPTION

~1~

IN THE INFINITIVE REALM OF the spiritual dimension, Sarah and John, proven souls, moved toward the Infinite One's Hallowed Sanctum. As kindred spirits, their accumulated knowledge, in all aspects of life, stretched far back across the multiple dimensions that made up the physical and spiritual universe.

While journeying through those spheres of knowledge, their life-spans had been fraught with temptation and uncertainty. In the midst of confusion, during their physical trials, both had leant upon the other, waiting in turn for each to reach the divine truth of the current experience. Now, spiritually bonded, they had finally passed into the Infinite One's Celestial Realm. Standing together at the threshold of a new challenge, they contemplated their mission ahead.

As mentors to a new-born spirit, the success of this assignment offered them the opportunity to achieve perfection, rewarding them with entry into the Infinite One's Eternal Kingdom. This divine task, promised an existence of sublime happiness in an infinite world, where such beauty went far beyond the imagination of even the most resourceful of minds.

The time had come, for them, and others similarly, to take on the responsibility for a new-born spirit leaving the Hallowed Sanctum. As divine guides to this young soul, the Infinite One charged them with the task of teaching and counselling it, during its voyage across the universe to infinity. From their personal experience, they knew the extent of the trials that each new soul faced; the seemingly endless struggle, it meant, for all young spirits to achieve perfection.

Sarah and John, proven spirits of immense understanding and feeling, were unable to suppress the thrill of approaching the Infinite One's Hallowed Sanctum. The intrigue and mystery surrounding it filled their souls with awe and wonder. This Divine part of the universe impressed one with a definitive, timeless existence: a part of the Infinite One's Eternal Land where the darker entities, even with all their subversive powers, would never dare approach.

Instinctively, one sensed its arcane beauty; forbidden to those who had not yet earned the right to enter. This timeless kingdom lay beyond the bounds of the physical universe. Embedded in the minds of each new-born spirit, the Infinite One placed the knowledge of its presence— the incentive that would fuel the desire in them to learn His truth of life.

While present in the spiritual dimension, the focus toward that eternal land was constant; every soul aware of what was required of them to enter it. But it was on the physical planes where the seed, which offered that opportunity, was sown. The chance was within reach of Sarah and John now, and would grow to fruition from the success of their protégé, under their mentorship.

~2~

Standing together, they gazed around at other guides, waiting for their charges to emerge through the pale, silvery mist enshrouding the Hallowed Sanctum. Their minds drifted back to when, as new-born spirits, they had left that Divine place. Their mentors had maintained a caring vigilance over them, enduring their trials as they stumbled on through each physical existence in their search for the truth.

The sphere of learning, where they finally accomplished their proven status, had been a world called Earth. Life on this plane had come close to annihilation; its inhabitants surviving countless, self-generated and evolutionary, catastrophic events. The salvation of this world; finally resulted from the successful uniting of its people. Drawn together as one civilisation, the subsequent view of the future revealed the demise that awaited them as divided nations.

Sarah and John had been two of many souls, whose level of faith had finally shone the light of truth across that world. As their journey there came to an end, that dawn of enlightenment had focused the people of Earth away from its physical aspects, leaving the spiritual attributes to govern life there. Sarah and John eternally sensed their guides with gratitude: the intensity of their feelings enhanced by the knowledge, their own success had secured the opportunity for their mentors to enter the Infinite One's Eternal Kingdom.

The caring template, in Sarah and John, was in place. It would provide them with the wisdom to guide their young spirit, and extend the hand of friendship to its future companion. Now the voyage to infinity was about to begin again for them, but as witnesses to the trials of another. No definitive time-scale existed to enter the Infinite One's Eternal Land. From their experiences, Sarah and John, knew, that if any universal gauge existed that could determine the period for their charge's success, it would be measured by the birth and death of celestial events.

Patience, forbearance, benevolence and obedience to the Infinite One's laws, were attributes that had been indoctrinated into all proven souls. It meant their entry into the Eternal Kingdom, could only be enjoyed in the knowledge, their young soul had succeeded. Sarah and John reflected back on the celebration of feelings that had overcome them, witnessing their mentors entering the Eternal Land. Embossed on their spiritual minds forever, that precious moment became their incentive; the promise of reunion and companionship in a land free of the misery that plagued the physical planes.

They gazed at the silvery mist of the Hallowed Sanctum; becoming aware of a gradual change taking place. Brief flecks of pale blue light were beginning to pierce its shimmering surface. As they looked on, these fleeting points of light were forming into shapes, some appearing to protrude away; drawing the mist out drifting around them. Emotions welled up in the waiting mentors, deeply touched by the divinity of the moment as witnesses to the Infinite One creating a spirit.

Countless more indistinct faces began to appear; their hazy contours, as yet, feathered into the drifting, silvery mist. None of the waiting mentors had ever experienced such a moment and gazed on— profoundly moved. The features, on the faces of the emerging spirits, were becoming more definite; their expressions revealing their growing awareness, as the Infinite One poured life into them.

John, touched by the expression of devotion on Sarah's face, sensed the affection rising in her; her soul, reaching out to a particular young spirit focusing its gaze on them. She was unable to suppress her maternal commitment toward the young, which had become part of her nature during their voyage to infinity.

The scene became even more enchanting, as the light, continually streaming away from the Hallowed Sanctum, silhouetted the pale, iridescent forms of the young spirits beginning to break free. In that divine moment, the chaotic life-styles existing on the physical planes, paled into insignificance— Sarah and John, reflecting back over their incarnations. Their physical minds had been insensible of this process, incapable of comprehending the Infinite One's true munificence. It was in moments like these that one sensed His love for the creation of life, spawned of His Hallowed Sanctum.

Each proven soul, waiting there, was conscious of the trust the Infinite One had placed in them— it represented an awesome responsibility. Now, in possession of His truth, they had pledged their allegiance to Him, destined to care for His young ones as others had done since time immemorial.

~3~

The endless void of the cosmos stretched away to infinity, as the young spirits took up their places before their guides. Sarah smiled down at the young soul standing before them. She perceived a presence of complete innocence; untouched, as yet, by any physical or spiritual aspect.

Sarah and John sensed their minds being probed by the young spirit, aware of a rationale that was inconsistent with physical new-born. They embraced the young soul with their auras; its voyage to infinity had begun. The initialisation onto its first physical plane still lay a short while in the future: it would be during this period that Sarah and John would teach, and prepare the new spirit for the challenges that awaited it.

As the young soul began to learn, it continually sensed them with its eagerness to begin. Gazing across its celestial horizon, John made out the first of seven physical planes it would journey through. It represented a world of mixed civilisations. Rife with suspicion and carnal desires, its inhabitants were presently living in an age dominated by cult practices.

The sinister atmosphere, existing in that world, had raised concerns in Sarah and John for their young spirit's first incarnation. From past experiences, their first encounter of a physical plane had been one governed completely by the material aspects available. The subsequent return to the spiritual dimension had been one of disappointment and regret for them. As they became aware of the Infinite One's plan, the wisdom, knowledge and understanding gained from their mentor's counselling, dramatically changed their approach to future journeys across the physical planes.

The material aspects available to their young one, would be the same. Before entering each physical environment, the knowledge the young spirit received from their counsel would remain in its spiritual mind as a resource. This would become the voice of conscience, and could provide a tool for Sarah and John to try and influence the young soul when incarnated.

As time passed, Sarah and John were satisfied their young spirit's preparation was nearing completion. During its first incarnation it would meet its companion, who would then partner it on the voyage to infinity. The bond that developed between them, could only be broken if either one chose to form a dedicated alliance with the lower realms. Any misdemeanours they committed in ignorance could be considered as part of the learning process, but once aware, would not.

The celestial plan was for new-born souls to form a partnership with another spirit and then, throughout the voyage, both could act as a resource for the other. There were no doubts in Sarah and John, that the first physical encounter would be a revelation to their young spirit. However, while viewing its physical life-span from the world of spirit, the choices it needed to make, when incarnated, were obvious.

When an erring soul returned from an unsuccessful material life, lost opportunities on that plane were then irretrievable, raising disappointment to insurmountable levels. In His divine plan, the wisdom and benevolence of the Infinite One allowed for a soul's transgressions, as the materialisation of its companion would also bring with it its own spiritual-guides. As an expanding group, they would provide a formidable resource to guide, and protect, both young spirits while they journeyed across their chosen physical planes.

~**4**~

The young soul was eager to learn, airing a positive attitude toward its plan. Sarah and John, however, remained cautious, knowing its voyage ahead to be fraught with all manner of encounters. Devious entities, bent on using these young souls, would try to tempt them with desires that could allow the dark legions to touch the physical plane. It was only through these innocent, young spirits, the dark entities were able to regain access to the pleasures of the material life.

Once beyond the point of inception, the young souls were vulnerable. While the knowledge of the spiritual world lay dormant within them, its existence would appear as if a fantasy on the physical plane. Sarah and John were confident they had done all they could; teaching their young one how to draw on the information from the world beyond. What they sensed from the young spirit encouraged them, feeling, the knowledge they had offered, raised the young soul's determination that nothing was going to sway it from its search for the truth.

The seed was being sown; the young soul now committed to that physical plane. The parent hosts were in place, and engaged on the procedure that would initialise the young spirit's access to the material life. As time raced toward their young soul's first incarnation, Sarah and John viewed the approaching event with a blend of excitement and trepidation. There was so much at stake, and where, in certain situations, they could find themselves powerless to do anything to help.

While the material aspect developed, the knowledge of the spiritual dimension receded; locked in the spiritual mind of the incarnated soul. Governed by time, the incarnate spirit would emerge in a physical state of profound innocence. The environment it entered then, would begin to indoctrinate it into the current civilisation's life-style. Throughout its infancy, so much depended upon the parent hosts; their teachings, reflecting their assessment of the morals practiced in the surrounding society.

Already logged in historical almanacs of this world, transcripts existed of a celebrated Divine Soul who had lived a life that provided a template of the truth. Over the centuries, the doctrines he had taught, diversified into differing beliefs. As the centuries passed, intolerance toward different opinions began dividing nations; creating issues that fuelled serious conflicts between beliefs.

John embraced Sarah's aura, sensing similar thoughts in her to his. Conscious of the dingy realms encompassing the world below, they perceived the dark entities engaged on their sinister activities.

Incited to act on this knowledge they bowed their heads, and prayed their young spirit would follow the Infinite One.

Safe in the security of the spiritual environment, Sarah and John watched the steady flow of other young souls returning to their guides. The solemn mood in those who had failed, told the story of the challenges that awaited their young spirit. They could only place their trust in the Infinite One: let His benevolence, understanding and wisdom influence their judgement as they guided their young one.

The day arrived; the young soul gazing up at them, emanating hope and anticipation of future success. Sarah and John embraced it, hoping their young one could develop the faith to breach the barrier between the spiritual and physical dimension, its success, then, would be assured. They gazed on, as the moment of conception drew the young spirit into the material life. The initialisation of the young soul's journey had begun. John panned his gaze across its celestial horizon; dark clouds were beginning to gather, causing him to fantasise again on what lay ahead of it in that life-span.

~5~

Time was of no consequence in the spiritual dimension, but for their young spirit now, it would be of essence. A sudden, overpowering feeling seized John, reminding him of how the real danger to all newly incarnated young souls, was that fleeting time factor. What complicated matters still more, was the fact— the dark entities were also aware of that.

The evil legions enjoyed the advantage on the physical plane, but their interest in the young souls was only focused there. Once back in the spiritual dimension, a young soul's life-span could be evaluated, and vital lessons learned. A soul's deeds could either shorten or lengthen its period to succeed, but what added to the joy or sorrow of each physical experience, was the knowledge that its deeds had either enhanced or compromised the progression of its companion.

The plan had been set in motion; the preparation carefully and conscientiously carried out. If future experiences for their young soul proved to be similar to those in their past, Sarah and John were ready to offer their counsel to encourage a bitterly disappointed, and disillusioned young spirit.

The two great spirits settled down to the prospect of watching and waiting, monitoring the society their young spirit was destined to join. The soul's choice had been a developed part of civilisation. The opportunities there, offered it a chance to extend compassion to the poor and disabled people of the world. Equally, it provided the means to develop indulgent, selfish attitudes that could lead it to ignore the plight of others.

The young spirit's destiny was now it's own to shape; the choices it made, on this first encounter, setting a precedent for the future. A blue-print of the divine plan was locked in its spiritual conscience, suppressed by its physical conscience. If it learned how to listen to the small voice within, it could open an access to Sarah and John and benefit from their vast knowledge.

Now Sarah and John were entering a dormant period, while the physical aspect of the incarnate spirit matured in the womb. They would use this gestation period to generate strategies, and address any potential threatening events planned by the dark influences; undoubtedly now, already focussing their attention on their charge.

During the period of their young spirit's foetal development, Sarah and John sensed an atmosphere of evil descend around them. It had been something they had expected, soon after the young soul's conception had taken place. The Evil One's minion began to make its presence felt; finalising its plan to challenge Sarah and John for the will of their young soul.

The minion, though powerless in the spiritual dimension, would prove to be a formidable adversary on the physical plane. As a staunch member of the dark legions, it preyed heavily upon the embittered feelings of failed souls: those, clinging onto material desires that had dominated their lives on the material plane.

The symbolic ladder that ascended to light and success, also descended into darkness and oblivion. But the Infinite One's door was always open. Should an erring young spirit slip back a few rungs on that symbolic ladder, the opportunity was ever present to reclaim what it had lost. But reclamation became harder to achieve, as the descent into iniquity increased; the communication with one's mentors, distanced by the sinister atmosphere existing in the Evil One's miserable kingdom.

Sarah and John gazed across the world below, sensing hope for their young spirit from the prayers they had offered to the Infinite One. Orburn was a middle aged world in cosmological terms. It had initially been seeded by an immensely sophisticated, morally structured civilisation, situated several galaxies away out in the universe. Like most mature worlds, it had suffered violent change imposed on it, both from its inhabitants and periodical evolution.

Celebrated chronicles describing Orburn's history, related how past civilisations had been steeped in cult-practices and superstition. It had now moved into an era, where an industrial revolution was advancing technology at a rapidly increasing rate. Throughout the history of the universe, this stage of development had overseen the demise of countless civilisations on many worlds; a lack of foresight, neglecting to plan ahead and manage the effluent from varying technologies.

As had been the case on so many worlds, Sarah and John recognised the decent into immorality occurring on Orburn, and the threat it posed for their soul's first incarnation. It was a major concern for Sarah and John, as this mood was currently spreading a sinister disrespect for the sanctity of life across Orburn. One aspect that helped to off-set this was their young spirit's parent hosts. Though not well-situated in society, they were sufficient enough in resources to maintain their lifestyle, but more importantly, they were conscious of their moral responsibility toward the young they brought into the world.

The Evil One's minion, now present, gazed intently at them: seen through mortal eyes, the apparition would incite terror into the beholder. Sarah and John pitied it, sensing an entity whose existence stretched far back into the mists of time. It was hard to imagine how this disciple of evil had once emerged from the Hallowed Sanctum. Since then it had faltered on the symbolic ladder, continuing its descent into the depths of the underworld. Surrounded by its legions, it aired confidence in its intent; many of its followers; failed souls that were rapidly slipping down toward that dingy kingdom.

Sarah and John deliberated over how there was little else they could do now. At present, the immense power they possessed allowed them few options upon that physical plane; the initial contact having to come from their young soul. The two proven spirits pondered over how Orburn was similar to their last world, Earth. A beautifully situated globe with so much potential, it stood as another testimonial to the Infinite One's creative power— the sole threat to His creations, humanity.

As with all worlds the means to recover was there, threatened only by the time factor. The steady flow of young spirits through it, offered the inhabitants valuable opportunities to take it up to a higher plane. And when on that day they achieved it, Orburn would be another celestial body in the heavens to expand the Infinite One's legions.

CHAPTER TWO

THE JOURNEY BEGINS

~1~

*

Jamie Hoskins, sat with his elbows on the back of the pew in front of him. Resting his chin in his hands, he thoughtfully gazed at his mother's coffin slowly disappearing behind the curtain. Only the year before, she had been sitting beside him as they paid their last respects to his father.

He let his thoughts wander back over his past. From the moment he had become conscious of his life, it seemed to have promised an existence full of opportunity. As time passed, a variety of misfortunes, had constantly plagued his life, and yet, the resources had somehow materialised that allowed him to rise above them.

The first real tragedy to involve his family had happened shortly after his birth. As an infant, the gravity of that event held little significance for him; destined to lie in the more sinister archives of his family's history as a poignant memory. Now steeped in a mood of morbid nostalgia, he contemplated his passage through life. Letting his mind wander back to his infancy, he reflected on the events as they had occurred, focusing on the one aspect in his life that had provided the resource to cope with them.

*

On the distant horizon, the rising sun iced the few clouds with its golden glow as they slowly drifted toward it. Sally and Carl Hoskins were preparing for the new day, while their baby son, Jamie, burbled playfully in his high-chair. Sally, was now in her post-natal period, and had planned a few weeks off to support Jamie after his birth. The mandatory period to oversee him into his infancy period, was the only practical option available; their financial status, precluding any possibility of her giving up work.

Carl finished his breakfast and gathered up his brief-case, pausing by Jamie. "I'll see you this evening, Chubby Chops," he smiled. He gazed slyly at Jamie, teasing a grin on the baby's face.

Sally listened contentedly as she washed up the breakfast dishes. Grinning at the faint reflection of them in the window pane, a car drew up outside. "Freddy's here, Carl." She nodded out the window at the car paused by the garden gate.

Rousing himself, Carl gave her a peck on the cheek. Lifting his coat off the hook, he swung the door open and looked back at her. "See you this evening." His gaze tensed a little. "Take care if you go out. You've only to read the newspapers to understand the risks."

"No worries! I'm not about to take any chances— especially with him." She gestured at Jamie, rattling his spoon in his bowl— still beaming the huge grin induced by his dad's attentions.

Carl closed the door and strode down the garden path, gazing at the lawn taking over the flower beds. Never a moment's respite, he thought, contemplating the mounting house and garden chores it meant for the approaching weekend. Shutting the gate, he waved at Sally; still smiling at him through the window with Jamie resting on her arm— the picture of them filled him with contentment.

They were not well off by any stretch of the imagination, but together on their small patch, their needs and desires were modest, focusing happily on their blossoming family lifestyle.

Carl tossed his case on the back seat, greeting Freddy cheerfully as he settled in. "You alright Fred?" he muttered nonchalantly. The lack of Fred's reply prompted Carl to glance up at him. The expression on his face looked strained, his eyes blood-shot; like those of someone who had been weeping incessantly or had suffered days without sleep.

~2~

Carl suddenly felt awkward, searching for the words to discreetly ask what the problem was. Over the past week he had noticed a change in Freddy, but it had never descended to this level. As the uneasy silence continued, Freddy seemed to pull himself together, making a move toward setting off.

Freddy paused again, his expression illustrating a deep meditation of thought. Suddenly, his face creased up as he rested his forehead on the steering wheel; tears streaming away from his eyes. "June's gone," he blurted out. "Taken the kids, and is shacked up with someone else." Freddy grated the car into gear and drove off. "It seems the affair's been going on for a year or two." The look on his face tensed as he stared out through the windscreen. "I still can't believe it. We had everything. Could I have done more for them, Carl?" he whispered incredulously.

Carl was stunned. No family had seemed closer. Two lovely children, their own house, and holidays each year. He clicked his seat-belt in; fumbling over what to say next. "I'm so sorry, Fred— I thought you two were inseparable. What has brought all this on?"

Freddy huffed a sigh. "She'd been in a mood since the beginning of last week, but wouldn't confide in me; I lost my rag in the end and we had a blazing row. I eventually stomped out and following my return later— you could cut the air between us with a knife."

Carl discreetly continued searching for the reasoning behind the bust up as they drove on, but there seemed to be more to the episode than Freddy was letting on. "It hasn't got to the divorce stage or that of the children's custody yet— has it Fred?"

"Damn right it has!" blurted out Freddy vindictively. "I can't do much about her. But I'm not giving up on my kids!" Freddy's words focused in Carl's mind, forming the picture of another family's fragmentation, and the lasting effect it could have on the children. The decisive tone in Fred's voice made any further conversation redundant on the subject, with Carl resolving to simply offer a shoulder for him to cry on.

He had known Freddy Collins since childhood; how it seemed their search for happiness had been a similar one. As Best Men at their subsequent weddings, their futures appeared secure. But fate, it seemed, gazed cautiously upon such happy unions, and like the ungracious entity it could be, had tested the strength of that relationship.

Freddy pulled up outside Carl's office and paused, gazing pensively ahead out through the windscreen as Carl got out.

Carl was at a loss to offer any words of comfort; the thoughtful expression cast over Freddy's face, continuing to illustrate his torment within.

"Listen, Fred," said Carl at length. "Let's meet tonight for a drink and a chat down the local; Sal will understand."

There was no response from Freddy as Carl gently closed the door. Freddy finally lifted his face and gazed up at him through the window— half-smiling with a nod, he pulled away. Carl watched the car disappear into the distance, deliberating on the mental turmoil Freddy was suffering.

As Carl walked toward the office-block entrance numerous scenarios drifted through his mind, concerned over what Freddy might do. Though not fully aware of the circumstances, it seemed that Freddy's wife, had shattered their family life in one foul swoop— it was so out of character for June. She had always come across as a dedicated mother. Only a month earlier, they had all gone off on a day out with the children.

It confused Carl; unable to put a finger on it. He felt there had to be some underlying reason that made June suddenly act the way she had. It led Carl to deliberate nervously over the fragile, intimate aspects of relationships; how the break up of his family would have devastated him. One's home-life provided security and respite from the trauma of routine life.

~3~

Several people bustled past him as the door swung too behind; a chorus of greetings coming at him from all directions.

"Carl! Carl, are you OK?" asked a voice, rising above the background jumble of conversation going on around them. "Carl!" repeated the voice, tinged with a little frustration.

"Oh! Hi, George," muttered Carl, gazing vacantly at him.

"You seem a bit stressed out this morning, Carl." George fanned through some papers in a file he was carrying as he spoke. Selecting a wad, he offered them to Carl. "That's the case I spoke to you about at the end of last week; it's turning into a dirty business. He paused, gazing more intently at Carl. "Are you sure you're going to be up for it today?"

Carl extracted himself from his thoughts as he took the papers. "Yes... Yes of course. Just had a bit of a shock." He gazed at George; letting his mind drift back to reality. "Sorry if I seem a bit vague." He slipped the papers into his briefcase and feigned a smile as he turned toward his office.

George stood, thoughtfully staring after him. "...Call me if you need any more info... Other than that; I'll see you for lunch..." Carl strode off waving his hand above his head, before disappearing into his office.

Sitting down at his desk, Freddy's dilemma edged back into his mind. Carl had worked for the social services for many years; his days, usually filled with all manner of human irritability. He had not given any thought to the previous offer he had made to Freddy; spontaneously blurting out the suggestion to spend the evening together. In Freddy's frame of mind, Carl needed to consider any support he offered with care, and not submit it as a counselling professional.

Carl gazed thoughtfully at the pile of files stacked up in the in-tray, teetering on the edge of his desk. Their presence indicated Freddy was not alone in his emotional dilemma, and when compared with most of Carl's other cases, a lot better off than some. However, this was no consolation. No matter what one's disposition was in life; to have your world crumble around you so suddenly was mentally unsettling.

Carl dismissed it from his mind, snatching a file off the top of the stack. He fanned through it, reading the tabulated dialogues that had occurred between his department, and a family under investigation for child abuse. Carl had long-since found the complexities generated by human nature, staggering: one's struggle in life could be complicated enough, without adding to the hardship of every day survival.

Moral decline, fuelled by misdemeanour that challenged ways to police behaviour within the populous, were threatening the family structure. Each day, the files that landed on his desk, revealed how doubts in society were raising discussions over the complexity and inadequacy of current legislation. An escalating number of individuals were challenging society's policing infrastructure, demonstrating, in their behaviour, a complete disregard for the rights of others.

Sally's mother, Emily, an ardent spiritualist, dogmatically expounded her beliefs and solutions during their frequent family visits. Her views irritated him; appearing too conciliatory toward the offenders. What incensed him still more: she based her opinions on a source he considered was fictitious.

He conceded she had a point, when she declared the responsibility for a lot of society's breakdown was due to the lack of parental guidance and discipline. But in contrast to her beliefs, the majority of his workload had to deal with brutal treatment directed against the infant population; little people, unable to defend themselves.

~4~

His office door suddenly burst open; George gazing at him anxiously. "Get off to the hospital quickly, Carl. You're mate Freddy's been involved in a car accident."

Carl jumped to his feet, snatching his coat off the back of the chair. "How bad is it, George?" he asked, as he hurried out the door and down the corridor, with George panting breathlessly behind.

"They haven't said much, other than he's in intensive care and asking for you."

"I'm not surprised. The poor bugger has no one, now his Mrs' gone off with the kids."

George looked a bit awkward. "She's there too."

Carl paused, gazing blankly at the front-entrance; his hand, thoughtfully hovering against the door-plate as he slowly pushed it open. "A guilty conscience no doubt. There's nothing I've got to say to her. It's all her doing. And now this event might've laid everything conveniently at her feet nice and legally."

George shook his head, placing his hand on Carl's shoulder. "It's happening every day, Carl. We know nothing of what goes on behind closed doors. I know he's a mate of long standing, but try to keep an open..."

"Don't lecture me George," muttered Carl abruptly. "You don't fully understand the bonds that exist between our families."

George withdrew humbly, raising his hands in a conceding gesture. "Try to think on it rationally though, Carl. You deal with cases like this every day. If it comes as any consolation, remember, you have understanding friends too who are willing to offer their help with intimate problems like this."

Carl nodded vacantly; the thought suddenly dawning on him, he had no car. He looked apologetically up at George. "Sorry, Mate... Don't suppose I could borrow your car— save waiting on taxis?"

George reached in his pocket for his keys and tossed them to him. "Make sure you don't join your mate, Carl."

Carl feigned a smile as he turned for the car, pausing briefly to look back. "Do 'us one more favour, George, give Sal a ring at home and brief her on what's happened. Tell her I'll phone her from the hospital."

George nodded again. "No worries, Mate."

During the journey, Carl had already passed judgement on June; filled with animosity toward her. His daily routines, when addressing the bitter, heart-rending situations that were placed before him, had always been dealt with in a mood of benevolence and understanding. As an unbiased observer, it was his task to help fathom out the reasons for family conflicts, and why it led the individual parties to adopt the actions they had taken. But this event was different. A sensitive choice loomed now of who to support, and had to be made between two life-long friends.

He pulled up into one of the parking bays outside the hospital intensive care unit and walked briskly in. Making straight for the desk, he noticed June sitting alone outside a closed door. He was unable to bring himself to look her in the eyes, as he gave his name to the practitioner in charge.

The Doctor summoned a nurse to show Carl into the room. As they approached, June rose to her feet, gazing intently at Carl. He paused, finally able to return her gaze. The look in her eyes unsettled him: expecting a cold unfeeling stare, he perceived a sense of humility and compassion in them.

"Can we talk after, Carl," she whispered. "Freddy and I have made our peace together." She continued to look penetratingly up at him with such an expression of hopelessness on her face; it diminished his bitterness. He nodded, and then followed the nurse into the room.

"We can only allow you a few minutes, sir," whispered the nurse, disappearing behind the closing door.

Carl approached Freddy's bed, gazing at the bandages dressing his horrific wounds. For a moment, the silence focused him on the tragic aspect of the scene. Watching Carl pull up a chair, Freddy forced a smile and began to speak.

"I've not been completely honest with you, Carl these past few years. It's taken an event like this to bring me to my senses"

Carl, though vaguely curious, ignored the statement. "You don't have to say anything, Fred; let's wait till you've recovered, then we'll have all the time in the world to discuss it."

Freddy's look intensified. "No, listen to me, Carl, I have to get this off my chest while there's still time."

"Fred! What's with all the drama? You're going to be fine," uttered Carl incredulously.

"Just listen! Carl. You have to understand. What I said in the car earlier..." Freddy paused, searching for words. "...What has happened between June and me is not her fault." Carl gave him an old fashioned look, as he continued. "I've been living a double life, Carl— I have another partner too."

Carl stared at him, convinced these were the ravings of a man not in control of his senses.

Speaking hesitantly, Freddy continued; airing an expression of confusion over what he was trying to say. "...David and I have been seeing each other for the best part of five years. June had some inkling I was meeting someone, but only recently found out the truth of my relationship." Freddy looked at him penetratingly. Carl turned away, focusing on the name, 'David'— dumbfounded over what he had just heard.

Freddy's declaration had cast a totally different mood over the room. The gay movement was gradually being accepted in modern times, but hearing this from Freddy, one who he had considered to be a dedicated family man, came as a complete shock. Carl found himself fighting off feelings of disgust that now portrayed his old friend in an entirely different light. How could he have, so completely, misjudged Freddy; someone he had known throughout his life?

His feelings instantly mellowed to sympathy toward June, considering her reaction to have been perfectly natural now. To learn of your partner's infidelity was unsettling in itself, but to lose them to a person of the same gender was humiliating.

He looked back at Freddy searchingly; wondering, now, over the reasoning behind his sudden outburst in the car earlier, which had clearly placed the blame on June.

"Why, Freddy? You two had everything going for you." whispered Carl, shaking his head— totally confused.

"I know what you're thinking, Carl."

"Fred! You can't possibly know what I'm thinking; I hardly know what to think myself." Carl gazed vacantly down at the bed. "It makes no sense to me as a family man, Fred." He looked at Freddy. "We'll never agree on the choice you have made, Fred. Whatever, you, and those like you say, it isn't natural."

"How can you be so sure of that, Carl? Are you telling me that it's not natural to indulge in friendship with someone— anyone?" asked Freddy.

"A friendship is natural enough, Fred, but not when it entails intimacies in a male to male relationship similar to those shared between a man and a woman..." Carl looked away; the confusion evident on his face. "...The logistics of the human process demonstrates to us that it is unnatural. If it *was* natural, in the present context of life, the human race would cease to exist."

"You don't understand, Carl," whispered Fred.

"No I don't, Freddy; not in light of what you've thrown away." Carl sensed Freddy was showing signs of distress, as their discussion became more intense. He rested his hand on Freddy's. "But our long-standing friendship requires I accept it in you, and merely add that I admire your courage in making a clean breast of it. But you'll have to be patient with me, and accept we are worlds apart on this subject."

Freddy nodded concedingly, settling back into a more relaxed mood: seeming to derive some comfort at having cleared the air between him and those close to him.

~5~

The nurse entered the room, gesturing for Carl to say his goodbyes. Carl rose to his feet and paused by the door to gaze back at Freddy dozing peacefully. What possessed him? he wondered, thinking of his young family. Outside, June was still sitting in the chair. She looked up at Carl, sensing, in his expression, a little more benevolence toward her.

"How long have you known, June?" he asked.

"I suspected it for a couple of years, but just recently as to the true nature of his relationship. I cannot rationalise it yet, Carl— it has come as a complete shock. But now I must think only of the good times. One thing I found particularly hurtful was how he convinced himself I had another partner; seemingly to try and justify his own infidelity."

Carl bowed his head. "I'm so sorry, June. I type-casted you along with some of the many devious characters that I meet in my job."

She nodded understandingly. "I think a lot of our close acquaintances blamed me. But talking to Freddy, something strange has happened to him during this event; it has unsettled him. It's extraordinary; we have never talked as intimately while we waited for you to arrive. It's as if he knows he's going to die, and has seen something that has made him want to put things right. Few people have the opportunity to return from 'near death experiences', but whatever touched him, has made it imperative to put things right between us. I don't know what he's said to you..." Carl went to speak, but she continued uninterrupted. "...Somehow he's been given this unique insight into what lies beyond— it's diminished all my anger toward him." She took a handkerchief from her bag as her eyes moistened. "It's completely changed his perspective of life, but I fear it's come too late."

June briefly related how the Doctors had told her the extent of Freddy's injuries now threatened his life. The massive internal bleeding had been difficult to manage during the emergency surgery— her face creased up as the morbid event flooded her mind.

Carl gazed sympathetically at her, embarrassed to raise the subject of Freddy's partner. "Have you seen...?"

She shook her head briskly, intuitively picking up on the sense of his question. "I believe he's been here. I don't know what passed between them... Say it, though I shouldn't, I don't really care."

Carl nodded understandingly. "Would you like me to stay with you?"

She seemed reluctant to answer. "It's kind of you, Carl, but no thanks. This is something Freddy and I have to finish together— one way or the other."

Carl parted from June, feeling more sympathetic toward her than he had on his arrival. Though Freddy's revelation had come as a complete shock, Carl had accepted it as his choice. Inwardly though, Carl was nervous, concerned over the question that now hung over Freddy's family, and how this break-up might affect them in the future.

Arriving home, he found Sally anxiously waiting to hear the whole story. She had offered to look after June's children while she was at the hospital, and had bundled them off to bed early to avoid discussing any of the sordid details in front of them. She listened intently as Carl related the event, finding her reactions similar to his.

Carl and Sally held open minds to life around them generally, but Sally's mother had very strict ideas on the family structure, offering little sympathy to anyone who deviated from the doctrines she adhered to. Carl contemplated her visit the coming weekend, and the incessant lectures on morality they would be subjected to when she found out about Freddy. Should Freddy succumb to this event with his life, it would offer her a whole new theme; expounding to all those around her the retribution that awaited him in the world beyond.

~6~

That evening, the subject of Sally's mother raised a little humour in the solemn mood, teasing a smile on Sally's face. She sensed, instinctively, the meditation of thought tracking through Carl's mind. "Now cheer up, dear, you know you enjoy her visits really."

He looked cockeyed and grimaced at her "Yeah! I suppose so. But it'll be your job to prime her by phoning before hand. Let her know what's happened and then, perhaps, she might get most of it out of her system before she arrives. How long's she staying for this time anyway?" Sally smiled sheepishly. "Oh no! Not the whole week," he anticipated gloomily, humorously burying his face in his hands. "I'll just have to spend it visiting Fred in hospital, help to speed up his recovery."

Sally smiled condescendingly. "Well, what else can I say, Carl. Since Dad died, and me being an only child, Mum's always on her own now." She grabbed his hand, gazing teasingly at him. "You *can*, of course, divorce me if you wish... you know?"

He looked at her slyly. "Don't tempt me." he grinned, as the phone rang.

Sally rose to her feet. "I'll get it," she muttered, disappearing out the door. He picked up the daily newspaper, attempting to untangle the mess that Sally had left it in. Catching fragments of her conversation on the phone, he listened, anticipating her return as she replaced the receiver with a ting.

The brief light-hearted mood faded, as he gazed at the sad look on her face peering at him from around the door. "Freddy?" he whispered.

She nodded. "That was June. Freddy died just a little over an hour ago. They had to rush him back to the operating theatre, but he'd lost too much blood. She gazed up at the ceiling, thinking of his children asleep in bed; picturing their pale faces when June had to tell them what has happened to their dad. She was unable to prevent the tears from welling up in her eyes. "Poor, Freddy," she sighed.

Carl nodded, staring vacantly out into the gloom through the kitchen window. "It's all come about so quickly. We read about these events in the papers, never really believing anything like it could happen to us." They sat together well into the evening, simply talking about all the good times they had shared with their two best friends.

The thoughts of Freddy's infidelity had faded, remembering him as the true friend he was. The whole affair had left Carl feeling that there was a strange atmosphere enshrouding the event of Freddy's passing. Something had induced him to make the decisions he had, and shatter the lives of his family. Was Sally's mum right, he wondered? Were there really invisible entities down here that sought to impose their wills on souls while in this life? The issues that had surrounded Freddy, focused on his decision to abandon his responsibilities in life. The fact he had chosen a male partner did not seem to matter in the final analysis. The disruption, it caused to the lives around him, would have been the same had it been otherwise.

For people like Sally and Carl, the family morals they inherently adhered to, within the human relationship, would always distance them from superficial emotions that bonded less sincere people together. Freddy had been a long-standing friend, and a devoted father to his children. But his personal desires, had finally over-ridden the moral responsibility toward his family that should have taken precedence.

Deep within Carl's subconscious, this event had raised feelings of insecurity. It had demonstrated to him how fragile the human relationship could be. He gazed up at Sally, as she solemnly washed up the supper dishes. The mood of the moment seized him, pledging to himself he would never neglect his family. They would always come first. He would share his life equally with his wife and young son; whatever the future held, they would face it as a single entity.

Suddenly, Emily's faith in the life beyond was beginning to intrigue him. He would discreetly hold an open mind. It would be folly to put any questions to her in her present, intense belief; she would undoubtedly embark on a campaign to brainwash him completely.

He rose from his chair and crept up behind Sally, slipping his arms around her waist. "I've never fully appreciated what I have in life until now," he whispered. "There has never been, and will never be, anyone else for me, but you."

She smiled coyly, gazing at his reflection in the darkened window. "And what's brought all this on, then?"

"I think you know, Sal," as she turned, letting herself sink into his embrace.

CHAPTER THREE

THE FIRST EXPERIENCES

~1~

F OLLOWING F REDDY'S FUNERAL, THE EVENTS that led up to his passing, haunted Carl and Sally for the rest of that year. To divert himself, Carl focused on his work; seizing every opportunity to go on job-related courses that were unknowingly boosting his career. As a result, this strategy concluded in a promotion that allowed Sally to devote herself to Jamie's upbringing. With Sally now a full-time mother and housewife, Jamie's future seemed secure.

***

In the spiritual dimension, John and Sarah had followed the events surrounding Freddy's passing. Freddy had been fortunate; given an insight, courtesy of his near-death experience, into the gravity of his deeds in life by his mentor guides. Before making his transition, his determination to put things right with those close to him, had gone some way toward balancing his achievements against his transgressions. Now, back in the spiritual dimension, he would be counselled by his guides to learn of the consequences of any misdemeanours; the ability to change them, no longer an option.

Sarah and John gazed over Jamie's celestial horizon, and saw fleeting, sinister shadows of events that would touch his life in the future. The evil minion stared intently at them both. It was confident of its plan for the future; the increasing immoral environment, surrounding Jamie on Orburn, favouring it. It drooled over the potential it sensed would become available in Jamie's life; the unlimited opportunities offering it the chance to spread its evil influence on this physical plane.

However, John and Sarah had the spirit of the Infinite One within them. The combined power the two great souls possessed; together, they had the means to outwit the minion. Though this power provided them with the capability to influence Jamie away from the threat of the minion; what complicated matters for them, was how they were to apply that resource. Jamie would have to listen to the voice within; be persuaded to forego moments of indulgence, premeditated acts of aggression, revenge or seduction that could manifest in him a blaze of rapturous feelings on the physical plane.

Once gaining access to Jamie's conscience, those decisions asked a lot of any incarnate spirit. With no real understanding of the importance of the life beyond, the physical mind could easily suppress the small voice within. In the infant stage of life, there was no baseline for incarnate souls to measure their conduct against. These moral attributes, primarily, had to be instilled into a soul's conscience by their parent hosts.

Jamie had chosen his wisely. Carl and Sally would instinctively adhere to their responsibility toward him, but the real assets in life, that offered clues to the truth, were experiences like those of Freddy's passing. Sudden changes in a soul's attitude, after a brief recovery from a life-threatening event, generated curiosity. To the discerning onlooker, these events focused on unanswered questions surrounding the spiritual life. Combined with the faith held by people, like Sally's mother, it could lead to awareness of the different influences existing in the dimension beyond.

John and Sarah gazed on as the minion merged into its band of followers; its cat-like eyes glaring unblinkingly at them. It seemed unconcerned, even after sensing Sarah and John's confident, meditation of thought. It raised anxiety in Sarah and John; not for *their* spiritual welfare, but for that of their young spirit. They knew the barrier separating the physical and spiritual dimensions could be breached by faith or remain impenetrable in ignorance. The choice to determine which, rested with each incarnate spirit. For Sarah and John it was theirs now, to watch, wait and hope, as their mentors had done for them during their voyage to infinity.

***

~2~

Jamie was growing up fast; the young spirit within beginning to learn the ways of the society it had been born into. During his infant period, Jamie had made many friends, but after moving into the primary school stage he had befriended Vicky Joseph. Sally found herself curiously paused by the window on many occasions, smiling at them playing together in the garden. She was inwardly touched by the innocence of their blossoming relationship.

As the years raced by, the bond between Vicky and Jamie strengthened; speeding them toward adolescence before those around them realised it. It was during one particular moment, while watching them from the window, Sally noticed Vicky's movements appeared a little erratic. It was not blatantly obvious, revealing itself more to the intimate eye that had gazed on regularly at them sporting affectionately with each other.

Passing it off as a strained tendon or ligament, Sally got on with her daily chores. A few weeks later, she was peering out the window again at Vicky and Jamie doing their homework together in the garden. Jamie suddenly reached out and took Vicky's hand, gazing intently into her eyes. Vicky's response was instant; her face, softened by a blush as she closed her hand around his.

The suddenness of Jamie's act had taken Sally's breath away, realising now, the true extent of the bond that had grown between them. She thoughtfully withdrew from the window, feeling her distant observation of them now to be an intrusion into their privacy, but the event had excited her. Though it was understood by both families that their children should finish college, her secret hope had been that Jamie would choose Vicky.

Sally, unable to wait for Carl's return home, phoned him at the office. His response was typical of a man; sporting with her elation, humorously chastising her at disturbing him in the middle of preparing for a case. Sally, however, excited by this new development, between Vicky and Jamie, sensed her call had raised his mood too.

Since that day, when Vicky had seemed a little unstable, there had been no repeat of any similar incident.

What supported Sally's hopes for Jamie's growing relationship, was, how she and Carl had suddenly begun to see a lot more of Vicky's parents, Brenda and Paul Joseph. It seemed a natural progression, realising soon after how much they all had in common. But, when Sally broached the subject of Vicky and Jamie, Vicky's parents always appeared a little pensive; never seeming to be openly enthusiastic about their future. Sally, keen on their children's growing relationship, was puzzled by Brenda's reluctance to comment; confused over why she continually led her off the topic.

It was on one particular day that Brenda suddenly popped in, using the pretext of a cup of coffee and a chat, as an excuse. As they talked, Sally realised the conversation was leading toward Vicky. She eagerly seized the opportunity to gossip over what was, undoubtedly, her favourite topic. But as they continued, Sally sensed from Brenda that all was not well.

Brenda gazed at Sally; her eyes gradually moistening with tears. "I don't know how to tell you this, Sally, but Vicky's future is uncertain. Paul and I have learned to live with it, but seeing Jamie and Vicky together touched our conscience: aware of the potential implications of Vicky's medical history, and how we could lose her in the future."

~3~

Brenda continued on with her story, describing how Vicky's early symptoms had made the accuracy of any diagnosis, difficult. There had been many events in the past where they had labelled her as inherently clumsy; passing it off with amusement. But their GP was particularly astute, boasting a long history in the treatment of motor neurone disease. His belief that Vicky was showing the early symptoms of Amyotrophic lateral sclerosis was subsequently confirmed from tests— it came as a great shock to them all.

Understandably, being a fatal condition affecting the motor neurone system, Vicky was terrified of the future; unable to rationalise her feelings toward the inevitable, degrading effects associated with this disease. As she accepted it, she gradually revealed how she felt it symbolised entering a dark tunnel with no light at the end. The morbid scenarios dominated her thoughts daily; fearful of the prospect of being left alone with none of her intimate family able to help her.

Suddenly Jamie appeared on the scene; it offered Vicky hope. But she felt it was a deception to string him along, before the debilitating affects of her condition revealed themselves. Though she appeared clumsy at times, she was still a lively and attractive, pretty girl. In an intimate moment with Jamie, she confided in him. But he was committed— whether or not the cards in life were stacked against her; the bond between them had been struck.

Sally stared at Brenda, stunned; all her hopes for the future suddenly crashing around her. "So it *is* confirmed, Bren?" she asked.

Brenda nodded. "In some scenarios, the specialist tells us that the many symptoms of ALS could remain absent for years, and then slowly manifest in loss of limb movement, speech..." she turned away, "...it's too horrible to think of."

Sally reached out, taking Brenda's hand. "Vicky, of course, has been counselled by her Doctor and has accepted it, has she?" asked Sally.

Brenda nodded again. "And, I believe she has discussed it with Jamie as well."

Sally gazed away toward the window. In that moment, life seemed to have cheated them all. Her dream of holding her grand-children, now suddenly so remote. But this was not to be her prime consideration. They had new friends they had been eager to share any joy with; was that bond strong enough now to share their grief?

Sally's expression softened as she smiled at Brenda. "Whatever we can do to help, you only have to ask."

Brenda was overwhelmed by Sally's comforting response. She and Paul had long-since accepted their lot, never believing the situation would arise where Vicky would attract the attention of a partner. Sally's words had come as an immense relief, suddenly allowing them to share the dreadful secret that had burdened their family for so long.

Rising from her chair, Brenda wiped her eyes and gently kissed Sally on the cheek. "...I had better go and do the shopping," she whispered, "Life goes on." Brenda sighed, as she made her way out into the hall.

Sally gazed at her; paused by the open door. "I don't know how, but I feel the bond between our children is something special. Let's not be pessimistic about the future. Think of it as a match made in heaven perhaps?" smiled Sally. Brenda nodded slowly, disappearing behind the closing door.

~4~

It came as some consolation to Sally to know that Jamie was aware of Vicky's predicament, but it had raised the curiosity in her; why he had not chosen to confide in his parents. Jamie, over the years, had matured into a passionate, independent young man, impressing those around him how it seemed he had grown up before his time. If he had been affected by the knowledge of Vicky's condition, any concerns he had were not evident on the surface.

His attachment to Vicky was increasing daily, planning their future as if a foregone conclusion. Sally feared he was shutting out the morbid reality, believing that Vicky's condition would never progress to the point where it could finally threaten her life. The physicians caring for Vicky were under no such delusion, and knew, from their periodical tests, the onset of the disease was inevitable, and that the consequences could affect her any time.

Ironically, it forced Brenda and Sally to focus their attention on Jamie, watching him from a distance as he and Vicky moved through college, and on into their final exam period. He appeared to isolate himself from the family; living in a world with Vicky, adopting an attitude that seemed to consider they were impervious to anything that could threaten their future.

If this turned out to be the case, it worried Sally, feeling that for Jamie to adhere to such a strategy was folly, leading him towards an emotional upheaval that could have an affect on his mind for the rest of his life. For anyone to deliberately ignore a threat that over-shadowed someone close, should they suddenly lose them, the consequences could be psychologically catastrophic. But for the time being, the exams were focusing them on studies that absorbed their attention, distancing them from the morbid scenarios. All their families could do was to wait, and hope the grim issue would remain unrealised.

Success followed success in the exams for Jamie and Vicky, with university beckoning near the end of that year. The radiant look on their faces confused those around them into believing that perhaps a miracle had happened and, what seemed unlikely, that the physicians had got it wrong.

In the months ahead, Sally, since the disclosure of Vicky's illness, had noticed how Jamie had got into the habit of frequently visiting his grandmother. Emily's beliefs, though common knowledge to all the family and friends, had never really interested him in the past. It was during one visit, while Carl was at work, Sally raised her suspicions with her mother. She felt Emily was with-holding something she knew about Jamie and Vicky. Sally had expected her mother to seize the opportunity to expound her beliefs and ideals, ranting on about how she would put the world to rights. But instead, she found her uncharacteristically silent on the subject— cunningly leading Sally away onto other topics.

Sally became frustrated, and gazed searchingly at Emily. "Mum!" she exclaimed. "Why are you being so evasive? Has Jamie said anything to you about Vicky and him, or not? Brenda and I feel as if we've been left out in the cold— what's going on— we *are* family you know!"

Emily looked confused, seeming to want to help, but not knowing quite what to say that would. "Sally, since Vicky's condition was made known to us all, it has affected Jamie in a deeply emotional way."

Sally gazed at her mother incredulously, somewhat taken aback at her statement of the obvious, and simultaneously, curious over the absence of her usual fire and brimstone approach to matters spiritual.

"Undeniably, Mum, and perfectly understandable. But..."

Emily shook her head as she cut Sally short. "I don't mean in the physical aspect; more the spiritual one, asking me questions on how one went about the prospect of healing someone." Emily looked away, the confusion on her face mutating to concern. "It worries me, Sally, as Jamie's request infers an ultimatum."

Listening to Emily had raised new fears in Sally. If she had understood her mother correctly, Emily thought Jamie was challenging the very source of life while making his request. Though the majority of the world's inhabitants ignored a belief in the Infinite One, an inner sense prevented one from openly directing ultimatums to Him. Jamie's devotion to Vicky had clouded his judgement, using his grandmother's gift to try and force the issue, rather than suppress his pride and make any requests with humility.

Emily's single-minded approach to anything spiritual had obviously been mellowed by Jamie's attitude, unsettling her on how to address the situation. Viewed remotely, by others not possessing Emily's understanding, it could easily place a question mark over Jamie's presence of mind. But when viewed from Emily's perspective of life, Jamie's strategy seemed to directly challenge the Infinite One. As far as she was concerned, it was jeopardising his spiritual welfare, and how she gave the advice she offered, placed a responsibility on her that could either compromise or enhance it.

Sally's acceptance in the existence of the life beyond was not as intense as her mother's, feeling that all this was nonsense. During the past they had tolerated Emily's beliefs, but this was the first time she had applied them to such an important issue. But, however, what Sally had heard, did confirm the mental turmoil that was going on in Jamie's mind.

***

Sarah and John recognised the event as the first real challenge to their young soul. The minion had not wasted any time; determined to seize this chance to get at them. Jamie had met the soul that was to partner him on his voyage to infinity; but the subsequent spiritual bond, which had arisen between Vicky and him, had played into the minion's hands.

Gazing over Vicky's celestial horizon, confirmed that her lifespan, on this occasion, was going to be a compromised one. In the future she would be the first to return to their band of guides in the spiritual dimension, and there, await Jamie to complete his period of incarnation— accepting his deeds as her own.

While Vicky remained on the physical plane, the opportunity availed itself to their guides to influence Jamie through her. As her life succumbed to the disease, and her transition approached, it would bring about awareness in her of the life after, and hopefully, help to settle Jamie's physical emotions. Emily's contribution to those guides beyond would be invaluable, but she was competing against medical opinions that considered the spiritual solution as unrealistic, and therefore, a dangerous alternative.

Jamie, blinded by his physical desires, would see no reason for the threat to his Vicky. It was part of the plan, when entering an incarnation, that one of the main attributes to be learnt was humility. The conditions that threatened human life could be avoided, as many miracles to heal those, suffering illness, had been demonstrated on countless material planes throughout the history of the universe. But even if Jamie had genuine faith, and could, with humility submit a plea to the Infinite One for her life, though such an act would confirm his belief, if it was part of Vicky's plan, it could not be granted.

For the ones left behind to rationalise this, there had to be an understanding of the life beyond. Ignorance of this fundamental aspect promised a life of bitterness in the material world. This basic understanding, of the relationship between the two dimensions, made up the entire syllabus in the physical universe. The solution had to come from each soul's faith in the spiritual life to discover where truth lay. As they journeyed toward infinity, from faith came the sudden realisation that companions had not gone forever, and created the resource to cope with set-backs on the physical plane.

Sarah and John could only look on now as Jamie approached one such crossroad. His love of Vicky had focused him on a choice; his grandmother's belief, or his strategy to bargain with the Maker for Vicky's life.

***

CHAPTER FOUR

VICKY'S LEGACY

~1~

WITH VICKY AND JAMIE, SPENDING most of their time away at university, the families had settled down to the business of getting on with their lives. Their earlier fears for their children had waned in light of the success of their education. Now in possession of their degrees, Vicky and Jamie's wedding banns had been announced, Emily, however, still had reservations, but kept them to herself, appearing to join in with the euphoria of the occasion.

Having completed their studies, Vicky and Jamie began preparing their new home, ready to move in after the honeymoon. Vicky's condition was being constantly monitored by her general practitioner, and the specialist he had referred her to. The numerous symptoms of ALS, presenting with similarities to other diseases, had originally complicated Vicky's initial diagnosis. Because of this, Jamie would not accept it. Watching Vicky enter her early twenties, where the sudden onset of the disease had manifested in so many other people, he felt the doctors had got it wrong.

The wedding came and passed. Sally and Brenda gazed at the photographs of all the smiling faces bearing witness to the happy day. Whatever happened now, they had something they would be able to look back on. The weather had made the day a summer event in all its truest traditions: not a cloud in the sky, birds singing in the trees, and all caressed by the gentle sigh of a warm breeze. As Vicky moved further into her twenties the first signs of her condition began to show. Her coordination gradually became more erratic; cups and plates spontaneously falling from her hands. It distressed Jamie to witness her growing frustration as she tried to cope.

He became over attentive, insisting he did everything for her. He stopped visiting his grandmother; seizing any opportunity to direct his increasing bitterness toward her spiritual beliefs. Any attempts to counsel him were met with irrational outbursts. It appeared to satisfy the need in him to express how he felt the powers beyond did not exist. That to utter copious prayers to an invisible entity, who he believed in his case had not listened, was humiliating.

As Vicky's condition deteriorated, Jamie became more moody, continuing to distress his family, who watched, powerless to do anything to help him. When Vicky's speech began to slur, it was the final straw, and he broke down in an intimate moment together.

He held her hand as he gazed intently at her. "Why is this happening? If there is an Infinite One, why *doesn't* he help us?" Ironically, his intense despair, on what was casting a shadow over their lives, was making Vicky accept it even more. As she became trapped in her body, the unselfish desire in her to help him, focused her away from the gradual onslaught of the debilitating effects of the disease.

The days turned to weeks and the weeks to months, Vicky, finding herself on many different medical regimes to try and relieve the symptoms of the disease. Where the disease's affect had been eased, the side effects produced offset some aspects of that relief. Jamie, however, consumed by grief, was inadvertently adding to her distress. A spiritual resource within Vicky was beginning to strengthen her resolve to cope with the situation. It fuelled the determination in her to get it through to Jamie; she had accepted what was happening to her.

Emily was intrigued by Vicky's strategy, raised in the regular conversations they'd had together. She sensed from them, Vicky was leaning more toward the spiritual, rather than the physical aspect of her existence. She was learning that her guides in the spiritual dimension were real and constant. As her life became more compromised, her spiritual understanding began to dominate; revealing clues as to the true reasoning behind why all this was happening to her.

Within a lifespan, so many unknown physical and environmental issues were involved, which could affect a change in the direction of a life. Because the spiritual solution had come across as Vicky's choice, Jamie's feeling for her obliged him to go along with it. The vague spiritual understanding between them now, however fragile, was enhancing the opportunity to make as much of their material lives together as possible.

Both the families gazed on, gaining a little hope from the understanding that was developing between their children. The person, who seemed to be getting through to Jamie, was the one whose material existence was threatened. Emily, however, continued to view the situation cautiously. She knew that if Vicky made her transition too soon, Jamie could relapse even deeper into his unjust recrimination of those in the world beyond.

~**2**~
***

From the spiritual dimension, Sarah and John contemplated how Vicky's predicament affected Jamie. Jamie's focus on the physical aspects of his incarnation had prevented him from seeing the bigger picture. When Vicky eventually made her transition, this picture would reveal her in all her spiritual glory: free of the degenerative effects of the disease that had stricken her on the material plane.

Her life's sacrifice, offered him the opportunity to learn humility. The feelings, that were present in him now, would have no value on his return to the spirit world, realising a lost opportunity upon him. With no understanding of the life beyond in the material life, it was a natural progression to vent one's anger on divine doctrines. All the while the attributes in life favoured one, the need to reason over a purpose for the physical existence seemed pointless.

While Vicky sustained life, there was a chance the spiritual guides could work through her to free Jamie from the grief that could so easily turn him away from the truth. The minion, the evil antagonist shadowing him in the dark dimension, had other ideas, sensing that the first victory was going to be its.

***

Jamie gazed at his reflection in the bathroom mirror, listening to the sounds of Vicky getting up. Even though she was steadily succumbing

35

to the effects of the disease, the medications for the present were keeping her fairly independent.

He lathered up his chin and began to shave, as a resounding crash echoed across the landing. He raced out through the bathroom door, finding Vicky sprawled over the bedroom floor, giggling. Her laughter settled the tension in him, having created all sorts of wild scenarios in his mind.

"What *are* you doing, Vicky? You scared the daylights out of me," he muttered, helping her up.

"Oh, Jamie, don't be so dramatic. I know I'm a worry to you all, but we must live and let live." She sat on the edge of the bed, gesturing him toward the door. "Go on! Don't just stand there looking like Father Christmas; get off to work, and earn loads of money for me to spend."

Her jocular statement enticed a smile on his face as he reached for her, rubbing his lathered chin into the side of her neck.

"Ooh! You beast," she squealed, wiping the smeared lather from her skin. "I'll get you for that."

"Yeah! Yeah!" he muttered confidently, disappearing out the bedroom door.

Sitting alone on the bed, Vicky pondered the gravity of the event. Her strategy, to settle Jamie's fear of her increasing instability, was gradually reconciling him into accepting her condition. The jovial atmosphere she created, lifted his spirits considerably, and helped to focus her away from her illness.

Sitting at the table, he tossed some cereal into a bowl. "What's your day going to involve then?" he asked, spooning liberal helpings of sugar over the cereal.

She gazed on horrified. "Ja...mie!" She muttered tunefully. "Too much sugar. You'll clog up all your arteries or end up like the side of a house, and then I won't love you anymore." He grinned, displaying an old-fashioned look. "Mum's coming over to take me out to lunch," she continued, feigning a smug smile.

"Alright for some," said Jamie, reaching for his coat hanging over the back of his chair. Taking out his wallet, he offered her a note. "There! Tell her it's our treat..."

She snatched the wallet from his hand. "Ooh! You old skinflint, that's not enough to feed a fly," helping herself to a couple more.

"Charming! What am I going to do for lunch, then?"

"That bag of sugar you've just spooned over your cereal should last you weeks."

He rose up from his chair, grabbing his coat. He buried his face in her neck, tickling and kissing her. "Be careful, and don't exert yourself today while you're out gadding about."

He disappeared, leaving her to get ready for her mum's arrival. Though her fall earlier had been due to a sudden loss of coordination, her tactic to treat it casually had set Jamie up for the day: in a strange way, it was also serving to suppress the fear in her of what the future held— increasingly strengthening her resolve to meet this challenge in life.

She was determined not to be pessimistic about her prospects. What gave her added confidence, was the daily proof of how much she was loved by her family. When the time arrived she would be unable to do anything for herself, they would be there for her.

~3~

The doorbell chimed, and she made her way through the hall to the front door. The beaming smile of her mother greeted her as she opened it.

"Hi! Mum," she said cheerfully, beckoning Brenda in."

"And, how's my little Cherub today?" smiled Brenda.

"Oh, Mum! How corny," replied Vicky, nauseated by her mum's doting greeting.

"Well, I must say you're looking radiant this morning, so you must be doing something right." Brenda watched as Vicky walked toward the kitchen door. "Have...Have you had any further signs... of..."

"Now don't start, Mum," retorted Vicky firmly. "We've all agreed to leave well alone, and trust it to the medics to make all the decisions. Where're you taking me today?" asked Vicky, quickly changing the subject.

Brenda stared after her, feeling somewhat squashed. "Yes... Yes! Do you remember that little steam railway Dad and I used to take you on years ago. I was speaking to a friend who says they've expanded it, building a restaurant at the end of the line; I thought we might go there today. You wouldn't have to..." She bit her lip, pausing to gaze at Vicky pouring tea into a cup— resisting the temptation to suggest she should do it.

"There we are," said Vicky firmly, pointedly handing her the cup and saucer. "Get it down you, and then we'll be off. The weather forecast promises a fine day, so it should make it a pleasant trip."

During the journey, Brenda relaxed, chatting copiously on the events of her week. Vicky nodded, adding the odd euphemism to the conversation while her mother rattled on. As always, the topics described her mother's boring lifestyle; ignoring any of her father's daily routines.

Since first being diagnosed with the disease, Vicky had found it necessary to be firm about her family's approach to her, and yet, not appear to come across ungrateful. She felt this strategy would allow her to hang onto her independence for as long as possible.

Her mother would have wrapped her up in cotton-wool; drowned her in suffocating compassion as her independence faded. Vicky felt her approach to the disease had educated those around her, setting a bench-mark for the future that would help to maintain her dignity.

The voice of her mother intruded back into her thoughts as she gazed out the carriage window onto the scene drifting by.

"Vicky, Dear! You're not listening to a word I'm saying."

"I am, Mum. But we're missing the scenery; look how it's changed."

"You mean, you're still able to remember that far back?"

Vicky glared at her mother. "There's nothing wrong with my mind, Mum."

"Sorry, Dear...," replied Brenda sheepishly. The carriage fell silent; both of them watching the small station approach. The atmosphere took on a more forgiving mood, as they gazed out on the beautiful setting surrounding the restaurant complex. The emphasis was on conservation, with walks leading the sight-seer to various wild-life habitats.

Vicky and Brenda gazed enraptured over what the owners had achieved. As they carefully descended from the carriage, they noticed a group lifting a man in a wheelchair down from one of the other carriages. The scene had obviously affected them, intoxicating the mood of the person in the chair similarly.

The look in his eyes, gazing out on that peaceful scene, spoke a language of its own. His expression revealed an inner joy that seemed to have transcended the physical barriers imposed on him by his condition. That moment, showed Vicky the important role a caring family played when helping to off-set the misery of a physically, stricken life.

Vicky gazed at her mother in humility, seeing in that soul in the chair, a future picture of herself. It sensed her with the notion of how her present strategy could appear as an affront to those supporting her. To cling to independence was important, but needed to be preserved with gratitude.

She gently closed her hand around her mother's. "I do appreciate how you all care for me, Mum," she whispered softly. "I want you to remember that when the time approaches that I cannot tell you, Jamie and the others, how much I appreciate what you all do for me— tell them for me."

Brenda's eyes moistened, gazing at the person in the wheelchair and then back at Vicky. She smiled, giving Vicky's hand a squeeze. "Come, my dear, let's eat. You must be starved."

"Thought you'd never ask, and Jamie said it's our treat..." Brenda made to protest. "...No arguments, Mum," insisted Vicky firmly.

~4~

The railway outing became a regular venue for Brenda and Vicky, with Jamie joining them on occasion. The theme of the conservation area brought one closer to nature, providing much pleasure from observing the variety of species there. The relief it offered to Vicky, helped to offset the side-effects of the countless medical prescriptions that were beginning to govern her life.

The balance between Vicky's desire to ease the concern in her family against their efforts to do everything they could for her, was settling into an amicable understanding. The society researching the disease, provided guidelines that helped to support sufferers from its onset, through to its final stages, but there was an unknown quantity. Everyone had a morbid fear of some aspect in life. It lurked in the back of one's mind, and could turn life's dreams into nightmares. For Vicky now, that was becoming a reality, slowly reducing her physical ability to amble freely in the world around her.

Though the developments in technology helped to address a sufferer's needs, they were unable to suppress the increasing feeling of insecurity, as the disease became more incapacitating. What really unnerved Vicky, was, the limiting affect on her astute, active mind's awareness as her body became unresponsive. Now that Jamie was beginning to see the problem in a clearer perspective, he was making it a priority to work out ways to help Vicky maintain a modicum of independence.

By far, the most important factor in any life was that of communication. In this particular field the technology was streaking ahead. Having achieved a degree in a career related to types of communication, Jamie was researching methods to help people like Vicky back into society. This task had led him away from the bitterness he had felt toward those in the life beyond; thanks to Vicky, he no longer believed they ignored them.

Over the next two years, the family rallied around Vicky as her symptoms reached the stage where she was unable to manage without help. Jamie wanted to give up his job and devote his days to nursing her, but it made no sense as the bread-winner. Emily proved to be the one able to lift her spirits constantly: Vicky, delighting in sitting in her wheelchair, listening to the tales of Emily's psychic experiences.

***

John and Sarah knew Vicky's mind was unaffected by the disease. They sensed her frustration; unable to respond to Emily's beliefs or reason over why some people had to suffer, while other lives remained untouched. But Vicky's soul already knew the answer. Her sacrifice was providing the means for others to learn the attributes, which would open up countless opportunities for them in the life beyond.

Though it would be viewed as no consolation to Vicky in her incarnate form, her sacrifice was enhancing her own spiritual existence. Her determination, to meet this challenge in life, constantly encouraged her to reach beyond her ability. As each day led her toward her transition, the acceptance of her condition was influencing Jamie back on course.

The minion was losing ground from the dedication shown by the two incarnate spirits, and the support they were receiving from their worldly families. At present, its options were limited, but when Vicky's celestial horizon closed in, and she made her transition, Jamie would find himself at an important crossroad. The desire to maintain contact with her, however, would secure his continued belief in the dimension beyond. The loving bond and conscientious way he had cared for her would, in future intimate moments, allow her to reveal herself in her spiritual form; confirming the relationship that now existed between them on their voyage to infinity.

***

CHAPTER FIVE

SPIRITUAL BEDFELLOWS

~1~

JAMIE GAZED ON DESPONDENTLY AT the queue of traffic reaching ahead; it was going to be another tedious trek home from work. He contemplated Vicky waiting for him; it being her mother's week to care for her. They had all come to the general understanding, that he would see after her in the evenings and over weekends: it was something he had insisted on, treating it as the highlight of his day.

He knew she listened while he chatted to her about his day. It was something her deep-feeling GP had encouraged, as her astute, receptive mind made it a highlight of her day too. He gazed at his watch, and then in the mirror at the traffic gathering behind. The time was dragging on, with no one seeming to be making any headway further on.

After the best part of half an hour, the queues were still static; it was obvious, some sort of traffic problem had occurred ahead. He contemplated the rush-hour, how he felt motorways provided invaluable access for business, but shared an affinity with Grand Prix race-tracks; people, taking chances in the scramble to get home as fast as possible.

Gradually, the queues began expanding into three lanes. He craned his neck, trying to make out the nature of the hold up. Suddenly, flashing blue lights of ambulances, fire-engines and police cars, their sirens wailing, sped up and down the opposite carriageway. People in front and behind were getting out of their cars, trying to make out the nature of the problem. As the emergency services took over, they set about clearing a way through to disperse the queues of traffic.

It was turning into a nightmare, with Jamie constantly thinking of Vicky back home. The family had got into the habit, that whoever was caring for Vicky could leave a little prematurely, believing him to be only a few minutes away. If the situation adhered to the norm, Vicky would have been unattended for the best part of an hour already.

He gazed in the rear-view mirror; the queues now stretched way back into the distance. The crash-barriers prevented any dramatic attempt to cross the central reservation and re-track back to exit the motorway— he was stuck with it. The fact they were moving forward at a trickle, confirmed to him the obstruction must have occurred before the next slip-road.

At last, the emergency services seemed to have made some headway, and were starting to filter traffic past the obstruction. All eyes were focused ahead, as an unimaginable scene of horror came into view. There had been a multi-car pile up. The state of some wrecks revealed how, following the initial impact, subsequent vehicles had ploughed one into the other.

Jamie gazed on in horror at the carnage strewn out over the carriageway. The buckled remains of the crash-barriers bore witness to the speeds some of the cars must have been travelling at. All the emergency teams were working flat out, extracting mutilated bodies from the tangle of metal. Jamie felt sick to his stomach as his section of the queue crept past, gazing at the wrecks that appeared to have been screwed up by some giant hand.

Covered bodies lined the central reservation of the carriageway; a harassed traffic officer, waving cars impatiently through the access cleared by the emergency services. The grim picture remained in Jamie's mind as he sped away, deliberating on how the quest to get home as fast as possible for some, had now taken a lifetime.

Blocking the grizzly scene from his mind, he entered his turn-off and made for home. He felt sadness for the lives left behind who would be touched by this tragedy. How the impatience shown by the deceased in ignoring the speed-limits, could almost have been viewed as an act of selfishness; shattering the lives of their loved ones waiting at home.

~2~

He drew into his drive behind Brenda's car, somewhat relieved to find her still there. Gazing in through the window, he smiled, spotting her sitting with Vicky. It was his turn now; suddenly focused on the thought of making his Vicky comfortable for the evening.

Brenda greeted him at the door, a pale look of concern on her face. "Jamie! I thought you had been involved in that horrific accident; it's all over the news."

He smiled as he walked past her toward Vicky. Resting his hands on the arms of her wheelchair, he bent over and kissed her. "Hello, my darling" he whispered. "Now it's Vicky time again."

Brenda smiled at them together. "Would you like me to stay and help, Jamie, as you've been held up?"

Jamie shook his head. "No. We'll manage," seeing Brenda to the door. "Thanks for your help. Has Vicky had supper yet?"

Brenda nodded. "Just her ablutions to do."

He closed the door, and smiled at Vicky. "Right," he grinned. "It's out with the plastic ducks and into the tub with you tonight, my dove. "Vicky's eyes seemed to dance and sparkle at his jovial gesture, sensing how lucky she was at having people so dedicated to her.

Should the opportunity have presented that allowed anyone to peer into Vicky and Jamie's life together, they would have seen nothing remotely promiscuous about it. It was one of those rare relationships where the spirit dominated. Seen through Jamie's eyes, Vicky still appeared as a beautiful young woman; the debilitating changes imposed on her body by the disease, invisible to him.

Having run her bath, he gently lifted her out of the wheelchair, and began mounting the stairs. "Either I'm getting weaker or you're getting fatter, so it's on a diet for you, my girl," he joked. Seeing to her essentials first, he tested the water before gently lowering her in. As he washed her, he chatted about work, and how he never missed a day there, researching new facilities that were being developed to help the chronically incapacitated.

The downside to accessing these new resources had been the expense, but grants were beginning to appear. To him there was no moral justification to hold anyone to ransom because of their affluence in life. There was untold wealth in the world, despite the fact most of it was pooled in assets to generate more, or cached in banks. Single-minded, uncaring people, intent on gazing the other way, were enjoying luxurious lifestyles; remaining blissfully ignorant of the suffering going on around them in the world.

He lifted her out, and then, swaddled in a towel, he carried her into the bedroom. Slipping her night-gown on, he looked into her eyes. "Now you're squeaky clean again?" he whispered. Supported by pillows, she gazed back at him; the expression in her eyes, weary from the effort of the event.

Though he worked tirelessly to make her life as comfortable as he could, the progressive affects of the disease were taking there toll. It distressed him to think about it, but he knew she was losing the battle. He could not bear the thought of life without her, but every day was increasing the physical and mental drain on her.

Their GP had already broached the subject, suggesting she might be better off in a specially equipped hospice. But Jamie made it clear; telling him the family wanted her to have the care she needed at home. If the end was to come soon, they wished it to be in the privacy of her own home, surrounded by the intimate members of her family.

None of them had any misconceptions of what lay before them; least of all Jamie. As Vicky deteriorated, both families suddenly found themselves looking to Emily, and the spiritual aspects of her belief. After Vicky's diagnosis was confirmed, Jamie had been particularly aggressive in his attitude toward Emily's beliefs, now, as the main focus in his life was slipping away, the spiritual solution seemed to offer him the means to maintain contact with Vicky.

~3~
***

Vicky's guides were preparing to receive her soul. They sensed from Jamie, an acceptance now of how her transition would be a happy release, and that his desire to keep her with him arose from the intimacy of their relationship. Though the physical and mental hardship of looking after her had never been an issue for him, it placed intolerable pressure on her.

Jamie's guides, Sarah and John, were delighted with the spiritual outlook. The combined efforts of both families, and Vicky, had developed the realisation in Jamie, not only of the existence of the spiritual dimension, but that one should not submit aggressive ultimatums to those within it. Once a plan had been invoked, it had to run its course governed by truth.

In the weeks ahead, Jamie's physical life would sink to an all-time low, as Vicky completed her first incarnation. The families of both young souls had played their part in full, and as progressing spirits themselves, could move onto their next individual incarnations with a clear conscience.

The minion had long since realised the redundancy of its present plan. There was no possibility of influencing Jamie directly, not even now the one closest to him was in the process of leaving the physical plane. But there were plenty more fish in the sea it could use to tempt Jamie— once he was free of Vicky. The minion's cold, unfeeling mind had already written her off. Its ice-cool gaze panned Jamie's celestial horizon, planning out a string of events that would prey on Jamie's loneliness and grief.

Sarah and John were not naive by any means of the imagination, and knew that they could not relax their vigilance for an instant. The minion's constant target was to gain access to the material life at any cost, but thanks to Vicky's earlier strategy to help Jamie accept her condition, it did not hold all the cards now. Jamie's bond to Vicky was so strong, it seemed incomprehensible that the minion could find the means to erode it. It fell to Sarah and John to ensure it would never get the chance to create that opportunity. However, it had many cunning powers at its disposal, and a team behind it that was equally equipped for the physical plane.

The true relationship that had developed between Vicky and Jamie, had given their guides a psychic option. In the times when Jamie would be exposed to the aspects of the minion's devious plan, Vicky would appear to Jamie in her spiritual form. The revelation these events would realise in him then, would rekindle all the feelings that they had shared when she had been with him.

*** ***

CHAPTER SIX
THE TENDER PARTING

~1~

DURING THE MONTHS AHEAD, VICKY'S condition became critical, developing dramatic changes that began to affect her breathing. Jamie dreaded going to work; believing everytime the phone rang it would be to summon him home. The nights passed as if an eternity, with Sally and Brenda insisting he went to bed, pledging to call him should the worst happen— he just laid there awake, thinking of Vicky.

It was one evening after his return home; he arrived to find the doctor present. Brenda and Sally were in tears, with Paul and Carl standing sad-faced behind them. A chill feeling swept over him, thinking Vicky had passed on, and there had been no time to summon him home. He rushed into their bedroom, finding Vicky very weak— hanging onto the threads of life. It was as if she had sensed her time had come, and had asked for this moment to say her farewell to him.

The doctor hovered in the background, slowly closing his bag. "There is little more I can do for her now," he whispered. "She's as comfortable as I can make her. I'll call round in the morning to see how she is. It's worth mentioning; there *is* a bed in the hospice if you wished to reconsider..." He could see none of them were listening. "...I felt I should...," his softly muttered words petering out. Picking up his bag, he wandered toward the door. Brenda offered a laboured smile, thanking him as she showed him out. He paused briefly to look back, feeling intuitively, his intention to review Vicky in the morning would be redundant by then.

Jamie fought back the tears, as he sat holding Vicky's hand. He knew she wanted to avoid a morbid atmosphere when her transition came. They had talked about it many times, during the early stages of the disease. Vicky's wish stemmed from the discussions she'd had with Emily; her knowledge of the spiritual dimension adhering to the belief now, one's transition was merely a doorway into the world beyond.

Emily had gently chastised Vicky on numerous occasions when she had referred to her future passing as 'death'. There was no such word in Emily's vocabulary. When the chains of the physical life dropped away, such a term was too harsh to describe a passing into the beautiful world of spirit.

Intuitively, Jamie felt his parting from Vicky was imminent. Had his desire to keep her as long as possible, prolonged her suffering? He buried his face in her hand; his tears trickling down through her fingers. As his emotion took hold of him, his beliefs faded from his memory; all that had passed between Vicky and him— lost in the physical mire of his inconsolable grief.

He lifted his face from her hand, and found her eyes gazing intently at him. They were sparkling again; alive with expression; seeming to tell him that their parting would be but an infinitesimal speck in time. What Emily had taught them was the truth, and that the time spent on the physical plane was no more than the bat of an eye, when measured against the spiritual life.

He managed a faint smile; her eyes continuing to dance and sparkle back at him, like they had done so many times before to relay her feelings. Instinctively, he felt she was calling in their pledge to celebrate her success in the physical life. Her period of incarnation had entailed years of suffering, but in rising above his confusion, his beliefs now had endorsed her sacrifice.

~2~
***

Sarah and John gathered around with Vicky's guides, as they prepared to receive her soul back into the spiritual world. As the night stretched before them, they sensed the mood of tragedy arising from the small group drawn together around Vicky. But the mood in the spiritual dimension was euphoric, celebrating Vicky's first incarnate achievement.

Passing into the small hours, Vicky's soul began to break free. The years her spirit had been incarcerated in that prison of flesh and bone, had imparted no lasting affect on her. The spiritual guides smiled, gazing on as her shimmering spirit rose out of the crippled shell of her body. She was drifting free now, released from the incapacitating affects of the disease that had stricken her on the physical plane.

In contrast, the sadness in the families below reached a climax, as they realised she had slipped away. Their grief prevented them from appreciating the real truth of Vicky's transition. She wanted to tell them all how happy she was; feeling as free as the wind over the sea and in the swaying branches of the trees of the forests. But there was one among the group on the physical plane, who could sense the essential truth of what had taken place.

***

Emily gently placed her hand on Jamie's shoulder. "She's at peace now, Jamie," she whispered. He tearfully gazed up at the faint expression of a smile on Emily's face, softened by the night-light. "You have nothing to reproach yourself over the care you have given her; we are all witnesses to that. Don't begrudge her this release from the suffering she endured all these past years."

As if to endorse what Emily had said, the spirit of Vicky appeared to her alone, sitting on the edge of the bed next to Jamie. Old spiritual campaigner, as Emily was, these happenings still touched her with a divine presence. The events that had led her to this moment had also taught her lessons, mellowing her strict views: liberating benevolent feelings in her that needed to be applied with them.

When the grief of Vicky's passing abated, Emily would teach them all how they could maintain contact with her. She would tell them there was no need of a morbid wake, but more how to celebrate the success of Vicky's life. Vicky's loss would undoubtedly linger on with Jamie; all the little intimate things persisting as memories, constantly making him reflect over their lives together.

The doctor was called, and duly arrived to certify Vicky's passing, sanctioning the necessary arrangements for her interment. By early morning, her body had been removed. Jamie gazed at the empty bed;

it was too much for him to accept, and he walked out into the cold, dew-ladened early morning air to spend some time alone.

Sally went to go after him, but Emily grabbed her hand. "Let him be," she said softly.

As Jamie walked, he was fighting off all his old feelings of how he felt life had cheated him; thinking over how many of his friends were enjoying the pleasures of parenthood with their partners. He symbolised himself as if walking on the edge of a precipice. To raise all those old issues again, could send him headlong into the abyss of confusion and bitterness that Vicky had fought so long to rid him of.

The sun was beginning to peer above the horizon, paling the dark blue sky above. A sense of peace descended upon him. It was as if Vicky was there walking by his side; voices from the past, seeming to whisper in the gentle sigh of the wind rustling the leaves in the branches above. It had been a walk he had often taken her on in her wheelchair. There had been no need of words; both of them feeling Nature's embrace in an early morning, magical silence.

He felt desolate now. Never again would she speak to him with her eyes, nor sense her thoughts track through his mind. He let himself drift back to their discussions with Emily. If she was right, Vicky would be enjoying a freedom even greater than his now. It offered him a little consolation, but the thought of life without her, now promised a lonely future, and one he felt obliged to accept in lieu of her sacrifice.

✳✳✳

In the spiritual dimension, Sarah and John watched as a jubilant Vicky walked by Jamie's side. She would never leave him now, waiting for his time to join her. Her first incarnation had set them on course for their voyage to infinity. It was now Jamie's responsibility, to ensure he played his part to complete the success of their first combined incarnation.

The evil minion stared at Vicky. She was beyond its reach now, safely back under the guardianship of her spiritual guides. Its greedy eyes turned toward Jamie. Gazing across his celestial horizon, an opportunity approached where Jamie would offer his help to someone. Engaged in a business that researched applications for physically incapacitated people, Jamie was being guided toward a meeting with a soul embittered by their lot in life.

The minion sensed how it could use Jamie's benevolent nature by placing him in sensitive situations; use the emotional hopes of those he was helping, to gain access into Jamie's spiritual relationship with Vicky. The Infinite One's laws could not be breached. Though Jamie had pledged himself to Vicky, whether on the material plane or in the spiritual dimension, the act of spiritually helping someone could easily be confused with material affection. This, in essence, was the minion's plan, and it hoped to lead Jamie into an emotional situation that could hold the life of a young soul in the balance.

***

CHAPTER SEVEN

JAMIE'S QUEST

~1~

SALLY TRIED TO PERSUADE JAMIE to return to the family home with her and Carl, but he declined. Though the constant sense of loneliness crowded in on him daily, the soul within him rallied, strengthened by those in the spiritual world beyond. He clung onto Vicky's memory; her presence evident from all the paraphernalia of hers he had displayed around their home. It distressed his mother, feeling that he was letting himself sink into a bachelor existence— he was still a young man.

But Sally's concerns were parental ones, and lacked the insight her mother, Emily, had in the power of the spiritual solution. Sally's level of faith was incapable of appreciating the understanding that had developed between Emily, Vicky and Jamie. That understanding arose from believing in the world beyond, allowing the soul to tap the resource available there. Emily and Vicky's relentless persuasion, had finally convinced Jamie to breach the barrier separating the physical and spiritual worlds; revealing how it could provide guidance to prepare them all for their inevitable transitions.

As the months drifted by, Jamie fell back into the mundane work-routines of everyday life. His colleagues found him approachable and chatty enough, but beneath that exterior, sensed his inner battle to come to terms with Vicky's loss. It was on one particular day his superior, Richard, called into his office.

Richard pulled up a chair and sat, gazing thoughtfully at Jamie.

"This looks a bit ominous," grinned Jamie curiously.

"Na! Not really. Nope! I haven't come to bore you with hard-core business today, though my desk is stacked up with new projects..." gazing at the pile of files on Jamie's, "...like yours. Of all the people working for our department, you are the only one with any real experience of caring for a chronically incapacitated person." Jamie nodded cautiously, as Richard continued. "During this month's departmental-board-meeting, we discussed a proposal put to us in a representation from a league of societies caring for chronically disabled people. Under their guidance, they invited us to participate more in the patient's physical care."

Jamie huffed a smile. "We've no medical or psychological expertise to administer in situations like that."

"No! No! Just let me finish. Like all similar companies, we have a long history of liaison with medics and carers. Not wishing to lay open old wounds again, you, in particular, have years of hands-on experience in the caring aspect." Richard knew he was touching on a sensitive point with Jamie, and would need to choose his words carefully. "What you and your family did, lifted Vicky's life considerably, and I know if she were here now, she'd want you to use that knowledge and expertise to help others. I may have been sceptical of the methods, and the course you and your family adopted, but we've not been gazing on blindly in our remote observations of what you've all achieved. The medical profession can testify to the intolerable pressures placed upon carers, and yet you shut yourself away now like a hermit— you're still a young man, Jamie."

Jamie smiled. "You're beginning to sound like my mother."

Richard conceded a grin. "I feel that, as incapacitated as she was, Vicky filled your life, as there seems no desire in you to enter into other relationships. It has raised the board's curiosity, wondering if you may have something to offer others like Vicky; on a purely platonic basis. This may sound mercenary, from the business point of view, but for us to get involved in this new project could expand our research programme; help us to generate new ideas that will lift the lives of these people even further."

Jamie gazed at Richard a little mystified. "We strive to do that anyway. It has always been part of our corporate manifesto to dedicate ourselves to researching new ideas for the chronically disabled. So where do you see us going from here, Richard, that would add to the services we already offer?"

"The board has asked me to suggest that you, Jamie, head a new department to develop ideas— what worked for you and Vicky, for example." They fell into silence as Jamie considered Richard's proposal; his suggestion, seeming to imply something more.

At length, Jamie looked up. "While using Vicky and me as an example in your profile, Richard, you've painted a very physical picture; the reality for us was quite different..." Richard made to speak, but Jamie gestured for him to let him finish. "... The spiritual solution, to which I believe you are referring, became a prominent part of our lives, and provided considerable comfort for Vicky over the years— and eventually, for me. In view of the current mood of the world, you know as well as I do how the spiritual aspect would be received generally."

A pained expression spread over Richard's face. "I know," he replied. "I'm way out of my depth on the spiritual subject."

Jamie sensed Richard's frustration from his deflated reply. "The essential question we need to ask ourselves here, Richard is, would people really accept it? Initially, my feelings for Vicky forced me to go along with her, as she seemed to gain a lot of hope from the spiritual solution. But I was as sceptical as you, and damned annoyed at my grandmother for filling her mind, with what I considered, was fictitious rubbish at the time. It wasn't until Vicky completely lost the coordination of her body that I realised what those beliefs were doing for her— that seemed a miracle in itself. It appeared to open up a whole new world to her, providing the means to accept life from within her crippled body. I don't know how, but I could sense the change in her the more she talked with my grandmother. It finally eroded my scepticism. But my over-all impression, to your suggestion, is that to embark on such a course commercially, might jeopardise the good name of the company."

Richard pondered Jamie's comments. "I know you're basically referring, again, to our past discussions. I admit then, there were times when I was unable to take you seriously. But over the years I've been privy to yours and Vicky's lives together; seen the difference it made to her for myself." Richard looked away, a little embarrassed over his confusion, and lack of understanding on the spiritual subject.

Their confidential discussion, though, was beginning to intrigue

Jamie. He doodled thoughtfully on a scrap of paper. "How could we go about persuading people, that the spiritual aspect provided a comforting solution, Richard? You can't force it on them. There are countless doctrines existing today, on this subject, which lie at the root of popular beliefs, and make people intransigent toward adopting new ideas."

Richard rose from his seat, offering Jamie a conjectured smile. "Well yes I know. That's why I'm going to leave it with you as a company minion to come up with some ideas."

Jamie gazed back at him; a sly grin breaking over his face. "Thought you might."

"Well, you and Vicky achieved it."

Jamie rubbed his chin thoughtfully. "See you for lunch. I'll give our discussion some consideration, but don't expect any miracles."

Richard nodded. "Thought miracles were common place with the spiritual solution." He grinned, disappearing behind the closing door.

Jamie sat quietly at his desk, contemplating Richard's proposal. The spiritual solution had worked for him and Vicky, but they had been given an insight into it by Emily. His grandmother had many years of experience behind her, and now, approaching her nineties, was becoming incapacitated herself. He felt unequal to her ability to withstand the ridicule she had endured in the past; the extent of her faith, rendering her impervious to opinions that questioned her presence of mind. But for commercial businesses to add a solution to their service, generally considered fictitious by the majority of the population, could lead to commercial suicide. He smiled thoughtfully down at his scribbled doodles. Richard had been shrewd indeed, in placing the buck with him.

During quiet moments, Jamie found himself deliberating on ways of how he could introduce the spiritual solution into the company manifesto. To simply tell people how much relief Vicky had gained from it, and the incentive it had given him to help her, seemed too much like a fantasy; but the fact remained, it had done just that.

⁂

Jamie's guides, Sarah and John sensed his scepticism, but they were unconcerned. From their perspective, it was all going to plan. Nothing was impossible for the spiritual solution; it only needed faith to believe in its existence and ability. Over the past few years, the change in Jamie's attitude toward life bore witness to the true value of Vicky's sacrifice. When Jamie finally encountered the disillusioned, stricken young soul, it would be at that point the minion would make its move; the true value of Jamie's resources, then, revealing their worth.

It had taken Jamie many years to rise above his bitterness over Vicky's predicament. Emily had been the rock on which their futures had been founded. When Jamie's moment arrived, he would be that rock. The purpose, for all he had learnt, would suddenly focus after his first meeting with that disabled young soul. The success of this quest would complete Jamie's first trial of this incarnation. There was no guarantee that the young soul would listen to him, but like Vicky, that soul's sacrifice was destined to offer similar opportunities to others, as Vicky's had.

***

~2~

A few weeks later, a memo arrived from Richard, asking Jamie to join him at a meeting. Run by one of the local disabled societies, the purpose of this inaugural meeting was to establish contact and discuss plans for the future. Jamie was nervous about it, as the theme of it focused on his and Vicky's story; and which had raised particular interest in the society's management committee.

The means to call in his grandmother, Emily was no longer an option, because of her great age. But in intimate discussions with her, he sensed her excitement for him. In this event, she at least saw the opportunity to turn peoples' attention toward the spiritual solution. Within the scope of her failing rationale she advised him, but the essence of her message came across clearly.

On the eve of the meeting, he sat in his study reflecting back over his life with Vicky. He pictured the eyes of those attending the meeting staring at him in anticipation. The beleaguered, overworked carers, with their despairing charges, undoubtedly hoped to hear new ideas that would lift all their lives. There seemed nothing tangible in the spiritual solution that would offer any real relief. How could he get across to them how it had worked for him and Vicky? Would his guides that Emily had spoken of, produce the rhetoric in him to get the message over?

He gazed down at his desk; the dim glow of the desk-light before him, diminished to shadows in the corners of the room.

He sat quietly, opening his mind to Vicky. "Give me the wisdom and the words to speak tomorrow, Dear One," he whispered. Sitting immersed in thought, he contemplated his request. It had been the first time he had deliberately made any attempt to ask help from those in the life beyond.

The silence crowded in on him, as he sensed a definite cooling in the air. The desk-light appeared to fade, dimming the furniture arrayed around the room, into shadowy outlines. The atmosphere took on a surreal mood that seemed to extend beyond the confines of the room. It was as if he had been transported to the edge of the world; sitting at his desk, gazing out into the infinity of space.

He felt a tingle of nervousness in his stomach; reluctant to look up and gaze around him. Gradually in the periphery of his vision, a soft blue light began to form on a chair in one of the corners of the room. He fought back his fear, drawing on all that Emily had taught him and Vicky on the subject of psychic presences.

The apparition began to intensify, taking the form of a human. Gradually he gazed toward the pool of light, and focused on the smiling face of Vicky looking at him. His heart leapt within, diminishing his fear of the supernatural, as a celebration of intense feeling welled up in him. For a moment, he just stared at her; the sparkle dancing in her eyes as before— she was just as he remembered her from their teenage years.

Suddenly, he heard her voice in his mind, vibrant and bubbly; like it had been when they had first met.

"Don't worry over what you will say at the meeting, My Heart," she began. "We will put the words into your mind. But now, this brief audience offers me the opportunity to thank you for the way you cared for me on the physical plane. It has given us a power beyond your imagination, and I am forever grateful to you, Dear One. I will never leave your side; just think my name and you'll sense my presence."

As the words faded, the apparition disappeared, leaving him gazing at the empty chair. The experience had touched him deeply, especially so, as it had been Vicky. All his fears had diminished during her presence; the visitation, representative of everything Emily had described to them about psychic phenomena.

He could hardly wait to tell Emily he had seen his Vicky: to have heard her voice was indescribable, feeling confident in relating the event to his grandmother, as she would understand. The objectives of the meeting had faded behind the euphoria of seeing Vicky, but it had achieved the determination in him to develop the resource Richard hoped for.

He turned off the desk-light and rose from his chair; the gloom, pierced by a thin shaft of light from the partially open study door. The eerie shadows created fantasies, seeming to enhance the psychic atmosphere; making him reflect back on the struggle Vicky endured in their short life together. He pondered again how she was just as he remembered her; young, lively and sparkly. There was no hint of the degenerative effects of the disease that had stricken her. This seemed, in essence, to be what he needed to get over to those suffering in similar fashion, confident he would now, with Vicky's help.

~3~

The next morning he was up at dawn. He had been awake most of the small hours, wrestling with rhetoric; imagining the type of dialogues he might find himself engaged in. Richard had arranged to pick him up around noon for a working lunch, allowing them adequate time to reach the meeting by two.

Feeling strangely calm and relaxed, despite his restless night, he gazed at his reflection in the bathroom mirror. He had given no thought on how the theme of this meeting should be approached; leaving it to Richard's suggestion that he would open it. But what had been even more extraordinary, was Richard's keenness to be present there at all.

As far as submitting to any belief in the spiritual world, his colleague, Richard had always been a rank outsider. For a while, Jamie had shared his beliefs, until Emily introduced him to the spiritual solution as Vicky's condition deteriorated. Now that this meeting had caused Vicky to reveal herself in all her spiritual glory; her visitation placed the purpose for it beyond doubt. There was no question of Jamie being persuaded the event was a figment of his imagination; all his physical senses refuted that now.

The more he contemplated the spiritual aspect, the more it seemed to present as fact. One of Emily's earlier statements had stopped him in his tracks. She had gazed at him with penetrating eyes, asking him to deliberate on the definition of the word 'inevitability', in the context

58

of their lives here; how it implied, everyone was destined to enter the world of spirit whether they liked it or not. Looking at it logically, there was no purpose in denying it.

It suddenly dawned on him that here was an irrefutable fact he could use— no one could avoid their future transition. To present this as a theme for discussion, might encourage people to view their beliefs realistically. But more than that, demonstrate how believing in the spiritual world revealed a continuation of life after the material existence.

Suddenly, the need for him to write long speeches seemed pointless. Was Vicky already filling his mind with what she wanted to get across? He would not dispute anything she wanted to say, as having experienced her transition; she could clearly see the purpose for the physical existence now.

Their whole plan had been revealed to them in the few years they had been together; the resources to complete it, materialising in ways they could never have imagined. The task facing them now was to convince others to follow their example. The means to enjoy life on the material plane was not guaranteed, nor was ones state of health. But everyone had an opportunity to make themselves a resource for others. Tomorrow, that chance would be offered to Jamie, as he related the story of the events involving Vicky, Emily and him up to Vicky's transition.

CHAPTER EIGHT
A FLIGHT INTO
THE SPIRIT WORLD

~1~

***

FROM THE SPIRITUAL DIMENSION, SARAH and John gazed on, cautiously optimistic over the success of the two young spirits. So far, Vicky and Jamie's plan was on course, despite the minion's constant attempts to influence them toward more devious aspects of life. Sarah and John were aware, however, that now Jamie was on his own, the task ahead for him would be a formidable one. But thanks to Vicky and Emily, he had the faith, and commitment, to help him achieve his objective.

Essentially, it was Jamie's mission to open the door to the spiritual world; demonstrate to those under sufferance, how to tune their minds to gain information from their guides. By teaching others how to use the mind as a conduit to liaise with those beyond, a stricken life could receive much comfort. By the end of his lifespan, it was hoped, that Jamie's revelations would have offered a new idea to many incapacitated souls, able to accept it on faith.

The evil minions were powerful entities; able to exploit the physical attributes weighing heavily in their favour. Through Jamie's and Vicky's level of faith, they had also given their spiritual mentors access to the physical plane. From beyond, their guides were able to provide the resources Vicky and Jamie needed to navigate the phases of their plan. Jamie's greatest advantage, however, was his awareness of Vicky in the life beyond, keeping him one step ahead of the minion and its followers. The minion's trump card, though, remained; undermining the ability of those, counselled by Jamie, to accept his revelations on faith.

***

Jamie gazed at the clock, and then out the kitchen window, as Richard's car drew into his drive. Strangely confident, he felt no sudden burst of nervousness; remaining relaxed about the approaching meeting. He swung the door open, greeting Richard: who stood beaming a smile back at him, poised in the throes of ringing the doorbell.

Richard grinned as he entered. "Ready to make history?" he muttered, gazing down at his watch. "I'm early, I know; we've got about three hours. Let's get off to lunch and discuss our strategy for the meeting." There seemed no hint of any concerns in Richard, that the ideas they were going to present might be viewed as fantasy.

Jamie picked up his belongings and locked up, following Richard to the car.

Richard paused with the key in the ignition, gazing up at Jamie. "You're very quiet, Mate. Not having second thoughts, are we?"

Jamie shook his head. "Quite the contrary, old chap." His nonchalant reply sent Richard off into copious descriptions of how he planned to open his address.

During the journey to the lunch venue, Jamie realised how serious Richard was on this event, listening to the topics he planned to use in his introduction. It confirmed again, from its theme; Richard's beliefs had undergone a dramatic change. Over lunch, Jamie was hardly able get a word in, as Richard rattled on with his plans for the future. Jamie sensed he would need to tone down some of Richard's ideas to add any sort of credibility to them, but it was encouraging to have someone so focused on his side.

En route to the meeting, Jamie tendered his own thoughts on some of the points raised in Richard's address. Any discreet criticism Jamie offered, raised an almost apologetic outburst from Richard; conceding the point without argument. Drawing up outside the society's offices, Richard leapt out the car, fumbling manically to extract the speech from his briefcase.

As they walked toward the entrance, Richard rested his hand on Jamie's arm, gazing pensively up at him. "When I agreed to this meeting, I may have been a little over-enthusiastic in my initial introduction, Jamie, but I've rationalised it, and know exactly what I'm going to say in my opening address." His statement raised an element of curiosity in Jamie. Jamie, however, felt confident that Richard would not have over-dramatised his and Vicky's story; running the risk of turning the meeting into a psychic fiasco.

~2~

They paused outside a door with 'Conference Room' in bold brass letters arrayed across it. Richard gently pushed it open, revealing carers sitting alongside their charges in wheelchairs. The atmosphere appeared relaxed, with the gentle buzz of conversation hanging in the air around them. A man and a woman had spotted their arrival, and were weaving their way through the wheelchairs toward them.

They smiled as they approached, stretching out their hands in greeting.

"Hi, Richard," uttered the man, turning toward the woman. "Let me introduce Sylvie Webber. She's our liaison officer. You're company has, no doubt, had dealings with her in the past." Richard nodded. "Aha!" exclaimed Dave. "So this is your medium friend, Jamie!" Jamie flashed a searching glance at Richard, who returned it rather sheepishly.

"Er...! Dave. This is Jamie Hoskins... Jamie, Dave Agar: The League of the Disabled Societies' chairman."

Jamie nodded, shaking hands with Dave, and then returned his searching gaze to Richard. "I think we need a quick chat before we get started, Richard," he muttered firmly.

"There's a room at the back where you can park your belongings." anticipated Dave. "We're all very curious to hear what you've got to say, Jamie."

Richard was visibly uncomfortable following Dave's *medium* comment, ducking Jamie's penetrating gazes.

Once inside the room, Jamie went for the jugular. "OK! So what've you said that's given them the idea I'm a practicing, spiritual medium, then?"

"Now calm down, Jamie..."

"Calm down, Richard? You know what they're all expecting out there now, don't you?"

Richard waved his hands manically in front of him; gesturing for calm. "Jamie..."

Jamie paced around the room, descending deeper into panic. "Richard you've dropped me right in it, and I trusted you when you said that I would only have to tell Vicky's and my story. Now I'll undoubtedly be expected to relay messages from uncle and aunty... what's-a-names— like in a one-to-one séance."

"Jamie, just give me a chance to sort it. Dave has made an erroneous assumption, that's all."

"I can't see any way out of it now, Richard," muttered Jamie, gazing frantically around the room. "Half the gathering out there are probably aware of it by now."

Richard gestured for calm again as he made his way toward the door. "Just leave it to me, Jamie: you'll see; I'll make it alright in my address."

As they entered the room, Dave and Sylvie had gathered the people together, and beckoned for Richard and Jamie to approach. While Richard made his address, Jamie gazed around at the souls in their wheelchairs. Past memories flooded back, suppressing his disillusioned feelings toward Richard. The distressing scene was a familiar one, having been a witness to Vicky's struggle against her illness. The distorted bodies, slumped in their wheelchairs, looked at him through eyes reflecting utter hopelessness; could his and Vicky's story possibly make a difference? He almost began to regret that he was not a medium, as his guides could tell their story better than him.

Richard continued with his address, correcting Dave's misguided assumption that Jamie was a medium. That, like them, Jamie had been alone with no knowledge or spiritual enlightenment to help him care for his young wife. He went on to describe how, over the years, a family member, with that knowledge, had revealed the spiritual solution.

As Richard's speech droned on, the focus was dropping away from Jamie. It settled him into thinking over what he was going to say. But as Richard continued, it occurred to Jamie; Richard was not leaving much meat on the bone for him. At length, after noting a few yawns in the audience, Jamie discreetly strolled forward and paused by Richard. Settling in a chair next to him, he subtly indicated his readiness to take over.

Richard gazed down, sensing, from Jamie's expression, that he should end his address. "Well I've rattled on enough," he concluded. "Now we'll hear it from the horse's mouth, so to speak."

~3~

A polite round of applause followed, with Richard acknowledging it as if he had just completed a rhetorical master-piece. Jamie smiled, watching Richard milk it for all it was worth. As Jamie sat there, a sudden strange feeling spontaneously swept over him. His face felt flushed and numb, sensing heat, with pins and needles spreading over it.

The unfamiliar sensation continued to intensify, raising insecure feelings in him. He began to panic, as his mind appeared to be disassociating itself from his body. He nervously clung onto his fading rationale, simultaneously curious over the weird happening: considering the morbid possibility that he was undergoing the onset of some bizarre, medical condition himself.

Suddenly, the uttered word, 'peace!' drifted into his mind. The solitary expression, impressed upon him Emily's past descriptions of the trance events she had experienced as a spiritual medium. How she had told him, that to succumb to fear, on those occasions, could terminate the trance procedure; realising a lost opportunity for that soul. One had to completely trust one's guides beyond, and so long as it was conducted with divine intentions, and for the good of others, there would be no risk involved.

A definitive sense of calm descended upon him, as he resigned himself to the event. The strange happening intensified, reaching a stage where he felt totally alienated from his body. It was not an unpleasant feeling; sensing a weightless, floating sensation. He gazed around at the faces looking on— their eyes transfixed toward where he stood.

He turned and looked at himself standing at the front addressing the gathering. His physical body had a strange, iridescent glow around it; like something was within him. He could see his mouth moving; as in the throes of speech, but perceiving no sound. Behind him were, Sylvie, Dave and Richard; their astonished faces portraying stunned expressions of amazement.

Turning his attention toward the main gathering he looked beyond them, making out the shimmering form of a woman standing alone. His spiritual mind, dominating now, instinctively enabled him to determine that she was Sarah— one of his spiritual guides. In that moment, he sensed the soul speaking through him was that of his other guide, John, her partner.

A celebration of sublime euphoria welled up in Jamie; reminding him of all that Emily had taught Vicky and him. This event had provided the physical proof that the true life was the world of spirit. That the realisation of this truth had resulted from faith and commitment, keyed to the beliefs he had submitted himself to on this physical plane.

Intuitively, Jamie knew that his guide, John, was narrating a dialogue of hope to the stressed-out carers, and their wheelchair-bound charges. How the sacrifice of suffering by some, offered others the opportunity to administer compassion. It was all part of the plan to achieve progress in the life beyond.

Gradually, Jamie sensed that his trance-address was drawing to an end, and gazed across at Sarah. She smiled as another figure began to materialise next to her. Jamie experienced a sublime burst of joy, as the unmistakeable, smiling face of Vicky gazed back at him. How he longed to be with her again; her absence, seeming to have made the task on the physical plane stretch away to infinity.

As the address closed, he sensed an inexorable power drawing him back into his body. His gaze fell upon a cord of pale light, appearing to attach him to it. Drifting back, he reflected over how there had been nothing surreal about what had taken place; everything was real.

As the process ended, he felt privileged to have experienced the event, intuitively feeling that this was going to be the first of many, in the future. Dave's earlier assumption that Jamie was a medium had now been confirmed; as much to his surprise, as to the others.

~4~

While Jamie recovered, he sensed, from the conversation around him, how the spontaneity of this event was the predominant topic under discussion. The blank expressions, on the faces of those in wheelchairs, could not conceal the sudden hope that had appeared in their eyes. Dave and Sylvie had been confused initially, but after conferring with Richard, understood that he and Jamie had also been taken by surprise.

Jamie found himself under siege with torrents of questions from the carers; eager to understand what they had witnessed. The whole event was clearly mapped out in Jamie's mind; answers to the questions, directed at him, coming spontaneously. The strange happening had not followed the usual criteria of trance mediumship; no one receiving personal information from past relatives that might offer proof of their presence.

The way in which Jamie had been taken over, supported by obvious changes in his manner, had placed the authenticity of this trance event beyond doubt. During the journey home, Richard was beside himself with excitement, describing how Jamie's trance experience had affected them all. He listened intently as Jamie related how he had stood outside his body; clearly able to see the effect the event was having on the group.

This, however, had not been the prime objective. The desire to offer a deeper spiritual solution had been the purpose behind the exercise. From the expression in the eyes of the stricken souls in their wheelchairs, Jamie had seen a glimmer of hope. But it was just the beginning. The questions hanging in the air now, asked; would their curiosity match his Vicky's courage? and whether they possessed similar courage to pursue the opportunities it could offer?

Jamie had a true ally in Richard. Suddenly touched by the events surrounding Jamie's and Vicky's lives, Richard's dedication to his job had gone far beyond the nuts and bolts of the practical aspects of it. He had been privileged to an insight into the world of spirit that he had never believed in all his life. He now felt himself to be part of Vicky's and Jamie's plan, offering an exciting future, not only for them, but also for the suffering, disabled souls.

***

From their celestial window, Sarah and John had made their own evaluation on what had taken place. Effectively, the spiritual values had to dominate; try to influence the physical aspects. The practical benefits this offered would help a soul complete their incarnation, and ultimately, reveal the importance of the spiritual solution before returning to the life beyond.

What was of prime importance then, was to exploit this knowledge.

The minion would, undoubtedly, encourage antagonistic, sceptical attitudes to undermine future successes of events like this. Vicky and Jamie had introduced an idea. That idea, suggested a possible means to explore the potential in people, where illness seemed to have taken them out of the arena. There was still much work to be done to maintain the idea's momentum, Vicky, Jamie and Richard had set in motion.

The miracle, Sarah and John were trying to achieve, pivoted on hard business attitudes going along with their plan. So long as their plan did not jeopardise the company's cash-flow or the integrity of its objectives, Richard's senior position would remain fluid. Through the efforts of those on the physical plane, the company would share the prestige for helping to fulfil lives struck down by terminally, incapacitating illness. Everyone needed to feel useful; no one knew this better than Vicky now. With the help of all their guides, and in tandem with Jamie's group on the physical plane, Vicky was determined to get this message over to them: Jamie's trance success had now increased the opportunity to achieve that.

***

CHAPTER NINE

A SAD ENCOUNTER

~1~

THE WEEK FOLLOWING THE MEETING, Richard continually frequented Jamie's office, using any excuse to raise a discussion on their psychic event. As the head of a new department, Jamie was expected to attend the monthly board meetings now. His first had been somewhat tense, realising how Richard's memos to the other board members, had been a little over-enthusiastic; colourfully describing what had taken place, during the meeting with The League of Disabled Societies.

As a witness to that event, Richard had sought to demonstrate the potential of how he felt this new idea might benefit the company. When first presenting his case, it raised an atmosphere of scepticism in the majority of the board. But after submitting a detailed report on responses, it intrigued them; settling some of their concerns on how they initially thought it might affect the business.

Having had the best part of two weeks to study, and consider the reports from Dave and Sylvie's meeting, Jamie and Richard knew it had set a precedent for any future ones. Jamie felt at ease with that now. One of the prime factors, which had helped to offset the fear of future trance recurrences, was the opportunity it gave him to see Vicky. In all consciousness, though, he was not going to allow this aspect to over-shadow what he instinctively knew to be the main purpose for the trance events. That resource was in place to provide guidance, and relief from the intolerable pressures, plaguing the lives of the disabled souls, and their carers.

There were, however, intransigent sceptics within the company, and Jamie found himself being indiscreetly scrutinised. Though he was impervious to their comments, it had convinced his grandmother, Emily, that he was being targeted by the darker influences. His parents, Sally and Carl, were also concerned, but not for Emily's reasons; more for the prestigious position they wanted him to build for himself in the company.

Jamie, however, was his own man; each day, seizing new opportunities that confirmed his direction in life. Reflecting on all his past experiences, it was obvious, that without Vicky's sacrifice, it was hard to imagine how their plan could have possibly got off the ground. But even in the light of that fact, without Emily's input, their plan could still have founded. The strategy, guiding Jamie in his life now was clear, fuelled daily by his belief that Vicky waited for him in the world beyond.

It was a bright, sunny morning that found Jamie making his way across the car-park toward the office entrance. A clatter of running feet behind caused him to pause and look back.

Richard uttered a breathless greeting, as he drew alongside him. "Hi! Jamie," he puffed. "Glad I caught you on the up; saves me sending you a memo later."

"Ah! Oh!" muttered Jamie suspiciously.

"Na! nothing like that, Mate. I've heard from Dave and Sylvie..."

"What! So soon?" queried Jamie, incredulously.

"It's almost a couple of weeks ago, Jamie. Now just listen. From the correspondence I've received to date, we made a big impact at that inaugural meeting, those present, asking us if we would make it a regular event..." Jamie made to comment. "... Now...! Before you start, Jamie, I've not committed us; merely telling them I would ask how you felt about the idea." Richard beamed an enthusiastic smile, anticipating Jamie's consent.

Jamie gazed at him thoughtfully; a teasing expression breaking over his face. "Well, Richie. I think I'm obliged to finish what you've started, then."

Richard huffed a smile. "Oh! Come on, Jamie. Be honest. You were taken with the event as much as I was. And what's more, Dave tells me that the word's gone out even further abroad, and that there'll be a few more present the next time— Sylvie's even suggested putting on a buffet"

Jamie grinned at Richard's enthusiasm. "Better put on my best bib and tucker then."

Richard sniggered at his patronizing reply. "Jamie! You're impossible. I'll see you later for lunch. I may have more details, and a few likely dates for the next meeting, by then." Still chuckling to himself, Richard peeled off and disappeared into his office.

~2~

The following weekend, Jamie popped into his mother's, greeting his father in passing; he, engaged on an errand for her.

Sally was pottering in the kitchen, preparing breakfast for Emily sitting out in the garden.

"Here! Make yourself useful, Jamie and take this out to your gran," she uttered.

Jamie took the tray, glancing out at his grandmother through the kitchen window. "You know I won't be back for at least an hour or so, don't you? Gran'll want a detailed account of everything I've been up to at work."

Sally grinned, shrugging her shoulders. "It'll be the highlight of her day, Jamie, as well you know."

Jamie gazed up in the sky, making his way across the lawn; it promising another warm summer's day. He pondered over how old and frail his grandmother looked, as she sat, dozing under the parasol.

Quietly resting the tray on the garden table, he gently shook her shoulder. "Hi, Gran!" he whispered.

The old lady opened her eyes, gazing up at him a little confused. "Jamie!" she muttered, with an expression of sudden recognition. "What a lovely surprise." She looked down and stared disdainfully at the tray of food resting on the table in front of her. "Your mother expects me to eat this, does she?"

"Come on now, Gran. What was it you used to say to me when I was a lad...?"

Emily gazed at him through narrowing eyes; a faint, knowing smile breaking over her face. "I know, Jamie. But when you're old and quaint like me, it's hard to generate an appetite."

"Well here's the deal, Gran. While you eat, I'll tell you what's going on with our new project at work." She grinned, wagging her finger in the air at his astute ultimatum.

He began reminding her of the events that had occurred at the inaugural meeting.

She stopped him immediately. "I've heard all that, Dear," she protested. "Haven't you got anything new to tell me?" Her sudden outburst revealed to him how her presence of mind still towered above her old age. "I'm not completely over the hill yet, Young Man." She started eating her breakfast with a relish that contradicted her previously declared lack of appetite.

He nodded, grinning at her perceptiveness. "From first impressions, Gran, it seems we've made a big impact..."

"Well, of course, I knew you would," she interrupted knowingly. " I always said..."

"Do you want to hear this or not, Gran?" he uttered, light-heartedly.

"She spontaneously reached out and put her hand on his, chuckling softly. "Just teasing, Dear. You know how I love to hear everything you're getting up to; especially when it's related to the beliefs we share."

Jamie described how the next gathering promised to be even more exciting. Those that had attended the first, seemed to be readily accepting the objectives of these meetings. But more encouraging than that, an exchange of opinions had substantiated the potential, of how it was hoped these gatherings would give purpose to the lives of all those involved. Leaving the practical aspects of communication and research to be dealt with by the company, Jamie and Richard were monitoring the responses to the spiritual solution.

The latter aspect was the more important factor, where if one managed to persuade people to achieve a real understanding in the life beyond, they would see for themselves how it offered lasting benefits.

Jamie chatted quietly, expanding further on his and Richard's plans for the future. How, everyday, Richard's born-again attitude was strengthening his own resolve. After a while, Jamie bent down and peered up at his inanimate grandmother; she was sound asleep. He sat there, gazing affectionately at her. What a wonderful old lady, he thought. He reflected how, in the beginning, it was her original counsel that had given purpose to his and Vicky's lives. And now, from that had grown the idea to offer that same solution to others.

He rose from his chair; a feeling of such love for her consuming him, as he gently kissed her forehead. He would miss her, as go she must when her time came. There was no hint of a doubt in him that she was spiritually prepared for her transition. After she had passed on, her staunch beliefs would stand as her legacy to them all. It amounted to a wealth of knowledge that was immeasurable in terms of the material aspect of life.

He sauntered thoughtfully across the lawn, pausing to turn for a last look at her, sleeping peacefully in the shade of the parasol. He sensed a desire to increase his visits. That feeling had not only been provoked by the necessity to exploit the time she had left in life; knowing his new-found psychic ability would provide future contact. It was more to offer her material comfort, as her physical constitution gradually began to fail.

He wandered into the kitchen, placing his grandmother's tray on the table.

Sally looked up. "How was she?" gazing at the empty plates on the tray. "I see you managed to persuade her to eat something."

Jamie nodded thoughtfully, turning to look back out the window at her. "Bless her heart," he whispered. "We'll all miss her."

"Oh! She's as tough as old boots," muttered Sally nonchalantly. "Yer Gran'll be around for a while yet."

Jamie gazed at his mother, dispassionately. "That's a rather unfeeling assumption to make, Mum."

Sally turned and looked at him searchingly. "It wasn't meant to sound the way it came out." She thoughtfully wiped her hands on the tea-cloth, offering him another cup of tea.

He shook his head. " No thanks. I've places to be, and things to do..." He paused. "I'm sorry if I seemed a little tense just then..."

Sally nodded understandingly. "Contrary to your beliefs, we love her too. Familiarity can sometimes breed contempt, but it's our ardent hope she'll be with us for a while yet."

Jamie smiled humbly. "Well, you'll be seeing a lot more of me, as I intend to make the most of the time she has left."

"Good," muttered Sally abruptly. "We'll start tomorrow— dinner for one?"

He gazed at the grin on her face, feeling boxed in by her shrewd, opportune invitation. "Yeah, alright," he nodded.

~3~

A week later, Richard dropped into Jamie's office, tossing a memo onto his desk. "Can't stop, Mate. Read it, and I'll see you later to discuss it over lunch." With that he disappeared out the door.

"Richard!" shouted Jamie, hurrying across the room, peering out the open door. "What..."

"Read it!" Bellowed Richard, disappearing into his office.

Jamie closed the door, vacantly gazing at the memo. He sat down at his desk, thoughtfully unfolding it. Dave and Sylvie had written down a series of dates, leaving it to him and Richard to liaise and choose one that suited them both.

As he read on, he noted the addition of a particular society caring for the chronically disabled; similar to the condition Vicky had suffered from. He contemplated on how it seemed Vicky had not wasted any time. He knew, from his experiences with Vicky, that these people had a real cross to bear. In the final stages of that disease, it was difficult to imagine how one could approach counselling anyone on how to meet such a challenge in life.

The plan involved trying to convince them they had something real to offer others. That despite their condition, there was a genuine part for them to play in society. His deliberations unnerved him a little. How could one realistically approach such a soul, when the person addressing them was enjoying a healthy, full life?

The paper crackled loudly as he thoughtfully folded it up. All the dates, listed, had suited him; more so because he had never developed any sort of social life. In the past, his daily routines had centred on Vicky's needs. Up until that inaugural meeting, he'd had no desire for any sort of socialising.

The day dragged on; his earlier deliberations continuingly intruding his thoughts. It had been touch and go with him; Vicky suddenly focusing on his bitter attitude, as their life together began to crumble around them. The theme of his thoughts reminded him of the complexities that existed in compromised lives, and those of the souls who cared for them. He considered he had been fortunate, as the few wonderful years he'd had with Vicky, secured the bond between them.

The more he contemplated the unknown future, the more the task he had set himself seemed to tower above him. That first meeting had made him the focal point. The subsequent communiqués, from

Dave and Sylvie, were filled with the curiosity and hope of all those who had attended. Inevitably, the next meeting would be different; he and Richard; also demonstrating the practical aspects that promoted opportunities for their company's part in the plan.

The next date had been set over lunch with Richard; in two week's time, Jamie's worst fears would either fade or be realised. If the spiritual solution eventually failed to be accepted, the whole plan would crumble, labelling him as an unfeeling eccentric who was leading the hopes of disabled lives into a world of fantasy.

There were no such feelings in Richard. Had the powers beyond, enlisted the services of another soul to assist Jamie? Richard could never replace Vicky, but his role each day was clearly supportive, like hers had been. With the meeting still two weeks away, Jamie focused himself on the practical aspects of his job; if nothing else, he could fall back on his managerial position in the company.

The leaps in technology were miniaturising the aids to increasingly, sophisticated levels. He deliberated again, on how his knowledge in the company's practical development might provide him with a way out. Each day it was graphically demonstrated how their achievements were offering sustainable relief to people.

As the meeting approached, Jamie's conflicting thoughts reached a climax; the over-powering feeling in him, asking— were these sudden doubts in the spiritual solution betraying Vicky's trust? He sensed he had gone too far with his plan: to abandon his quest, now, before it was rejected, could invoke the same reprisals, perhaps even more so, because of the deflated hopes of those under sufferance.

That evening, he waited in his study, anticipating a visitation from Vicky to bolster his flagging courage, but there were no familiar signs of a psychic presence. He suppressed his disappointment; the feeling persisting, it was down to him to overcome his personal inadequacies. His guides, and Vicky, had proved their presence, and how they were ready to help. It was theirs to manage the spiritual aspect, but his to do likewise on the physical plane. If he was unable to display confidence in what they were all trying to achieve, simply because the players on the material plane had changed, then the whole edifice what they were trying to build, could suddenly collapse around them.

In those thoughts, it dawned on him, that the issues worrying him were those his grandmother had lived with all her life. Was it possible, that such a frail old lady had demonstrated strength and leadership that was paling his into insignificance now? He knew, instinctively, it was confirmed everytime they spoke: that the purpose for her great age was to, perhaps, be there to set him on his destined path.

These few thoughts began to settle him. There seemed no need for any psychic presence now; another conflict within him had been suppressed. To contradict his assumption, the air cooled around him with Vicky appearing; smiling and nodding her head, as if to endorse his conclusion. No words were spoken. No words were needed; Jamie, aware of what was required of him, and more settled in himself to accept the direction he was being inclined towards.

~4~

The week, leading up to the second meeting, passed, filled with the boring aspects of business. Linked to these aspects was Jamie and Richard's spiritual solution; the company, the foundation on which all their future hopes were being built. While locked in his office, Richard was a business guru, managing the statistics, financial assets and resources of his company department. However, at the end of the day, the prospects of business were placed in folders and locked away in filing cabinets.

Richard stood up and stretched himself. This was the weekend he had waited for, impatient to meet the people who had showered so much acclaim on them. Clearing his mind of memos and meetings, Richard closed up his office and hurried out into the car-park. Even if Jamie had wanted to avoid him, it would have been impossible; Richard, as always, there waiting by his car.

Jamie smiled as he swung open the door. "D'you know. If you weren't there one day, I think I'd have to phone the police to report a missing person."

"Oh very droll," grinned Richard, resting his elbows on the roof of Jamie's car. "You know perfectly well why I'm waiting here, and in particular today— the auspicious weekend has arrived at last."

Jamie opened the car door and tossed his brief-case on the back seat, gazing back up at Richard. "What's the plan tomorrow, then?"

"Same routine as the last time, I thought." Richard stared at Jamie; a provocative grin breaking over his face.

"Thinking of your belly again, or is there something more devious going on in that scheming mind of yours, Richard, that warrants another discussion over lunch?"

"Well, I hoped *you'd* enlighten me on that." Jamie settled himself in the car, as Richard wandered around to peer in through the window.

"You know as well as I do, Richard, how we were all taken by surprise the last time." He thoughtfully slipped the key into the ignition. "I'm sure the team beyond have something planned. Until then, we'll just have to wait and see."

Richard nodded, smiling. "Not giving anything away, eh?"

"Nothing *to* give away." Jamie gazed out through the windscreen. "My plan is to follow their lead." He looked up at Richard. "But we musn't let our enthusiasm run away with us, and forget who we are doing this for."

Richard gazed back at him curiously. "The disabled, of course."

"True! We want them to benefit," smiled Jamie. "But let's not forget our Maker." Silence descended on Richard; the grin, slowly fading from his face as Jamie backed his car out. "See you tomorrow," gestured Jamie through the windscreen.

He looked in the mirror, aware of the penetrating gaze directed after him from Richard. A sly grin spread over Jamie's face as he turned for home. A little food for thought does no one any harm, he pondered.

The next morning, Richard was bright and early, but appeared a little reserved.

Jamie sensed the change in him, as they walked toward the car, attributing it to their parting dialogue the evening before.

"You OK! Richard? asked Jamie.

Richard gazed at him humbly. "I've been contemplating the meaning of your last comment yesterday evening in the car-park."

Jamie nodded; Richard's statement confirming it to be Jamie's acknowledgment of the Infinite One. "And!" There was no reply. "We need to respect the entities we are dealing with, Richard; ensure that when we open ourselves up to them, they're the right team."

Richard nodded slowly. "But what you said seemed so poignant." A thought dawned on him. "There's no sort of risk to us in what we're doing, Jamie... is there?"

Jamie smiled. "Not in the way or for the reasons we are doing it. I do, however, feel it's a token of respect to offer our thoughts and thanks, by acknowledging the team leader now and then." Jamie felt a warm feeling rise within for those few words. How Emily had drummed it into both him and Vicky, gifts from beyond should never be taken for granted.

~5~

As they pulled into the society's office complex car-park, the lack of parking spaces illustrated the increased interest, in their project, since the last meeting.

Dave suddenly appeared at the office entrance, waving them forward. "We've saved a place for you round the back."

"A few people have turned up, then," muttered Richard, gazing across to the packed, over-spill car-park.

Dave nodded. "Sylvie's in a bit of a quandary; she's had to rethink her buffet."

Jamie followed after Dave, while Richard parked.

Pausing outside a door, Dave beckoned him in. "This was the room you had last time. I'll leave you to settle in, as before, and see you later."

Alone in the room, Jamie felt a definitive presence; sensing all the familiar psychic characteristics near to hand. There was an overpowering feeling rising in him, that the events in this second meeting were going to go far beyond their first. From the brief exchanges, he'd had with Dave, he had learned that two chronically disabled members had been inspired by the last meeting; expressing the desire to write about their lives.

This news supported the practical aspects of his and Richard's plan, but revealed to him overall, how the spiritual solution was, perhaps, beginning to reach into the minds of some of those disabled. The carer's support would still be needed to deal with the physical aspects of a developing project, but the origin of the story would come from the active mind of their stricken soul.

This was just the beginning, thought Jamie. Would this be enough to produce the incentive to live a life compromised by disease? If companies like theirs embraced such minds and expanded their research into new areas; the possibilities seemed endless.

The door swung open, revealing Richard's expression of amazement. "There's not a square metre in that conference room that isn't occupied," he declared. "I suggest we mingle and chat with people for a while; suss out the general mood among them to confirm their hopes for these meetings." Jamie agreed that the idea made sense, but felt within that the team beyond wanted to have their say first. This, Jamie suggested, could provide the topics for discussion after.

As they walked out into the huge conference room, Richard's previous idea to mingle would have been impractical; wheelchairs and seats for the carers, tightly lined side on against one another.

Jamie leant over to Dave. "If this is going to be the norm, Dave, we'll need to rethink the venue," he whispered.

"It's already in hand," smiled Dave.

Settling into his seat, Jamie listened to Richard begin his address, simultaneously sensing the initial onset of the trance sensations. He smiled to himself, thinking how not a moment was going to be wasted by the team beyond. Though this event was only his second experience, he almost felt a veteran; letting his senses slip away as before— finally gazing at himself, waiting for Richard to complete his address.

~6~

As Richard finished, Jamie's guide began speaking, picking out souls in the audience to emphasise the points he wanted to get across. Jamie looked around the room, his gaze falling upon one particular crippled soul sitting alone in her wheelchair. He sensed an atmosphere of utter despair enshroud her; watching as two spirits materialised behind, impressing upon him, they were her guides.

He could sense there was no spiritual communication between them. The young soul, trapped in her physical world, had given up hope. More alarmingly, he sensed her intent to seize any opportunity to take her own life. Ancient religious doctrines expounded the folly of this. That life, given by the supreme entity governing the universe, was a gift in any shape or form. Whatever the cause or however useless it appeared on the physical plane, there was a purpose for it.

He sensed the challenge she offered. Intuitively, he felt this to be part of his quest, as without the sacrifice of souls like this, the opportunities to learn the essential truths in life would not be there. It was not his right to cast judgements on anyone, but if she could tell her story, it would undoubtedly benefit others. Clearly though, what would be the crowning achievement of her life, would be to simply live it.

The two spirits turned and smiled at him; the look in their eyes, seeming to endorse his meditation of thought. Lurking beyond them, he saw the faint outline of the minion sent to win the will of their young spirit. He gazed into its eyes, firmly transfixed on him. It would be so easy to generate hate for such an entity; its sole endeavour, to use any incarnate soul to access the physical plane, regardless of the misery inflicted.

His thoughts wandered to Emily, suddenly feeling a surge of confidence burst out through his soul. She was strong in spirit, and had sought to pass that attribute on to Vicky and him. Jamie gazed resolutely back at the hideous, contorted countenance of the minion: having sensed his thoughts, its expression appeared less confident. Jamie's determined spirit glowed brightly; he, Vicky and the team beyond, would do everything possible to prevent Gwen from falling under the influence of that minion.

Though these revelations in the spiritual dimension were occupying him, he was unable to suppress the physical aspects seeping back as he began to recover from the trance. His guide had concluded his address, leaving Jamie completely aware of its theme, as before. But still uppermost in his mind, was the plight of that incarnate spirit.

With people milling around him, he looked over toward where she was sitting. Still slumped in her wheelchair, by the door, she offered no interest in the event currently being enjoyed by her contemporaries. Her carer gazed inanimately ahead, seeming to have abandoned any attempt to communicate with her.

Jamie began to make his way toward them, acknowledging the occasional comment from those he passed. Suddenly, her gaze fell on him approaching. He paused, giving her the opportunity to decline his intended introduction. In a moment, she quickly manipulated her powered wheel-chair, and disappeared out the room. Her carer rose from her seat and made to go after her, pausing briefly by the open door to gaze back at him. She shook her head slowly before disappearing through it.

Jamie was not put off by this first failure, but sensed from beyond that he would have to be patient. Though that soul was chronically disabled, the astute mind within had demonstrated the ability to manage her wheel-chair confidently enough to avoid strangers. But, for the time being, common sense told him to leave it to the carer's counsel.

Merging back into the crowd, he was soon swamped with a torrent of questions curious about his trance ability. What was it like? How did one go about achieving it? Was there any danger to the host spirit? Later on, after the meeting had been closed, Sylvie joined him. "I saw your earlier approach toward little Gwen Davey."

"Unsuccessful approach to her," corrected Jamie.

Sylvie gazed toward the door, "There's a tragic history involved there. I hope you weren't discouraged."

Jamie shook his head briskly. "Oh no! I'm far from discouraged. If anything, more determined."

He went on to describe to Sylvie his hopes for the future, and she responded by filling him in on the details of Gwen's demise. The picture she gave him, described the most intimate of fears Vicky had experienced during the onset of her condition, and confirmed that he had, indeed, met another challenge in life.

CHAPTER TEN

A CLOSE CALL

~1~
***

JAMIE'S TRANCE ABILITY, WAS OFFERING Sarah and John a physical connection with the material plane. Essentially, this increased their ability to meet the dark influence on more equal terms. In the future, there would be many souls at different levels of evolution directed to Jamie, some, novice spirits like him. The lives of these souls were vulnerable, targeted by the minions and their supporters, searching for the opportunity to seize their wills.

To prepare Jamie to meet this, his early life reflected a stream of encounters that had strengthened his will. Now possessing direct contact with his team beyond, the minion shadowing him was finding it difficult to apply any influence over his physical mind.

From the spiritual perspective, support from the team beyond was expanding at an increasing rate. Each incarnate soul, involved in Jamie's plan, had two guides. The accumulating focus of power, this meant, would be insurmountable. However, on the material plane, certain conditions needed to be present to release that power.

With Jamie's increasing knowledge, he was learning how to apply his will to help others. The trance events shared this knowledge with others, but to benefit from it, souls like Gwen would have to accept their situation; open up a liaison with the world beyond as Vicky had done. Sarah and John knew Jamie's determination to help any stricken soul was only half the battle, as the choice of direction in a life, whether right or wrong, was down to the incarnate soul.

The way ahead for Gwen seemed set to teeter over the precipice of failure, as she would come close in succeeding to her wish to end her life. The feelings were running high in those beyond; following their charges acting out the drama taking place below.

Led by Sarah and John above, they watched their incarnate spirit, Jamie, conceive a plan he hoped would help Gwen achieve a successful, physical incarnation. It was of no consolation to him; knowing that if Gwen succeeded in prematurely ending her life, there would be no affect on his spiritual progression. Benevolence, however, was an essential attribute to be learnt on the physical plane. Jamie had already demonstrated his humility after losing Vicky. The opportunity presenting now, with Gwen, was providing the means for him to achieve compassion.

***

During the week following the second meeting, it was agreed, by all parties, to repeat them every two months. Dave and Sylvie had moved the venue to a large, local community centre, with parking facilities to match. Attached to Dave's letter to Richard, Sylvie had slipped in an envelope addressed to Jamie. Richard, of course, was bursting with curiosity when he popped into Jamie's office to deliver it.

He gazed at Jamie, smiling provocatively. "You're a fast worker. What's going on between you and Sylvie then, Mate?"

Jamie tossed his eyes up to the ceiling, tutting at Richard's indiscreet innuendo. "Don't read anything into this. It only relates to the brief conversation Sylvie and I had about one of her disabled clients."

"Maybe, but don't throw any opportunities away, Jamie. Sylvie's quite a dish. I'm sure Vicky wouldn't begrudge..."

"Bye! Richie," interrupted Jamie, impatiently waving him toward the door. "Anyway. How d'you know she's not already attached?"

Richard grinned. "Aha! A glimmer of interest I believe?" Jamie picked up a file and made to throw it at him. "Alright! Alright! I'm going! See you for lunch. You can fill me in on any juicy details then." Richard disappeared out the door, leaving Jamie cogitating over his pushy remarks.

Richard's thought began to intrude in on him as he sat there. He conceded that it would not contravene any marital or doctrinal laws, if he were to take another partner. What made it difficult to explain to anyone, even to his intimate family, was that what forbade it was the extent of the bond that had existed between Vicky and him. He contemplated the possibility of someone having designs on his affections; it made him nervous, especially gazing at the unopened letter from Sylvie. He slipped the paper-knife along the envelope. 'Strictly business,' he muttered to himself. 'Strictly business'.

~2~

The theme of Sylvie's letter briefly related Gwen's story, but suggested they discuss it over dinner one evening in more detail. He pledged to himself that Richard would not know about this until after the discussion had taken place. The letter was informative, business-like and to the point, with no reference to any personal aspiration.

Jamie, during lunch with Richard later, frustrated his persistent attempts to extract the letter's content from him, he, finally concluding Jamie's evasiveness as some sort of confirmation of his affectionate intent. Jamie rose from the table, gazing down at him. "I'm not totally void of sensitivity or humour, when it comes to romanticising and sharing a joke. But Sylvie's letter airs concern for one of her charges, and hopes we'll be able to do something to help prevent a potential tragedy there."

The smile drained from Richard's face, gazing at the stern expression on Jamie's. "Whe...When did you learn about all this?"

"The last meeting. You were too busy feeding your ego with responses from all your doting fans." Jamie smiled to relieve any tension generated by his comments.

"But... I... No! Jamie?" spluttered Richard. "Everyone knows the focus was on..." He paused, gazing at the vague look of amusement breaking over Jamie's face. "*Touché*," muttered Richard, concedingly. "Very cute, I'm sure." He gazed up at Jamie. "Point taken..., but I'm still interested to know how you make out there, and even more curious over how Sylvie plans to use our project for this case."

"I'm not sure she knows herself, but she'll keep us informed. From my first experiences, it promises to be a monumental task to gain the confidence of this young woman. I shall know more about the reasons, why, after I've met with Sylvie;" Jamie, muttering it was in the lap of the gods, as they ambled out the canteen together.

Back in his office, Jamie read Sylvie's letter again; the date and time for the dinner-meeting, she had left to him. He was not going to waste a moment. Picking up the phone, he arranged to meet her the following evening. The humorous moment, shared with Richard previously, faded from his mind; preoccupied now with an image of the despairing Gwen Davey.

He reflected over how the majority, at that last meeting, had two or three caring relatives around them, but Gwen, only a single carer. There were several possible reasons. Gwen's intransigence against accepting help from anyone, even close family or some form of deranged, mental affliction. If the latter, it could render any future help he might offer, inappropriate.

~3~

During their dinner, Sylvie's story revealed the heart-rending account of a young life, which appeared to have had no chance from the beginning. Gwen had lost both her parents in her early teenage and then, shortly after, succumbing to a rapid onset of the disease. An elderly aunt had undertaken the responsibility for her initially, but had, soon after, become incapacitated herself.

What was believed to have contributed to Gwen's bitterness, leant toward the absence of the caring, intimate family environment. Gazing toward an unproductive, empty, lonely future, there seemed no incentive to carry on. Several attempts to end her life had been prevented, but she viewed these acts to have impinged on her rights; an interference that was unjustly prolonging her agony.

During Jamie's meeting with Sylvie, they discussed many new communication devices that were coming available for chronically disabled people. Though it was Sylvie's job to liaise with companies that provided medicinal and mechanical resources for the disabled, she was curious to learn more about his and Richard's new ideas. Despite Gwen's reluctance to face life, Sylvie felt she came across as an intelligent young woman, possessing an astute mind that was capable of achievement with the right support.

On the whole, the evening had gone well. Sylvie had convinced Jamie she was taking what he and Richard were offering, seriously. As had been Jamie's experience, during the past, the spiritual solution was always being used as a last resort. The authenticity of his psychic ability had remained unquestioned; undoubtedly, courtesy of the

84

team beyond, with few doubters coming forward from the first two meetings.

The initial phase, to help Gwen, would be to use future meetings to simply try and get through to her. It was Sylvie's hope, that where all the physical strategies had failed, the spiritual solution would find an access through into Gwen's world. The next meeting was still a few weeks away; Jamie, Richard and Sylvie, using the time to sift through all the feed-back from the first two.

In his office, and at home, Jamie found his mind constantly wandering back to Gwen. How dreadful it must be, he thought, to be trapped in an unresponsive body; no family contact to reach out to for comfort. The familiar feeling of Vicky around him, endorsed his thoughts, sensing him that all was going to be well— he just needed to be patient.

It was some weeks later, reading a communiqué from Dave and Sylvie, he learned that Gwen had made another attempt on her life; it came as a bolt of lightening out of the blue. As he read on, the event shared an affinity with a story his grandmother told him had happened while he was a baby. At the time, he had viewed his grandmother's psychic views as being unrealistically surreal.

During his infancy, a great friend of his parents had suffered fatal injuries in a car crash. With Emily's experience and spiritual understanding, the discussions she'd had with his mother and father, Emily believed their friend had experienced a near-death event. The dialogue in Dave and Sylvie's communiqué was describing how, like his parent's friend, a strange change in Gwen's personality had taken place. It set Jamie wondering over the possibility; had something similar occurred to Gwen?

***

Gazing down from the celestial window, Sarah and John knew of special circumstances existing, which Jamie was unaware of on the physical plane. The magnanimity of the Infinite One allowed two conditions for direct interference from the spiritual dimension. When the sources of darkness clearly had an unfair advantage or a proven spirit was to play an important supportive role.

Gwen's medical history certainly satisfied the first. It differed, however, from the friend of Jamie's parents. Gwen's life, up to the present, had few connections with any real experiences that could have influenced her. However, there was more to Gwen's incarnation, which those around her on the physical plane were aware of. Sarah and John knew she was a proven soul of immense age. Called upon by the Infinite One to support Jamie in his first incarnation, her assignment, was to create an opportunity that would help him to achieve his life's plan.

The nature of her mission was by no means unique on the universal material planes. Without the sacrifices of these knowledgeable spirits, the opportunities, for novice souls to learn, would never become available. In the years ahead, Jamie's trance ability would gradually focus him on this truth; but it would not mean he had been privileged. The ability to liaise directly with those beyond, had been achieved by applying his faith.

If Gwen succeeded in taking her own life, the implications of this were clear. The true purpose for her existence would be revealed after the transitions of all those, whose lives had been touched by her. On the physical plane, her disabled condition clearly displayed her physical need. It was the relentless agony of her suffering, then, people had to address to benefit from her sacrifice.

On Jamie's return to the spiritual dimension, another disclosure would surprise him. Richard, the friend that had suddenly become so supportive, was a proven spirit similarly placed. Richard's apparent scepticism had offered Jamie the opportunity to confirm his faith. Like Gwen's, Richard's spiritual existence stretched far back into the mists of time.

During their voyage to infinity, there had been several incarnations for both Gwen, Richard and their partners. Having earned their positions in the Infinite One's kingdom, there was one final task that He asked of them. It was to make the ultimate sacrifice, and briefly return to the lower physical planes to help others achieve entry to His divine world.

The enactment of those two proven souls, to play out their roles, had to be convincing. The portrayal of ignorance, joy or misery in their lives was real; their reactions to situations confronting them, affecting their future in that world, similarly. There was a long way to go for Jamie to achieve that level of success in his incarnate periods. As a result of his and Vicky's first endeavour, they had gone a considerable way toward building up a sound knowledge, and where, as proven souls, their experience would offer similar help to others.

Unaware of the full truth of this plan, learning of Gwen's continued attempts to end her life had unsettled him. From his brief trance excursion into the spiritual dimension, and the laws he was unable to fully appreciate governed those there, he felt it imperative, to somehow, break into her world and help her. Gwen's recent near-death experience had appraised her of Jamie's current level of success. Once back on the physical plane, this knowledge was suppressed, but had made her a little more responsive toward his desire to help her.

Sarah and John, however, were well pleased with the ongoing success of Jamie's plan. Increasingly revealed to him, with each fleeting, trance-visit made into the spiritual dimension, his increasing achievement added to his determination. Though the minion had not been slow in seizing the opportunity to exploit Gwen's disadvantage, the governing protocols in the spiritual world were stringently observed. Across the multi-dimensional universe, the Infinite One remained unchallenged. When an incarnate soul followed his directives, his protection for that soul was assured.

✻✻✻

CHAPTER ELEVEN

ENDEAVOUR GWEN

~1~

It had mystified Jamie, initially, how Gwen managed the attempts on her life. Her condition, at the stage Vicky's had been, should have prevented her from doing anything for herself. Sylvie's explanation revealed how new technology placed opportunities in her hands. In the beginning, there had been a steady decline in Gwen's capability. Her astute mind rationalised what the future held, and realised that she needed to seize the chance to end it while she still had some capability.

The soul endeavour for her carer then, was to keep her from self-harming herself. In reality, Gwen, totally succumbing to the disease, had gone some way toward relieving the pressure on her carer. This morbid scenario, whether viewed fortuitously or not, was short-lived with the development of powered ambulant devices. Carefully planning her last suicide attempt, she had cast herself into a river; almost drowning; but was rescued by a passer by.

Jamie gazed at Sylvie's report. The administering authority's conclusion had necessitated the decision to place Gwen in care, deeming her subsequent change in attitude as a ploy to mask future attempts on her life. It was an intolerable situation. Gwen now, was not only a prisoner in her body, but had lost any modicum of freedom she'd had.

Cases like Gwen's, were fuelling growing arguments, within the chronically disabled populous, focusing on a person's right to end their life. There were two main opinions, though, which were clear. From the law's perspective, it was currently viewed as a criminal act for any person to assist another to end their life, irrespective of whether or not it was based on compassionate grounds. From the religious viewpoint, individual doctrines were fairly diverse, but the majority decreed, the sanctity of life should be preserved.

Jamie found himself delving deeper into the aspects of euthanasia. One fundamental thought dominated and prompted the question; who was responsible for the origin of life? If the answer to this question rested upon the individual, then clearly each soul could exercise the right to terminate their existence. From ancient ecclesiastical doctrines, however, an intransigent principle existed that viewed suicide as a cardinal sin.

The beliefs that had been indoctrinated into Jamie revealed life as a gift from the Infinite One, and there to be shared with others: that all aspects of it were part of the challenge in the physical existence. It was inconceivable to Jamie, that the suicide solution should even have been discussed between Vicky and him. Though he was unable to share her physical suffering, he had eventually blended his life into hers; providing a purpose for her to struggle on. But more importantly by achieving this, he had helped to focus her away from her suffering— fulfilling both their lives.

Jamie's dedication to Vicky, honoured one of the principles the Infinite One intended should govern life on the physical planes; it contradicted the idea that Gwen had no one. This principle stated that humanity had an obligation to share, not only the material wealth of a world, among its people, but also their lives. Essentially, the compassionate decisions, made by the governing body for Gwen's future, had failed to address her innermost needs.

Jamie contemplated the possible directions his life could have taken, had he not chosen Vicky. Though he knew their lives to be part of a plan now, it never ceased to amaze him how it had all come to fruition. Pondering these few thoughts, confirmed the impact an individual life could have on another. If Vicky had chosen the decision to terminate her life, for reasons of fear or neglect, the opportunities, she was destined to offer him, would have passed on with her. It raised such a feeling within, when realising now, how their choice would enhance their future reunion in the dimension beyond.

Meditating on these thoughts, he sensed the beginning of a

strategy that might help Gwen. As each experience came to fruition, his plan was becoming clearer. With Vicky in the spiritual dimension, and him on the physical plane, between them, they possessed the complete answer. The events of Gwen's recent demise, had complicated the issue a little for her, but with Sylvie, Dave and Richard's help, the way ahead did not appear insurmountable now.

~2~

These revelations, in Jamie, were in effect what his guide, John, had focused on during his trance addresses. It was Jamie's objective now to apply them to the physical aspects of their spiritual solution on the material plane. The trance events, of the first two meetings, were gradually being referred to as séances; the theme of those events, appearing to give them a little credibility. As a result of his personal experiences, with Emily and Vicky, he was convinced the spiritual solution was the complete answer, not only for Gwen, but for humanity in general.

Jamie thoughtfully closed up Sylvie's report. She had assured him, that Gwen would have sufficiently recovered to attend the next meeting. Still the best part of two weeks away, it gave him space to plan. Ultimately, it was up to Gwen. She had gone some way toward convincing Sylvie and Dave she'd had a change of heart, but the governing authority dispensing her care, viewed it suspiciously. They held the one ace card; possessing the legal backing to prosecute anyone, who helped someone like Gwen, to end their life.

Two weeks later, it was an intrepid Jamie that joined Richard for the next meeting. Quietly contemplating what lay ahead, he ignored Richard's usual patter of conversation during the journey.

Richard fleeted a glance at Jamie as he drew into the huge community centre's car park. "What's the theme of the trance going to be today then?"

Jamie grinned at his relentless requests for trance previews. "Who says there's going to be any trance...?" Richard made no reply; leering a frustrated smile at him. "... It's up to them." continued Jamie, gazing around at the packed car park, "I'm sure they'll not disappoint anyone. But my mind's focused on our young Gwen— if she's here."

Dave met them at the entrance, welcoming them to the new venue. "I thought this place would be big enough, but it might be we'll have to think again, if we attract many more people."

For a moment, Jamie was lost to the conversation, scanning the rows of people in wheel-chairs with their carers.

Spotting Sylvie talking to Gwen's carer, he placed his hand on Richard's arm. "Will you two excuse me for a few minutes. I need to break a little ice." He smiled at the confused looks on their faces as he walked away.

He made his way through the crowd, pausing to acknowledge greetings offered to him. The nearer he approached Sylvie's group, the more his gaze focused on Gwen; it proving impossible for him to suppress a sudden eruption of nerves. Earlier, he had pledged to contain his feelings, pausing a few metres before them to compose himself.

He gazed around. It seemed that everyone's eyes were focused on him; his mind, a complete blank. What unsettled him more, was he had learned that some observers from the carers authority had been invited to this particular meeting; Jamie, assuming pessimistically, most would be sceptical.

He let his hands drop to his sides, and walked toward the group. Suddenly, he felt the soft sensation of a hand close around his. He looked down, but there was nothing there. The touch intensified; the nervousness, draining out of him like water down the plughole in a sink. Vicky's voice, softly speaking in his mind, was all it needed to restore his courage.

Sylvie smiled as he approached. Bending over Gwen, she introduced him. "This is Jamie, Gwen," she said softly. There was no response from Gwen, but like Vicky's had done in the past, her eyes, spoke to him in a language of their own. He looked up at Sylvie; she anticipated him. "She can hear what you say, Jamie."

Gazing down at Gwen, her eyes impressed him with the question, where do we go from here?

"Indeed," he muttered softly, "where *do* we go from here, Gwen?" He stood up and smiled at her. The ice, he had symbolised as the barrier standing between them, had been broken. He gently rested his hand on hers. "Let's hear what the team beyond have to say, and then we'll try to understand what's happening in our lives." He walked away, pausing briefly to look back; her gaze, still transfixed on him.

Richard's opening address faded, as Jamie went into trance. The familiar scene of astonished faces had now mellowed to acceptance, listening to Jamie's guide speaking. Instinctively, he knew the message was for everyone, but a dialogue he would be able to expand on with Gwen.

Jamie felt his confidence building, contemplating the success of these first few meetings in such a short space of time. Watching from his perch in the celestial realm, he became aware of several shapes materialising above the gathering. It amazed him to see how the spiritual team had expanded. Simply by joining with others on the physical plane, it had increased the spiritual aspect ten fold.

The group smiled, and sensed him with their delight and good wishes at his continuing success. Everywhere was saturated in light, save one dark smudge; instinctively he knew what lay behind. It unnerved him to picture the entities, waiting for him to falter in his quest. He felt, that to deliberate on such thoughts was not a complete waste of their precious time; serving to keep them constantly aware of the minions' presence, and intent.

Recovering from his trance, he sensed the audience's curiosity over what they had heard. Gazing out over the gathering, he felt the extent of the communal atmosphere that had grown from these few meetings; the stricken ones, with carers alike, joined together, irrespective of physical ability. He knew this was the true power of the spiritual solution.

He eventually made his way back to Sylvie and Gwen's carer, finding them tucking into the buffet provided, with Gwen's carer pausing occasionally to feed Gwen her specially prepared meal.

He took the plate offered to him, smiling curiously at Sylvie. "I can't imagine how you've managed to cater for so many people, Sylvie."

She grinned. "Just one word— volunteers!" He nodded concedingly; her reply, highlighting his belief— to unite, is to achieve.

~**3**~

To help Gwen, he would have to establish a means to communicate with her. Body language was out of the question. On the technological horizon, computer software development was demonstrating new, exciting solutions. Intuitively, he felt this aspect would be difficult for Gwen to master; now in the final stages of ALS.

If he was completely honest with himself, he had few ideas on how he was going to progress with Gwen. She was at the stage, where life had become meaningless. If she had been a creature of the world, the only humane option would be to end it painlessly. He felt Gwen was his guinea pig; he, searching for a solution to help her complete her life, and one that would set a precedent for others in the future. This was not the time to let himself succumb to doubts; answers to problems had mysteriously manifested during the past. Viewing it from the practical perspective, he was just a cog in the machine of life, and duty-bound— to simply keep turning.

Over the weeks ahead, Jamie continued to develop his friendship with Gwen. Sylvie gazed on, advising him on the methods they used to communicate and respond with their charges. But Jamie intuitively felt there had to be another way. Over the years, he had spent many hours in discussion with Emily, delving deeper into the spiritual solution. How were methods of communication achieved, then applied when there was no physical ability. Her replies always seemed unrealistic; requiring a discipline to train the use of the mind that appeared to border on fantasy.

Using him and Vicky, as an example, she made him reflect back over their lives together. When communication between them eventually was lost, he began to sense Vicky's needs through his mind. He had always thought this to be as the result of the intimacy, and familiarity that had grown between them. Emily's reply had been emphatic, describing how that assumption was precisely the cause, which kept the majority of human relationships isolated in those situations.

The need to consider it again had never arisen after Vicky's transition, until Richard's new project, but the whole concept of probing minds seemed intrusive. He'd had no secrets from Vicky, unconcerned at the prospect of her accessing his mind— after all, they were man and wife. But Emily got around that angle by using the intimacy existing within a family circle as an example. She compared it to ancient doctrines, describing humanity as being one huge brotherhood, with minds morally disciplined to higher planes of thought.

It amazed him; she seemed to have an answer ready for all his queries— everything was possible when applied to the spiritual solution. 'There was so much to learn,' he had said to her one day. 'What shall I do when you're gone?' She had replied, gazing at him with an expression of amazement. 'You! A trance medium; asking me that?'

He smiled to himself as he sauntered down the road, turning into the tree-lined drive of Gwen's home. The beautifully kept gardens filled the air with scent, raising the thought in him, that to lose one's liberty to a place like this could have its compensation. The air was still; the fleeting glimpses of sunlight through the canopy of leaves above, cast shimmering, mosaic patterns of light on the ground as he walked.

Rounding a bend, he broke out on the long approach toward the great house. Standing as a witness to an era of indulgence for the privileged few; in contrast to the poverty and deprivation of the poorer classes, it now served the needs of those who had succumbed to life's infirm challenges. In these modern times, it had raised countless debates in him over whether such extravagance, today, really served the needs of its inmates efficiently. On days like this, however, no one could begrudge the comfort it offered to those struck down by debilitating, terminal illness.

Halfway down the approach-road, he spotted Gwen in her wheelchair; her carer, sitting behind crocheting. He paused to focus on Gwen, who just sat there, gazing at a bird gliding above her on the wing. In that moment, he imagined the yearning in her was to be as free as that bird. It conjured up the feeling in him of how he felt life to be so cruel; displaying to Gwen all that it appeared to have cheated her of.

For a while he stood there, simply looking up at that bird, gradually sensing it's freedom. It was as if he was remotely sharing the sensations it was experiencing. But there was something more about the moment that intrigued him; was that remote feeling, coming from the bird, affecting Gwen similarly? He felt the question rising in him; had Emily been right again? If he could develop all that she had said was possible with the mind, and Gwen, similarly, the communication aspect could be resolved.

The solution seemed too simple, as he set off toward them. Suddenly, as if to confirm his thoughts, Gwen turned her wheel chair to face him; seeming to have sensed his presence. It set his mind wandering on how the general consensus of opinion, in the medical profession, agreed, that lost functions in parts of the human body generated enhancements in other areas. It had always amazed him to deliberate on how nature's backup systems were so resourceful.

He sent out mental greetings to her, but there was no response. He remained undaunted, pledging to persevere with this as an experiment each time he visited her. He felt it better to keep this idea to himself, initially; not out of any risk of future embarrassment to him, but more to establish a criterion to pass onto others should it succeed.

***

Jamie's guides, Sarah and John, were the source of his inspiration, and which would be confirmed in the future, as each aspect of it manifested to reality. This next phase of Jamie's quest, would gradually raise an awareness in him, of how there was much more to the physical life than what was understood.

The human form was a mass of flesh and bone; a sophisticated bio-machine, whose wonders were beyond mortal ability to replicate. In the tangle of vessels, neurones and matter, which made up the brain, there was a link to the world of spirit; this was the real driving force that could influence the physical life.

In that amazing, neurological complex; a conflict of conscience governed a soul's material decisions. The promise of what waited there offered a symbolic key that could unlock the means to succeed, both in the physical life, and the one beyond. This short period on the physical plane was so precious; only a soul's continued ignorance, and denial of the spiritual solution, deprived them of the real benefits that could lead them to true happiness.

As Jamie's experience, and trance liaisons with those beyond increased, his ability to achieve life's essential attributes was limitless. It was through liaisons, like those, that the more stricken aspects of humanity could be suppressed, and realise the true potential of each soul on the physical planes. When Jamie finally managed to break into Gwen's world, Sarah and John were confident; that moment would begin to reveal her potential.

***

CHAPTER TWELVE

A TRIAL OF MINDS

~1~

THE AFTERNOON PASSED PLEASANTLY ENOUGH; Gwen seemingly a little more attentive to the comments directed at her. Since Jamie had arrived on the scene, she had undergone an uncanny change of mood. From that day on, whenever Jamie found himself in her presence, he sensed intermittent, intrusive thoughts probing the periphery of his mind.

During every meeting, Gwen's eyes constantly searched his. Initially, it unnerved him; aware of an atmosphere that almost bordered on the occult. But it never impressed him with any evil tendency, more the intention in Gwen to seize this opportunity to try and break out of her physiological prison.

As the weeks passed, Sylvie gazed on silently, watching Jamie gradually gain Gwen's trust. Sylvie had approached this new concept of spirituality for invalidity support cautiously, suppressing her earlier sceptical concerns. Now that some benefits appeared to be manifesting, the decision she had made to try out this new idea seemed justified, especially in view of the feed-back they were receiving.

The meetings were now taking place at regular intervals; Jamie's trance address, the high-light of each event. It was several months after, following his introduction to Gwen, that Jamie found her increasingly occupying a large portion of his time. Sylvie monitored the situation with growing concern, as there appeared to be a clear sign of Gwen's growing attachment to Jamie. This sign was not indicative of any physical desire, but leant more to the secure family aspect Gwen had been deprived of in her younger years.

Catching sight of Jamie, enjoying a rare moment alone, Sylvie raised her concerns with him.

"The transformation in Gwen, Jamie, has been phenomenal, but it worries me to see her so focused on your presence." She paused, searching for the words to describe her fears. "She lives one day to the next, and only emerges from out of her shell when you're around."

Jamie smiled. "You think she is forming an attachment to me then?"

"I don't know what to think, Jamie. I believe what I fear most, is that we might lose all we've gained by misreading these people's responses to the opportunities we're trying to generate for them."

"I don't feel there's anything to concern ourselves over..." Sylvie went to comment, but Jamie smiled; raising his hands in a gesture to continue. "...Just consider the logistics of our existence here, Sylvie. These are intelligent people, whose lives have been compromised by their disability. We are trying to introduce a new concept into their world that requires mental discipline. They are learning how they can apply their minds and draw on the immense resource that is waiting there."

Sylvie stared at him with a confused expression. "You must be patient with me, Jamie. Sometimes I know you're right in what you say, but on other occasions, I cannot suppress the sense of fantasy in what we're doing; this feeling constantly dogs me. We are asking people to believe in an existence that has, for centuries, been considered a figment of the imagination."

"What else is there for them in life, Sylvie? I don't tender that question lightly or suggest the solution we are offering is an alternative. Nor do I imply that what we're doing will totally liberate them from their suffering. We are enjoying a freedom these stricken souls can only dream of; essentially, I want to find a way to share that freedom with them.

It is difficult for me to describe what it's like living with someone totally disabled; subjecting them to the daily humiliation of having everything done for them. But if I was given the choice to spend that period of my life with my wife, Vicky, again, I would jump at it. She gave me such a feeling of fulfilment. The physical relationship we enjoyed, led us into a complete, spiritual union."

"I'm not dismissing what you've said, Jamie, but in my present understanding of your objectives, my concerns are for Gwen's feelings"

Jamie nodded. "Then it's similar to the feelings I also experienced in my early years. It is what I have come to believe this life is for; to learn about what really matters. If Gwen wants to form an attachment to me, then I, for one, will respond. There's no physical or emotional risk here, just the need to be there for them. We can't guarantee success with any soul, as the first move has to come from them. However, when that move is made, there's no time for doubts in us."

Sylvie smiled sheepishly. "What you've said, today, has humbled me. It focuses me on my lack of understanding of what you're really trying to achieve here."

Jamie grinned. "It's as I said...; no time for doubts. You've made yourself part of the team, and one who has willingly played out their part since joining us— no one can do this alone, Sylvie."

She gazed at him, thoughtfully. "Vicky was indeed, a lucky girl."

"Your statement leads me to the very point I'm trying to make, Sylvie. Both Vicky and I were lucky; reaching an understanding that went beyond the bounds of our physical relationship. The subsequent spiritual bond, which manifested between us, helped to off-set the restrictions Vicky's condition placed on our lives." Jamie gazed intently at Sylvie. "My hope is that if it worked for Vicky and me— why shouldn't it do so for others? Richard and I, as individuals, may have conceived an idea, but it will need a united, physical and spiritual effort to bring it to fruition."

A modest smile broke over Sylvie's face. "I am learning little by little. I begin to see the practical benefits when applying your spiritual solution."

~2~

Leaving Sylvie cogitating over their brief discussion, Jamie made his way across the room to join Gwen and her carer. Settled beside Gwen's wheelchair, he began to appraise her on what he had been up to since their last meeting. Suddenly, as clear as if someone was standing next to him, a soft clear voice spoke in his mind. Instinctively he looked up at the carer as the source, finding her still immersed in her crocheting.

He turned back to Gwen; her eyes transfixed on him. The soft voice spoke again, asking for a response. He was confused and yet curious; having to convince himself that he had heard something. Around him, the buzz of conversation merged into an indecipherable jumble of words. He gazed into Gwen's eyes— still transfixed on him.

"I know you can hear what I'm saying, Jamie." The statement stunned him, seeming to confirm that he could be experiencing some form of mental contact with Gwen.

The spontaneity of this event had caught him off guard. Even though his plan was to develop extra-sensory use of the mind, what now seemed to have become its sudden reality— surprised him. Had Gwen overcome the despair induced by her condition? Suppressed her bitterness, which now seemed to have transformed her desire to accept any form of help?

Resulting from the trance demonstrations, during his meetings, the general feedback was gradually conceding to his belief in the presence of some form of life beyond. However, the level of faith that was necessary for anyone to receive knowledge from that source, and then apply it to any practical use, was still an issue that varied among individuals.

In reality, Jamie's initial introduction, to spirituality, had been an uphill struggle for him. Possessing a deeper understanding of the spiritual infrastructure now, Emily had taught him why individuals had to learn for themselves, and how it was his task to simply present his case. Out of the blue Gwen had suddenly committed herself; it had revealed an extraordinary turn of events. From a point in life, where she had been determined to end it, she was now showing the desire to become an active part of their team: to Jamie, it was another indication that the spiritual solution was working.

What seemed to have occurred today, contradicted the meaning of impossibility for Gwen. It had mutated to the questions of, what had they learned, and how could they develop this technique in the future? He smiled; a blend of excitement and confusion over which way to go next— Gwen, appearing to have taken the lead. The spontaneity of the event had loosely confirmed the possibilities for his thought transference idea. It had produced some exciting evidence for him, which, if substantiated in the future, could lead physically handicapped souls into active roles: helping him develop techniques that corresponded to his spiritual solution.

In the context of what they had been trying to accomplish, Gwen had suddenly become the teacher. Even at this initial stage, Jamie viewed the event as a gigantic leap forward. Though the brief responses, he'd had from Gwen earlier, seemed inconclusive, they needed to be reviewed carefully. In anything remotely connected with the spiritual aspect, one had to seize the initiative quickly; strategically assess the impact it could have on others before declaring it.

What Jamie needed to consider now, was the best way forward to develop, and how to apply the technique. Did one simply form sentences as thoughts, and then project them? It had all happened so unexpectedly. The questions confused him, seeming to force him back behind the familiar, communication barrier that enshrouded people like Gwen.

"It is more simple than you think, Jamie."

Her spontaneous statement, again, appeared to confirm that she had read his thoughts. The voice had come across confidently, seeming to have already gone some way toward releasing Gwen from her isolation; whatever resources were required, appeared to be in place. Instinctively, he felt the ability to develop this gift was, again, tied to spiritual belief. This raised the age-old stumbling block that posed the question; would others realistically accept it on faith, enough to develop it? As with everything spiritual, there would be no proof offered to anyone; the first move having to come from the individual.

~3~

Reflecting back over Jamie's life, what seemed even more incredible; was how all the prophecies his grandmother had made, were coming to fruition,. During earlier years, Emily's spiritual beliefs had been hard to accept on faith, now, having learnt to liaise with his guides beyond: was he being led toward applying those same beliefs to physically communicate with stricken people like Gwen? More intriguingly, were there mysterious resources, locked up in the dormant part of the brain, somehow keyed to the spiritual dimension?

Each day was a revelation to Jamie, producing some new aspect that was helping him to soften hard attitudes toward the spiritual solution. It brought on an irrepressible feeling that his plan went much deeper than he had realised. He meditated on these thoughts; Gwen's eyes searching his. Her sudden achievement had more than met him halfway, and she was now expecting him to reciprocate. He reflected over the logistics of what had taken place, considering again, was it to simply generate what they wanted to say in the mind, and then physically focus on the recipient?

"It is as easy as that, Jamie;" the soft clear voice, drifting into his mind.

There were a myriad of questions welling up in him from this event— would his grandmother have the answers to them?

"Do you need answers now, Jamie?" queried the voice.

If Gwen was sensing his thoughts, then her question implied a logic his confusion had distanced him from. The accuracy and spontaneity of the responses, he was sensing, were going beyond coincidence. Despite the fact the exploration of this type of communication was currently under research in various scientific faculties; the implications, and sudden degree of success in their experiment, had encouraged him to pursue it.

For the moment, he decided to remain silent on their achievement, at least until they'd had time to evaluate the true extent of what had taken place. One aspect was clear, though; Gwen's input, in spite of her disability, had been on an equal footing to his. This thought, towered above all others; implying there could be equal opportunities for everyone possessing faith in the spiritual solution.

The future now offered the opportunity to develop this technique for others, and with a soul's commitment, go some way toward proving there was a potential role for everyone in society. Richard and Sylvie had their suspicions that Gwen and Jamie had been working on some joint venture, and though intrigued; suppressed their curiosity. As the months passed, that memorable day was to remain as a landmark for Gwen and Jamie. Working together, they became more fluent, proving the technique to be within reach. The next step was to encourage others first, to develop their beliefs in what the spiritual solution offered, second, generate the faith they had in it to achieve what Jamie and Gwen had.

~4~
***

In the spiritual dimension, Sarah and John were well aware of where human limitations lay. To apply any aspect of the spiritual solution, an individual had to accept the existence of the world beyond unequivocally; this would always prove to be the governing factor. Jamie, counselled and guided by Emily during the past, was now applying that knowledge to help lift Gwen out of her despair. Gwen's acceptance of the spiritual solution was leading her to an understanding, which, effectively, was giving some aspects of her life back to her.

From these thoughts, John knew that the extent of Jamie's and Gwen's success would remain with them, the fundamental reason, again, spiralling down to the demand for proof. This constant need for proof was the barrier raised when seeking solutions that required an adherence to faith. To the onlooker; extra sensory techniques appeared surreal, as no one could see into the minds of people like Gwen or Jamie. For Gwen to openly confirm the success of their experiment, any recipients needed to develop their minds similarly.

The Infinite One's laws governing the universe were unrelenting— there were no short-cuts. Even though Sarah and John had access to the material plane through Jamie, a soul's free-will still governed the outcome. In the complexity of the mind, this confrontation between the spiritual and physical disciplines came face to face. It was when the dark influence entered the equation the creation of a conflicting triangle complicated the issues, stacking the odds against spiritual mentors like Sarah and John. There was no alternative. They had to trust in Jamie's capability to use the wisdom they had instilled into him; try to increase his knowledge of the spiritual solution. The faith, however, to draw on the power of the Infinite One required a commitment only Jamie could apply.

Gazing across Jamie's celestial horizon displayed his and Vicky's current progress on their voyage to infinity; the future still remained a daunting prospect, as Sarah and John had expected. With several physical planes still ahead of Jamie and Vicky, the assignment for the two spiritual mentors seemed, at times, insurmountable, even when viewed from the security of the spiritual dimension.

Though Jamie's and Vicky's plan was on course, it was imperative that Sarah and John maintained their vigilance and periodic assessments. As long as Jamie continued to use the spiritual resources offered to him, the bond between them all would keep their plan secure, and on course.

The evil minion scanned the rest of Jamie's years on this physical plane, as in the future a new challenge loomed. Faced with many compromised souls, tormented by the trauma of chronic disease, the desire to end their lives would continue to hold the sanctity of life in question. John sensed that Jamie's present following would be infiltrated by those agonising over resentful feelings toward his spiritual solution— an ironic re-enactment of the bitterness he had felt himself during his early years with Vicky.

To Sarah and John, in possession of the truth, the answer required to address the question of voluntary euthanasia was clear. On the physical plane, the only tool offered to Jamie was the story of an historical Divine Life. It fell to him to define the reason why that Divine Soul chose to endure untold agony, rather than use his power to end his suffering.

***

CHAPTER THIRTEEN

THE REVELATION

~1~

When Jamie finally revealed the extent of his and Gwen's mental communication success to Sylvie and Richard, the news was received coolly— it suppressed his feelings of achievement a little. He had expected sceptical responses from those new to their ideas, but not those established in them. It had to be conceded though, that Gwen's vacant expression offered no clues to what she was thinking, and therefore no visible proof to substantiate their claims: coupled with the fact, there were always going to be issues with experiments that involved development of mental ability.

A week later, the topic was raised again between Richard and Jamie in his office. Richard had popped in to discuss a job he had passed on to Jamie.

With the business concluded, he gazed at Jamie ruefully. "I'm sorry, Jamie, if Sylvie and I seemed a little reserved in our response to your project with Gwen— there was no offence meant" he pleaded.

Jamie continued to browse the file he was holding, and then looked up; grinning at him. "Yours and Sylvie's prerogative, and no offence was taken." Jamie let the file slip through his hands onto the desk, and gazed thoughtfully at Richard.

Feeling a little uncomfortable, Richard posed the question. "How is it possible to convince others there has been any level of success, Jamie, in mental communication with someone who cannot physically respond? It was different with your trance events, as..."

"How do you see it, then?" interrupted Jamie abruptly.

The question hung in the air as Richard, suddenly taken aback by Jamie's curt reply, stared back at him.

"Well... It seems... Well one feels intuitively that..."

Jamie stopped him short, feeling a little slighted by his statement. "You astonish me, Richard. After all we've achieved, and now to suddenly produce doubts at this stage. Past experience should've made us all aware: that the criterion governing the spiritual solution offers no physical proof. To state otherwise to those willing to open their minds, is to perjure the truth. Achieving any modicum of success requires absolute honesty, in what we're doing, and unquestionable faith."

Richard gazed at him, a little confused, feeling his dedication to the project had been questioned following Jamie's brief lecture.

"Let me make my point more clearly then, Jamie. Contrary to your current opinion, there's no question of any doubts in me, but you have to concede, surely, that when we started this project, we planned to apply logic to our methods: try to explore ways that offered some small aspect of credibility to support what we are offering."

Jamie sensed a prickly meaning in Richard's reply, feeling that his implied 'lack of faith' in Richard, had been presumptuous.

"OK then! So what is your point, Richard?"

"Well," began Richard. "Using Gwen as an example, it has dawned on me that only a few months earlier she was set on ending it all. Now suddenly, something has motivated her, which is plain enough for us all to see. It has already raised some curiosity in our community meetings, which prompted me to put the question to you today. Could this motivation be viewed as a form of testimony; attributing it to the project you and Gwen have applied yourselves to?"

Jamie stroked his chin thoughtfully. "I'm sorry, Richard. My attitude must have appeared a little assuming just then... Let me think on it a while, and I'll get back to you later."

Richard rose from his chair and paused by the door, casually resting against the frame. "I agree we have to err on the side of caution, while seizing all the opportunities we can, but we must consider the impact our projects will have on those we present them to...." Richard smiled artificially as he disappeared.

Jamie doodled thoughtfully on his notepad, contemplating the essence of their brief discussion. It was unlike him to have come across so overpowering. To view aspects of life rationally was an essential part of his work. It was not that he felt his attitude to have been reprehensible, but was he developing a too singular approach to their spiritual solution? They had all joked over Emily's fire and brimstone way of applying her spirituality, but his criticism of the spiritual movement during the early stages of Vicky's illness had made Emily rethink the intensity of her beliefs.

~2~

A communiqué from Sylvie, a few days later, notified him that a group of chronically invalided people were planning to attend the next meeting. The note was fairly brief, but Sylvie, aware of the mood of the group, sensed there was more to their intentions than the note revealed. Richard had also received a similar communiqué, and wandered along to Jamie's office to discuss it.

Pushing the door ajar, he peered in, finding Jamie gazing despondently at the huge stack of files teetering precariously in his in-tray. "Hi, Mate— got time for a chat?"

Jamie rubbed his eyes and squinted at Richard. Nodding thoughtfully, he closed a file; dumping it into the out-tray. "Only another thirty to go," he muttered gloomily.

Richard grinned as he pulled up a chair. "Well it's coffee time anyway now; I passed Connie's trolley a few doors down along the corridor, she'll be along soon." He pulled a slip of paper from his pocket, waving it in the air at Jamie. "What do you make of Sylvie's communiqué then?"

"Not really had time to study it," He thoughtfully juggled his pen through his fingers gazing at Richard. "Should we make anything of it?"

"Aha! In one of our reticent moods today are we?"

Jamie smiled, nodding toward the pile of work waiting in the tray on his desk. "Well, wouldn't you be?"

Richard tipped his head concedingly. "Yeah! Know what you mean. Anyway, forget that for the moment. I've been doing a little research on the group who are going to join us at the next meeting. There's nothing sinister, but it seems we are going to meet up with some pretty firm ideas, and attitudes, on the subject of our spiritual solution."

Jamie nodded slowly. "Did you think our project was always going to be a bed of roses for us then— everyone agreeing with the solution we're offering them?"

"Well... No... Not really, but it's as well to keep ahead of the opposition, so to speak. How do *you* think we should approach it then? "

"We don't."

"Jamie, you're talking in riddles again. We can't just stand there staring at each other all evening."

"Richard, old friend, we don't force anything on anyone; let them come to us... in effect that is precisely what they are doing..., isn't it?"

Richard thought for a moment, an enlightened expression dawning over his face. "Yes... I suppose it is." He slowly shook his head. "A comprehensive understanding of what our spiritual solution entails, still evades me."

"I wouldn't go so far as to say that, Richard; I find your approach positive— couldn't do without your support now."

Jamie's statement visibly lifted Richard's mood as a knock rapped on the door.

Richard spun around on his chair, greeting the tea lady, Connie peering in around the door. "Two coffees, Connie; heavy on the cream and sugar for me, and just cream... for Jamie?" Richard gestured the question at Jamie, who nodded.

Connie placed the cups on the desk, and then disappeared out the door.

Jamie thoughtfully stirred his coffee. "Now where were we, Richard; ah yes! Let me see if I can set your mind at rest over this approaching meeting. What do you believe is going to happen there?"

"I would imagine we're going to meet a few resolute people... indignant, perhaps, over us pushing ecclesiastic values at them, in our project, while we enjoy healthy lives."

"...And," continued Jamie, "some who'll probably derive a little satisfaction in telling us to mind our own business, as we have no real idea of the extent of their suffering. If that should turn out to be the case, we cannot argue with that." Jamie raised his cup to his lips and paused; seeming to meditate on whether to take a sip. "However, Richard I think our strategy, for the time being, should be to just listen. Try and ascertain their mood, and reason over their desires to end their lives. What appears to make matters more difficult for us, is the fact, the law supports our endeavours to preserve life; that ice-cool directive, inflaming attitudes. Ultimately, it falls to us to convince those, set on ending their lives, that they have a role to play in life, and then try to persuade them what that role is."

~3~

The days leading up to the next meeting, found Jamie reluctant to draw on the advice he had offered Richard. Similarly, if Dave and Sylvie had any reservations on this next meeting, they had not mentioned it in their communiqués. To add to Jamie's predicament, there was a current dispute raging over the news, discussing the rights of stricken people to humanely end their suffering; the advice from beyond, however, remained emphatically against it.

The evening before the meeting, Jamie sat alone in his study. It had been on a similar occasion that Vicky had appeared to him; settling his concerns for the first meeting. After an uneventful hour, the silence seemed to preclude any repeat of that event. He went to rise from his chair, as Gwen's voice spoke in his mind.

"Jamie! I sense your restlessness this evening; it's so uncharacteristic of you."

He sank back down into his chair. "We've never been faced with such determined attitudes like we will be tomorrow, Gwen."

"That isn't quite true, is it Jamie? Just think about it for a moment."

Her statement mutated his concerns to curiosity. "I don't understand what you're leading up to, Gwen."

"Jamie! Don't I count for anything? If we're honest with each other, my situation was as dire as some of those we'll meet tomorrow: perhaps even more so, because of my repeated attempts to take my own life. If it wasn't for you and your group, we might not be having this conversation now"

Jamie considered her point. One of the sole purposes, of his group, was for them to offer practical help to chronically, seriously ill people. The reality had reached the stage, now, where Gwen was counselling *him* on how to address bitter attitudes, arising from stricken people like her.

"You're perfectly right, Gwen. You put me to shame, but the obvious isn't always evident to us."

"It thrills me, Jamie, to think of a future possibility that I may be able to talk intimately with those close to me; to share moments of fear for comfort. Be able to confide in others, and feel I have a vested interest now, and an obligation to help you convince people of how your spiritual solution opened up my life."

Jamie was touched by Gwen's thoughts, sensing his thanks to her. Their mental exchange had been brief, with its content, providing relevant aspects that had answered many of his concerns. The dialogue prompted him to reflect back over the past, and how it had seemed Gwen would never respond to their group. The solution, however, was not theirs alone. A contributing factor had been Gwen's near death experience. It was partly due to that insight, which finally helped to persuade her to rethink her attitude toward life.

Instinctively, Jamie felt her experience had been a special case of divine intervention. It was unrealistic to assume such a dramatic event was a mandatory part of every soul's solution, but, effectively, it had given him a partner on the inside.

As he sat there, the familiar cooling in the air around him heralded a spiritual presence. In the chair opposite, a pool of hazy, blue light began to materialise, taking the shape of Vicky, smiling at him. He sensed the purpose for the visit instantly; her presence, endorsing the theme of what had passed between Gwen and him that evening.

This visitation had been another spontaneous event induced by his mentors. It clarified an issue that implied, there was no question of judging how other souls chose to manage their lives. The instinct, the Infinite One embedded in every spirit, reminded an incarnate individual of their responsibility to Him: a responsibility to become aware of the historic story of a Divine Soul's life-span, on their world. Jamie's group, having accomplished a spiritual understanding, it fell to those like them to share that information. Simply by adhering to the Infinite One's plan, they honoured the covenant that existed between each soul and Him.

~**4**~

Early the next morning, it was a blurry eyed Jamie that squinted sleepily at his alarm clock sounding off. It was far into the night before he had got off to sleep; his mind, generating a myriad of fantasies on the dialogues he might find himself engaged in at the meeting later.

Staring at his reflection in the bathroom mirror, he concluded, it would need a minor miracle to achieve anything presentable in his appearance. After shaving and showering, his mind started to come together, and he sat down to breakfast; occasionally gazing out the window for Richard's car.

Their plan today was to relax and discuss a strategy on how best to approach the new group. He felt their introductions would present no problem; the crunch coming when they introduced their spiritual solution, addressing those intent on lobbying for voluntary euthanasia.

Having been confident and enlightened earlier, on how the subject of their spiritual solution should be broached, there was a distinct lack of ideas in Richard now. Clearing away the breakfast things, the sound of the newspaper dropping on the door-mat sent him out to retrieve it. The usual depressing headlines confirmed the continuing, downward trend to immorality: the theme of events, described in the daily articles, similar— only the names of the offenders changing.

Jamie sipped at his tea, morbidly wondering why he bothered to buy a newspaper. However, one had to keep track of events in the world: it served no purpose to bury one's head in the sand like an ostrich. He contemplated how the unrest, going on around them, was hard enough to bear for anyone enjoying good health. When shut up inside an unresponsive shell of a body, it could enhance the sense of misery ten fold. This was just one factor, which fuelled the intent in anyone to get out of it, let alone those suffering chronic illness.

A shadow flashed across the table from the kitchen window, followed by the door chime sounding off. That will probably be Richard he thought, rising from his chair.

Swinging the door open revealed Richard's beaming smile. "Hi, Jamie," he uttered cheerfully. "Really looking forward to this meeting," He wiped his feet and hung up his coat, as Jamie closed the door behind him.

Jamie grinned, ushering him towards the kitchen. "Seeing it from the spiritual perspective at last, eh?" His remark referring to Richard's mood in the office earlier in the week, seeming to contradict his statement now. Jamie placed the kettle on the hob, pondering his own nonchalant mood; sensing him with irony over the feelings that had dogged him throughout the night.

Richard drew up a chair. "It wasn't that my faith in our work had faltered, Jamie, as you seem to imply...," pleaded Richard. "... more about seeking methods that could add a little credibility to our objectives. The issues we may face now are far more complicated, as we're up against resolute attitudes; convinced of their rights to do as they wish with their lives..."

"Which is the truth of the matter," smiled Jamie.

Richard shrugged in a gesture to concede the point. "As I see it, Jamie" he continued. "There appears to be only one option open to us, and one we must think carefully about how to present."

A brief silence ensued, as Jamie became intrigued. "Go on then." he mumbled curiously.

"I believe we've no choice but to base our approach on the doctrines endorsed by historic deeds, demonstrated during the life of our Divine soul, centuries ago." Richard sounded a little unconvinced; talking about an entity, whose existence he had given little thought to for most of his life.

Jamie felt a little deflated over the proposal, sensing, from Richard's statement, he was really seeking confirmation from him for the idea. Essentially, Richard's solution risked employing all the old symbolic euphemisms from the past. Though gems of truth, when viewed in the climate of modern-day life, their values came across as surreal.

In the reality of their situation, Jamie wanted to find a practical way into the minds of these people; try to discuss the issues in life, logically. This had worked with Gwen, but only after she had made the first move. The historic, Divine soul, who had lived centuries before, had provided a template for everyone to follow; the story of the appalling abuse he endured, during his brief life-span, standing the test of time.

Over the centuries, his decision to benignly accept his persecution had raised curiosity among people; leading them to reason over the underlying knowledge he drew on throughout his life. To believe in the doctrine he taught required complete faith. In today's moral climate, Jamie hoped logic might moderate people's desire for proof, leading them to answer the questions that historic being's life raised in them for themselves.

Jamie and Richard became embroiled in their discussion; gradually developing a strategy on how they could logically, and credibly present their case. Relating it to the needs of those in their group, they began focusing on a solution that asked them to consider fundamental aspects of that Divine soul's teachings, linking it to modern-day conditions. There were two basic categories that illustrated the difference between chronic disability: those that were hereditary, and those self-induced.

From the practical perspective, there was no difference between the levels of suffering— what separated the conditions was their onset. Jamie and Richard were learning that an irrevocable, physical deterioration, inherent from birth, seemed to lean toward a soul's sacrifice on the physical plane. It was gradually revealing a partnership with the Infinite One that provided the means for others to learn His truth. In essence, these souls were the unsung heroes and heroines of humanity, offering valuable opportunities to their fellow beings to learn the Infinite One's truth.

For those afflicted by misfortune, while engaged on life's challenges, it simply illustrated the ever present risks, on the material plane, if one exceeded the limits of their endeavours. From the care perspective, the doctrine taught by that Divine soul ignored the cause, asking people like Jamie to care and counsel everyone under sufferance regardless.

The real message, that was gaining momentum, focused on a covenant each soul had made with the Infinite One before entering the material existence. If one looked at life logically, one perceived fleeting opportunities in it that could touch a soul during its period of incarnation. Just like that Divine soul, whatever spiritual strategy was deployed by one in their incarnate period, there was a price to be paid.

In the absence of spiritual knowledge, the compromising disabilities that befell people, on the physical plane, appeared insurmountable. It was then the covenant with the Infinite One came into being, asking those souls enjoying freedom in life, to show compassion and share some of that time to help others. Increasingly from his trance experiences, Jamie had not only witnessed the true benefits this meant for people like Vicky and Gwen, but how it increased everyone's chances to successfully complete their voyage to infinity.

***

Sarah and John were steadily revealing more intimate purposes for the physical life to Jamie. Under their guidance, it was falling to him, and his group, to pass on that information in as credible a way as possible. Jamie, because of his relationship with Vicky, had reached the stage now where he would always respond to stricken people like

Gwen. His success, however, ran deeper than that, arising from a sound, responsible, family environment, which had been generated by those who had overseen his entry into the world. Jamie's choice, to have finally listened to that small voice within, had diverted him from a life of misery and self-pity. His reward now, was the privilege of sensing the joy of people, like Gwen, at being able to participate in his venture despite their disability.

***

CHAPTER FOURTEEN

TO LIVE OR NOT TO LIVE

~1~

BELIEVING THEY WERE BETTER PREPARED for the new group now, following their recent discussion, Jamie and Richard made their way to the meeting's venue. During the journey, they found themselves immersed in a tense atmosphere; their minds, continuing to fantasise over the response they thought awaited them.

Richard broke the silence first as they pulled into the car-park. "Why do I get the idea we're attending our own execution?"

"Bit dramatic, isn't it?" muttered Jamie. "Thought you said you were looking forward to this meeting?" Jamie gazed at him, feigning a smile.

"And you believed that?" grinned Richard sheepishly.

Jamie thoughtfully peered out through the windscreen. "Somehow I don't think it's going to be as bad as we're imagining it will be." He looked across at Richard. "Think about it. What's the worst scenario? Telling us we're a bunch of hypocrites... stop interfering with people's lives?" Jamie shook his head slowly. "Those who feel that way probably won't even bother to turn up."

"Unless they want a good moan," suggested Richard pessimistically.

Jamie continued to gaze vacantly out over the car-park. "Throughout history, whenever people have tried to help one another, there's always been a downside to some aspect of it." As if Richard's negative remark had just registered, he turned and stared at him. "Why are you being so frustrating today, Richard?"

Richard avoided the question, by pointing to Sylvie and Dave waiting at the front entrance.

Jamie wagged his finger at Richard. "Don't think you've heard the last of this, Ole Friend," he smiled, closing the car door.

As they walked toward the entrance, Dave disappeared within, leaving Sylvie to welcome them.

"Nice day to get roasted," stated Richard cynically.

Sylvie looked curiously at him, and then at Jamie.

"Take no notice of him, Sylvie," muttered Jamie, venturing in through the doors.

As they walked, Sylvie briefed them. "Contrary to what we all expected, there seems to be a very tranquil atmosphere within." She paused, thoughtfully gazing down the corridor. "There are, however, two severely disabled young people there, and who I think may prove to be too much for our spiritual solution."

It heartened Jamie and Richard to hear Sylvie so positively committed; now personally expressing herself as part of their project.

"Is Gwen there?" asked Jamie.

"Of course I am;" the prompt reply drifting into his mind.

Sylvie grinned. "There's no need for me to answer that, is there, Jamie?"

All three paused outside the door. Despite their previous discussion to psych themselves up for the meeting, it was a pensive Jamie and Richard that followed Sylvie into the hall.

Many familiar faces sprang into view as Jamie gazed over the gathering, settling on Gwen next her carer.

"You know what we have to do, Gwen?" focusing his thoughts on her."

Her response was instant. "I'm always ready to do whatever I can to help, Jamie."

"Good! We'll talk later, Gwen."

Jamie and Richard made their way through the crowds, acknowledging old friends, until they suddenly found themselves approaching the new group. The carers seemed a little reserved, undoubtedly conscious of the ongoing discussions, debating the rights of their charges to legalise compassionate euthanasia.

Gazing over the group, Jamie focused on a young man and woman at the front— the message in their eyes appeared forbidding and determined.

Sylvie gently rested her hand on his sleeve, inclining him toward them. "This is Emma and Joshua, Jamie." She smiled hesitantly as she made her introduction. "They've recently come under my jurisdiction..."

Jamie suddenly felt compelled to squat down between them. As he rested his elbows on each wheelchair arm-rest, he perceived the presence of his guides draw close. Letting his gaze drift between Emma and Joshua, a sudden feeling passed over him, sensing from it, nothing was impossible for his spiritual solution. Time, at least, was their ally, courtesy of the legal system, however much that fact inflamed the situation, he would overcome it.

As Jamie crouched there, he sensed strong feelings probing the periphery of his mind, like those he had experienced with Gwen. As had been the case with Gwen, he knew Emily and Josh could hear him, but thought it unlikely those feelings were arising from them yet. However, reflecting back on Gwen's case, she had been the first to mentally contact him. He deliberated again on some medical journals he had read that described how the body compensated for lost organ function; could the same apply to the brain, when the practical aspects of communication were absent in chronically disabled people?

~2~

This initial meeting, would undoubtedly bias towards the current legal issue under discussion, and because of this, sensed the particular importance attached to it. Squatting there silently, Jamie experienced none of the usual sensations indicative of his trance event, but intuitively felt the presence of the team beyond. As forbidding as this meeting promised to be, it had raised no inward concerns in him; just a discreet awareness of the need for delicacy in any dialogues.

He had been vaguely aware of some ongoing extra-sensory perception research, in various institutes elsewhere, but their success, so far, had been viewed sceptically. He hoped that from his and Gwen's success, his spiritual solution would prove to be the missing link.

Drawing up a chair to rest his aching knees, he began to speak. "It isn't my intention to bore people with doctrines that relate intransigent, divine laws, but more to seize the opportunity to enlighten them on how our spiritual solution can, and has, opened up stricken lives. To make it work, however, requires a soul's commitment, and complete faith in what I'm about to tell you all." Emma's and Josh's eyes, along with the rest of the group, remained transfixed on him; their gazes giving nothing away.

Taking his story back to the beginning, he described how he had become embittered, watching his young wife slowly descend into the grip of a debilitating, incurable disease— eventually losing her to it. He related how Vicky's illness took control of their lives, describing her courage as she accepted her condition. Despite her fears for the future, she used her disability as a means to try and address his bitterness; making him look more positively at how it was affecting him.

Her illness sent him into a frenzied search for the resources to support her. It was after he became obsessed with this search, a suggestion was made to Vicky that she should explore a spiritual solution. The spiritual alternative, traditionally, had offered some mental relief to terminally ill people, where modern medicine was no longer a viable choice. One of the benefits that seemed to surface, leant toward how it appeared to settle a soul's fear of death, helping them to accept their future transition from the physical plane.

Still consumed by his bitterness, then, Jamie went on to describe how the spiritual option appeared unrealistic to him, feeling Vicky's needs required prompt, practical help to meet the increasing onset of the disease. His disenchantment with the dimension beyond, and his obsession to create as comfortable an existence as possible for Vicky, superseded all else.

This unrelenting search for resources continued to dominate him; unaware of the mental stress his attitude was placing on Vicky, as she increasingly became more incapacitated. Finally, it reached the stage where Vicky lost her physical ability. He watched the control over her life progressively drop out of her reach. It was then that the spiritual solution was introduced to her again, but more intensely by his grandmother.

The significance of that introduction, made him rationalise Vicky's situation more realistically, realising what his grandmother's spiritual solution was doing for her morale. It made him appreciate how his bitterness and pride had ignored a resource that was, effectively, increasing precious moments with her. Vicky had finally found relief in a resource he had been too proud to acknowledge. Because of blind misjudgements, he had failed to fully understand the practical benefits attached to the power of spirit.

Jamie's love for Vicky had been his final salvation, making him view their future together more humbly. The lessons they had learned, would become a resource they could take with them into the life beyond: it was knowledge that could be cached in the spiritual mind. Now that Jamie understood how the spiritual solution had benefited Vicky, he was applying it to others: gradually revealing a new potential for people like Gwen, and where they could compete on equal terms, irrespective of physical ability.

Through this experience, he had learned that when applying the mind spiritually, it awakened dormant facets of it, revealing pathways into the world beyond. The continued development of mental ability, gradually substantiated the link the mind already had with the spiritual dimension: effectively, disclosing an understanding that this was the real world, and a method of how a soul could access the knowledge there.

With a clearer outlook on life, Jamie described how the more he explored the spiritual solution, the more it revealed to him that everyone entered the physical plane with a plan; However that plan manifested, it represented an opportunity given to a soul by the Infinite One. If a soul accepted this, then to allow physical aspects and human emotions to interfere with its completion could lead to lost opportunities that would never be repeated on that physical plane.

He went on, describing how his spiritual solution had helped Gwen. Tuning her mind to the spiritual world had opened up those dormant pathways in her brain. Able now to mentally speak to him, Gwen was gradually developing an ability that would allow her to teach, and enlighten others on the spiritual solution. Jamie continued, describing how the material values in life had diminished in importance— logically leading him toward higher things.

He became passionate as his address drew to a close. "The spiritual solution focuses us on one beneficial, practical resource in our physical existence—our minds. It has been said that the power of the mind can move mountains. If we genuinely believe that, then one can step beyond any physical disability that encumbers a life on the physical plane."

Jamie reached out and took Emma's and Josh's hands, gazing

into their eyes. "It is people like you, who offer those like me, the opportunity to learn life's truth. You are the unsung heroes, and heroines of humanity. It is not my place to criticise or judge how people should conduct their lives here, but we have a duty to the Infinite One to help one another. I see it as my duty to tell everyone, that should a soul decide to prematurely end their lifespan, be-it for whatever personal reason, pause a while to consider three things. Our historic Divine soul's sacrifice; the completion of their own life-plan, and the opportunity they offer people like me to learn life's truth."

~3~

Silence descended over the disabled group and their carers, as Jamie slowly rose to his feet. Only time would tell, whether, what he had spoken about would trigger any response from them. The picture he had painted of the spiritual dimension would appear surreal, when viewed from the practical perspective: while the material values dominated, they would mask any potential to believe in his spiritual solution.

With a parting gesture, Jamie wandered off with Sylvie to mingle with their other group regulars.

Sylvie, deep in thought as they walked away, intermittently gazed up at Jamie. "The more I listen to you, Jamie, the more I feel the proof I've searched for in the past, about the life beyond, seems to have been unnecessary." She clasped her hands together as she became engrossed in her thoughts. "The theme, you and Richard use to present your case, appears to ignore the need for proof by looking at life logically; it is the sense of that applied logic that teases at my imagination. As I see it, you've been shrewd in the way you address people; never emphatically making any statements on your spiritual subject that implies the need for proof..." she paused, "... in fact; seeming to place the ball squarely in the opposing court."

Jamie smiled at her curiously. "And, has it convinced you?"

"I'm not sure," she muttered thoughtfully. "That statement might confuse you somewhat, in view of the support I've given to the project so far." She looked vacantly ahead as they ambled through the crowds in the hall. "I think I'm beginning to see the bigger picture a little better now, and how you are using your knowledge to focus us on reasons why we should live out our lives here."

Jamie nodded. "There are so many factors in the equation that can affect us here, Sylvie. One of the most prominent criticisms I hear is directed towards the Infinite One. Generally accepted as our maker, it is in that context that confusion arises. He is a constant target for those under sufferance, the question repeatedly asked; why does he allow so much suffering on the physical planes...?"

"It's strange you should mention that," interrupted Sylvie. "It's a question that has dominated my thoughts for years... Why does he allow it?"

Jamie smiled. "Perhaps it's down to human frailty— we need a fall-guy. Seriously, though. If we think about it logically, He gives us free-will for a reason while down here. Should we accept that to be the case, does it make sense then to take it away when the chips are down? If we concede to the truth that we are the architects of our lives down here, and that should someone believe their way is better and takes up arms to implement it— is that the Infinite One's fault?"

Sylvie thought for a moment. "But then, Jamie, that still implies that the innocent and the creatures of our world will always be destined to suffer."

"You tell me you've looked at the bigger picture, Sylvie, and yet you have still not understood. When you measure the transience of the physical life against the infinitive Infinite One's eternal life, to exploit your fellowmen in the physical existence gains you nothing: that fact alone, should illustrate the purpose of His divine plan. When we return to what is essentially our real home dimension, the physical values will have no bearing there, but how we have conducted our lives down here— will. If we can accept that scenario, then the reason why the Infinite One does not intervene, becomes clear."

Jamie smiled, pointing to Richard and Dave approaching.

Sylvie remained thoughtful. "It all seems so confusing and unfair."

Jamie shrugged "Only if you view life singularly from the physical perspective." Sylvie gazed searchingly after him as he joined Richard and Dave.

***

Sarah and John, in the dimension beyond, smiled with satisfaction after listening to Jamie's words. The success of their young spirit's first incarnation was going beyond their wildest expectations. The minion, hovering in the background, had continually been frustrated by the constant support from the team backing Jamie on the physical plane.

The whole plan could so easily have turned pear-shaped, after Vicky had been struck down by her illness. Jamie had been saved by his deep love for her. Gazing beyond her physical shell, he had been touched by the beauty of her spirit; from that moment, he was destined to see only her spiritual make-up.

The most prominent aspect, that had put him beyond the clutches of the minion, had been Emily, his grandmother. Her task now was complete, and as Sarah gazed over Jamie's celestial horizon, she saw that Emily's transition approached. However, even in light of that event, it would still leave no opportunity for the minion— Jamie was strong in spirit now. From Vicky's past visitations, he had realised that Emily, like Vicky, would take her place among the team beyond.

For Jamie, his spiritual plan had long-since become a reality to him. He would obviously miss the presence of his companions on the physical plane, but Sarah and John knew he had not lost those team-members' help. Having breached the barrier between the physical and spiritual planes, that understanding, now, would allow them all to work as one team.

The current tasks facing Jamie, required him to focus all his spiritual energy on the challenges that were approaching. The only concern Sarah and John sensed from Jamie's projects: would those under sufferance listen to him? He came across as a fit young man, enjoying life. The advice he offered, could appear as an affront to those caged in decaying, disease-ridden bodies— it was in this context, the minion, constantly sought to seize opportunities.

In view of Jamie's continuing success, his guides, Sarah and John, were ever more confident that he would find a way, even though the choice to accept his offer of help, always rested upon those he counselled. What the situation he faced now equated to, shared an affinity with their historic, Divine Soul when he had asked his Father to amend his divine plan, but not as he had wished it.

The knowledge that Divine Being possessed of the life after, made the threat on his physical life of little consequence to him. The suffering he endured from the physical scourging, however, was painful and mentally debilitating, but by adhering to the completion of his plan, he had left a clue that pointed to the eternal life, and the presence of the Infinite One.

Sarah and John could see that a sense of that divine plan then, shared an affinity with a soul's request for compassionate euthanasia to abort their plan in these modern times. In that ancient garden, aeons ago, the temptation to request the easy option was as real today, but there were other factors in the equation to consider. Jamie's solution, was not simply to sympathise with and comfort those stricken souls, but to try and find a way to help them live out a fruitful life in society.

This latter part of Jamie's objective, Sarah and John felt, was the most important aspect attached to his team-plan: it sealed the covenant that each spirit had with the Infinite One. Sarah and John gazed down through the celestial window on their young protégé. The knowledge Jamie had gained during this, his first incarnation, had been unprecedented, and had substantiated his mentors' confidence in his ability to complete future phases of his own plan.

***

As the meeting approached its conclusion, the lack of response from Emma and Josh raised no concern in him. They had a cross to bear, and he would understand if the pressure of their spiritual plan reached the stage where it became intolerable. However, he would not give up, and hoped Gwen might be the team-asset who could make the difference to get through to them.

CHAPTER FIFTEEN
AU REVOIR— NOT GOODBYE

Following the closure of the meeting, there had been little response from the new group. They appeared to have offered no criticism to what had taken place; chatting casually with some of the regulars, which Jamie found encouraging.

While Jamie had gone about his business, he reflected on how he had been constantly aware of the occasional penetrating gazes directed at him from Emma and Joshua. Gwen had spoken to him, after the meeting, about how she planned to try to access some of the group's minds. He had given her his full support, but warned her to be patient. Though their intentions would be honourable, the question of an individual's privacy had to be the prime consideration.

Richard and Sylvie confirmed they had received no feedback from the new group, seeming to chat benignly with the regulars, as if Jamie's address had never taken place. Jamie, however, had already concluded, that any level of response would hinge on Emma's and Josh's acceptance of his spiritual solution, as a result of the subsequent evaluations they ventured to make on it.

Gwen, however, was excited at undertaking the first task in her new role, able to update Jamie fluently now, using their newly developed extrasensory powers. Jamie had sensed her increasing enthusiasm from their periodical exchanges: curiously, it was fuelling a belief in him that there was more to Gwen's presence on the physical plane than he had originally been aware of. The arcane thought, tied in with an impression of how he felt all those, who were manifesting into his group, seemed to have been selected from a band of spirits chosen to become involved in his plan.

What intrigued him even more, was a gut feeling that some mysterious liaison, with a divine, supreme entity, had counselled them all prior to their physical inception: since his first trance experience, concurrent experiences were beginning to provide answers to many of these questions.

Daily now, the reality of the spiritual dimension was taking preference over the material life for Jamie. Regular meetings had become an essential part of his routine, providing him with a constant liaison with the spiritual world, but more than that, how the world beyond was providing them all with real practical benefits in the physical life.

Pulling up outside his house he bade Richard good night, thoughtfully watching his rear-lights fade into the night. Pausing by the front gate, he deliberated on how not everything he had hoped for, at the meeting, had been achieved. The fact the new group appeared to listen, offered a glimmer of hope for the future, but it was important they understood that the doctrine he followed conceded to their rights as individuals. It was their choice to evaluate the information presented, and his part to simply pass on what he had learned.

~2~

The front gate whined on its hinges as he passed through, closing it quietly behind him. He paused before the front-door; his bunch of keys jingling musically in his hands as he searched for the latch-key. While he was standing there, he became aware of the telephone ringing in the hall within— it intensified his search.

Flinging the door open, he dived for the phone.

Muttering the number, he announced himself. "Jamie Hoskins here."

"Jamie! Thank heavens. I've been trying to get you for the past hour."

"Mum! I've already told you where you can reach me, when I'm at these meetings— haven't I?"

"I tried there... Just missing you... It's..."

"What's up, then?" interrupted Jamie.

"It's your Nan. She's taken a turn for the worse, and is not expected to live through the night... she's asking for you, Jamie."

Despite his staunch beliefs, the news raised a chill feeling in him. Though this phone call had been expected, its sudden reality had come as if another bolt of lightening out of the blue. What was even more relevant: it meant that one he had depended upon for so long was about to leave the physical arena. It had been something the whole family had expected; the reality of the event, now, making him feel particularly vulnerable.

His mind wandered, suddenly filled with intimate memories that reached back to his childhood...

"Jamie...? Jamie... You still there...?" queried Sally.

He surfaced abruptly from his thoughts, jarred out of them from the sudden sound of his mother's voice. "Yes...," he murmured hesitantly. "Yes... I'm on my way."

"Drive carefully, Jamie. Nan says she'll wait for you."

Jamie raced out the door, slamming it behind him, focusing on the definitive meaning behind Emily's words. Throwing open the drive gates, he ran back to the garage; oblivious of the clanging up-and-over door crashing up against its guide arresters. Hurrying up the drive, he impatiently glanced up and down the road, before speeding off.

It was a weird journey, he, seeming to drive his car remotely. He had experienced something similar years before. Shortly after leaving his parents' one evening, he had been conscious of passing through their drive-gates and then setting off up the road. The next thing he remembered was turning in through his own gates. He had sat there in the drive, trying to subconsciously map out his journey home. Unsuccessfully, he had searched his mind for the familiar landmarks he should have passed, but that night had remained a complete mystery up to the present day.

Drawing up behind his parent's car in the drive, he rushed towards the front door. As he approached, it swung open, revealing his mother's shape, looming as if a ghostly apparition, shrouded in shadows cast by the porch-light.

Sally kissed him, pointing to what had always been a store-room. "She's in there; as we had to move her downstairs, Dear..."

Jamie nodded, making his way toward it.

~3~

Gently teasing the door ajar, he peered in. Emily was laying peacefully, a night-light on her bedside table suffusing the room with a soft, gentle glow. There was no sense of drama or sadness; more an atmosphere that seemed to celebrate Emily's obedient, dedicated service to the Infinite One.

Jamie quietly pulled up a chair, slipping his hand into Emily's. "Hi, Nan," he whispered.

Slowly opening her eyes, she turned and gazed at him. "Jamie! You managed to come and see me."

"Course I did, Nan." He squeezed her hand gently. "Do you honestly think I would miss the opportunity to say goodbye to my favourite Nan, after all she's done for me?"

She grinned teasingly. "I'm your only Nan, as well you know, and what's with the 'Goodbye'?" she queried softly. "That sounds much too final. From the archives of the spirit world, *au revoir* is better suited." With a faint, humorous expression, she gazed at him. "Haven't I taught you anything, Dear?"

He smiled. "I ought to have known better, eh, Nan?"

She gave a slight nod. "You see! You're not going to get rid of me that easy, my lad. You're stuck with me now: and just you be aware, I'll be watching you from beyond."

Bending forward, he gently kissed her on the forehead. "It comforts me to hear you say that, Nan."

"Jamie," she sighed. "The pleasure's been all mine, my dear." Her expression tensed a little. "Even with all you have learned so far, Jamie, you still cannot fully understand the magnitude of the power Vicky and you have amassed in spirit. As I approach my transition now, I've seen for myself what it means for us all— so exciting, Jamie— so exciting."

"You must rest, Nan; save your strength..."

"Rest!" she interrupted. "There's still so much to do... So much we must do to help you complete our plan. No time for sadness... Partings are so brief... and life so short on the physical planes..."

He clasped both his hands around hers, as her voice began to fragment. Turning to peer behind him, he made out the shadows of his and Vicky's parents, Sally, Carl, Brenda and Paul, standing by the door.

Suddenly, Emily's hand tensed within his. "Oh, Jamie," she whispered. "We are all going to be so very happy together..."

Jamie bowed his head, as her last word slowly faded into a long, soft sigh— then she lay still.

It was too much for Sally, who left the room to be comforted by Carl.

Brenda and Paul quietly approached, gently resting their hands on Jamie's shoulders.

"We're so sorry, Jamie. We know what she meant to you, and to us as well— such a wonderful old lady." With that, they silently withdrew.

Jamie sat in the stillness of the night, looking down at his Nan; the vacant gaze in her half opened eyes confirming to him that her spirit had flown. He slowly reached up and gently closed her eyelids. Though grief-stricken by her loss, his tears would not come; as if she was standing over him, and in her own inimitable way, ensuring he endorsed all she had taught him about the world of spirit.

It was far into the night, before Jamie rose. Carl had called the doctor, who had initiated the procedure that would begin Emily's interment. Jamie accepted his mother's offer to remain with them for a day or so, but feeling it more for her benefit than his.

Sally's commitment to her mother's belief had been far less in comparison to Jamie's, and offered little relief to settle her grief now. Emily knew this would be the case, and rather than a wake, had asked Jamie to arrange a family gathering that would celebrate her life. It was this last gift to her family Emily hoped would confirm all she had believed in. Jamie, at least, understood the reasoning behind her request. It was Emily's legacy, that from her dedication to spirit, everyone, touched by her life, would understand that the world beyond was real.

~4~
***

The celebration in the spiritual dimension went far beyond that on the physical plane. Emily's contribution had been immeasurable, setting Vicky and Jamie on a path through life that would lift the lives of countless souls, Jamie was destined to help. Taking her place alongside Sarah, John and Vicky, Emily felt the Divine Spirit of the Infinite One embrace her soul.

She revelled in the joy of a moment that was enriching her spirit. Now, approaching the end of her own voyage to infinity, she had taken on the dark legions and set two virgin souls on a successful course in their first incarnations. Sarah and John were well pleased. Without Emily's guidance on the physical plane, things there could have been very different.

The strength of Emily's faith had provided the means for Sarah and John to access Jamie on the material plane. Emily's reward now was a reunion with her partner, Simon; one, who had been her constant companion on the seven physical planes they had journeyed across. Together, once again, they would join Sarah's and John's growing band of spirits, and watch Jamie successfully complete his first incarnation. On Jamie's return to spirit, the final task for Emily and Simon then, would take them to the Infinite One's Hallowed Sanctum. There, as thousands before them, they would receive into their care, a virgin soul to mentor on its journey to infinity.

***

THE FOLLOWING DAYS AFTER EMILY'S passing were fairly sombre affairs, despite Jamie's efforts to lift the family spirits at her celebratory evening. Reflecting back on that day, in his office one morning, the celebration had turned into a wake, as Emily had feared it would. He felt it to have been pointless to direct the finger of blame at anyone, attributing the low morale to Emily's popularity. Even now, as he sat there immersed in thought, Emily still seemed to be running the show.

Jamie felt a sense of relief when contemplating his trance ability: it had arisen under Emily's guidance, enabling him now to sense all his past companions around him. Emily would never be forgotten. She had left an indelible mark on their lives that emphatically directed them all to the Infinite One. Jamie gazed down at the array of family pictures on his desktop; it fell to him now to endorse her belief, and get on with the task of making that information available to others.

Staring at the in-basket on his desk brought him back to reality with a jolt. Life goes on he thought, snatching a wad of mail off the top of the stack of files. He gazed at his gran's picture again; imagining, for a moment, her chastising expression if anyone dared to question her belief. He smiled to himself, as he slipped the paper-knife across the first envelope.

CHAPTER SIXTEEN
THE FIRE WITHIN

~1~

OVER THE NEXT FEW DAYS, the full gravity, of what had taken place during that meeting, began to filter back to Jamie and Richard. Gwen's initial efforts to make thought contact, with Emma and Josh, had been frustrated, due to their resolute mood, and soon after, she'd had to confide in Jamie to suppress her disappointment. He knew these were early days yet; the technique they had evolved together, presently unique to them alone.

From the transcripts of ancient doctrines, it was understood, that if incarnate souls contravened the laws of the Infinite One in ignorance, their transgressions would be forgiven. Once they became aware of the truth, any transgressions then, would rest upon that soul's conscience. Jamie conceded that this definition came across as prohibitive, appearing to apply an ultimatum in an unsympathetic, threatening manner. It was his endeavour to help people, and not bully them into accepting the doctrine that he now adhered to in his life.

The message, however, that continued to come over from Emma and Josh was clear. Despite the advanced condition of their disease, they remained focused on their singular quest, persevering with their intent to help legalise compassionate euthanasia. For the first time, Jamie felt insecure over what he was trying to achieve. Each day, discussions taking place over the media, debated the compassionate issue of a soul's right to end a stricken, physical life. More alarmingly to Jamie, the dialogues, occurring in those controversial discussions, were becoming increasingly distanced from the doctrines laid down by the Infinite One. In light of that fact, it was placing growing limitations on the endeavours of groups like Jamie's.

One benefit of modern medicine made it unnecessary for a soul to make their transition in agony; this aspect, at least, could help a soul to complete their plan. However, to concentrate on this factor alone, defeated the strategy Jamie was applying himself too. It spiralled down to focus on the transient life-span on the physical plane, where the time-factor compressed the period, needed to get this message across to help others achieve their goals.

Once again, the confusion arose from a lack of understanding of the relationship that existed between the physical and spiritual dimensions. From the knowledge and insight Jamie had received from Emily of the life beyond, he was able now, to use that information to exploit every second of his physical life. Strangely enough, no one, as yet, had passed the obvious judgement on him. How, by enjoying a fit, healthy life, it was not possible for him to appreciate a soul's agony in their struggle against insurmountable infirmity.

The task ahead seemed set to diversify into new challenges, but the fact remained. Before a soul could rationalise their life realistically, there had to be an awareness of the two dimensions, and which one of them was the real world. To answer that question, Jamie had applied logic to his approach during the past; viewing it now, there had seemed no better method. Once an incarnate soul accepted the reality of the infinite spiritual dimension, the trials of the physical existence paled into insignificance: enabling a soul to meet each challenge faced in life more resolutely.

However, Jamie's spiritual solution, by tradition, would continue to come across as a surreal alternative; constantly looping around to the same requirement— faith. He was not only destined to continue to come up against intransigent attitudes, but also, suffer from increasing technology that was speeding up the pace of life generally. In many circumstances, this latter factor added to the demise of stricken souls, isolating them even further from the infrastructure of life.

Meditating on the problems he faced, he sensed alien thoughts intruding his mind. "Gwen... Gwen is that you?"

Her response was instant. "No Jamie. But I too have been sensing some thought-patterns these past few days, and have followed it with interest."

"Dare we hope it's coming from the new group, and in particular, Emma and Josh?

Gwen fell silent for a moment. "As you know, Jamie, my initial efforts there have been frustrated so far... as you said, when you counselled me over my disappointment back then— we can only continue to present our case."

"True, but time, now, is a commodity we can ill afford to waste, Gwen," insisted Jamie.

"I agree," she replied. "But neither will it help if we try to force the issue, Jamie. When I last met with Emma and Josh, I was impressed by their indignant expressions at being lectured on the morality of life, sensing me with how those morals were buried in history that didn't appear to equate to these modern times."

"That's always been the case with ancient doctrines, Gwen, but it doesn't diminish their values; just high-lights the importance of how we need to present them..." He thought for a moment. "...I'm sure that if we continue to try and persuade them to consider life logically, our spiritual solution will eventually provide the answers."

"Well, Jamie, it worked for me. However, in my case I did take matters into my own hands, somewhat. Emma's and Josh's group are trying to change the system... Leave it with me, Jamie. I'll persevere with the plan."

It was like someone had suddenly switched a light on in his mind. "Maybe that's it, Gwen? Coming from someone in the same, chronic predicament as them might raise their curiosity. It could create the desire in them to explore the reason behind what made you take hold of your life, despite your illness. In this context, Gwen, you seem to have made yourself indispensable."

A short silence followed. "...I've never looked at it in that light before, Jamie."

"Keep me informed, Gwen."

Their brief exchange had temporarily suppressed the pessimistic view of the current topic; that last idea, leaving them deliberating on his sudden revelation.

The next meeting was a little over two weeks away. The hope of any positive development from Gwen's and his last thoughts, largely depended on the mood of the new group, but he was unable to suppress the optimistic feeling, something would. He wondered if he was becoming too enthusiastic when offering his help. Though he conceded it remained the choice of the individual soul, if they chose to say no! Was that to be an end of it?

~2~

The next morning, Jamie, was sitting at the table eating his breakfast, watching the early-morning news on his kitchen television. The usual depressing topics would have bored him, if the issues they represented were not so serious. Pouring himself another coffee he casually gazed up at the clock, satisfying himself he had plenty of time before leaving for work.

As he sat there, the news presenter moved on to the topic of the ongoing debate on compassionate euthanasia. He listened to the differing views, as the various group-representatives discussed and opinionated on the points put forward. The theme of the discussion made him reflect on how his spiritual solution would be viewed; pessimistically feeling it would be regarded as an insensitive, unsympathetic alternative. Again, what was glaringly obvious, about the whole interview, was how it seemed to completely ignore the existence and doctrines of the Infinite One.

Rising from the table, he cleared away after breakfast and left for work. He wandered into his office and settled down behind his desk, beginning the task of sorting through his mail. As he fanned through the wad of letters, the bland appearance of one stood out against the official, traditional format of the rest.

He thoughtfully placed the others on the desk, and gazed at the 'Personal' inscription in one of the envelope's corners. Slipping the paper-knife across the top he took out a single leaf of paper. Crackling loudly, as he unfolded it, he began to read. His heart missed a beat when he realised the letter was from Emma's carer. Though the letter began officially, the main body of it adopted a more sociable theme.

*

Mr J Hoskins
Sunrise Disability LTD
Seal Industrial Est:
The Weald
TR18 1EK

Mrs. Jane Bayman
Bel-View
Seal
The Weald
TR14 5EF

Date: 20th July 2010.
Ref: Meeting Response.

Dear Mr. Hoskins,
Since our first attendance to your meetings, it has taken these past two weeks to evaluate what you are endeavouring to achieve for those like Emma and Josh. The feelings of myself, and those of some colleagues, initially leant toward a blend of sceptical and indignant conclusions. However, reflecting back over what you said, and how you applied your information, has been a source of continual discussion among us all since then.

The purpose of my writing to you is two-fold. First, what you touched upon, during that meeting, impressed us it was reminiscent of an understanding, we believe, had to have arisen from practical experience; I, along with a few others, would like to learn more. Second, however, I feel I should warn you that there are those who look upon what took place, unsympathetically, and are critical of your beliefs.

I am convinced there is no tendency towards malice attached to their attitude, simply distressed at watching their loved-ones suffer. Over the years, they have conceded to their disabled family member's wish to end their misery. It is difficult to express any opinions on their decision, only to try and understand the feelings of all the parties involved.

Perhaps we could meet to discuss, in more detail, your objectives for the future.

Yours sincerely,
Jane Bayman.
Carer to Emma.

133

*

~**3**~

Jamie sat, thoughtfully gazing down at the letter. Slowly folding it up, he reflected back over the early period of Vicky's illness; how it had been his bitterness, in contrast, that had dominated him. Seemingly insurmountable at that time, his enlightenment had arisen from the patient dedication of his grandmother's guidance, and where it now fell to him to apply a similar understanding to the attitudes Jane Bayman had referred to.

As he sat there, he pondered over how neglecting to understand a situation from other peoples' perspectives, was where conflicting opinions could arise. To be so sure of one's objective, could produce tunnelled views of life. To Jamie now, the way ahead was obvious. Having committed himself, the proof of his solution had come from the faith he'd developed. To apply what Emily had taught him, the latter part of his life, now, involved persuading others to take that step; confident they would realise similar opportunities.

One of Jamie's intimate fears contemplated the weight of responsibility, which rested upon the shoulders of someone who manipulated people's lives with their faith. It was unnerving to wonder whether one's belief, which was unsubstantiated by proof, was right. His grandmother had inclined her beliefs toward ancient doctrines, and had passed that choice onto him. In the final analysis, one fact eased his concern a little, feeling the receiving soul had the same choice; either to ignore his offering, or accept it.

This debate in Jamie, arose from the ever-present desire in him that wanted everyone to succeed. Unlike his grandmother, he had no grown family to pass on his belief; the persistent feeling he would never have children, having dogged him throughout his life. In his present situation, it had given him freedom, and now he was using that freedom to focus on his fellowmen. All the assets he had amassed, pointed him to that objective now: benefiting from the conscientious upbringing, the teachings of his grandmother, Vicky's acceptance of her illness, and now, the appearance of stalwart companions to help him.

Gwen's lonely, crippled existence had provided her with the excuse to opt out of life. Her lively mind had been frustrated by her condition, unable to create the opportunity to kick-start any form of productive existence. Her choice to listen to Jamie had developed dormant aspects of her mind, and had opened up new horizons for her. Jamie could see his fears were unfounded there. She had the potential now to access the minds of those like her, while Jamie, and his supporters, dealt with the physical aspects.

Though Jamie's most intimate thoughts had established a soul's right to accept or refuse help, he still felt it should not discourage him from making future offers. Emma and Josh, however, were a new challenge; their situation differed from Gwen's. They had engaged their minds on a quest that contested a law they considered infringed upon their human rights. Jamie could see that if he could redirect that fire within them, it could release a potential like that, which now existed in Gwen.

Each day was revealing how the developing role of the mind was able to breach the frontier separating the physical and spiritual dimensions. It confirmed to Jamie, how Emily had been a spiritual medium who had differed from others. She had focused on the bigger picture, one that related to the relationship between the two dimensions. Emily had not been bothered by the loss of companions; she knew those souls remained constant beyond. She was more concerned for the world's future, and how every incarnate soul on it had a decisive role to play there.

CHAPTER SEVENTEEN

A CRY FROM THE DARK

~1~

THE LIAISON BETWEEN JAMIE AND his spiritual guides, Sarah and John, had become as natural as the daily dialogues he found himself engaged in with his colleagues. Gwen was exploiting her newly developed mental ability to the full, confiding in Jamie; constantly updating him on her progress with Emma and Josh. Her help was proving invaluable, causing him to wonder over how he had ever managed without her in the past.

It was during one particularly dull morning, after being settled by her carer, that Gwen found herself gazing out the window, watching the clouds drift across the sky. She was deliberating on the report she had just sensed out to Jamie, when she suddenly became aware of fragmented, intrusive thoughts penetrating her mind. Jamie and Gwen had no other mental contacts at present, due to the infancy of their technique, so they were familiar with each others mental approach; Gwen, instinctively sensing it was not Jamie.

She became excited, as had been the case on several previous occasions— only for those sessions to conclude in disappointment. She sent out strong thoughts she hoped were focusing on Emma and Josh; inviting them to try and read her mind. Waiting in silent anticipation; the seconds turned into minutes. She repeated her request, when suddenly; she became aware of someone trying to access her mind again.

Gwen was cautiously excited, feeling that at last she was bordering on a possible breakthrough. There was no time to ask Jamie for help, fearing she might lose the thread of this possible contact. She began to pick up fragments of words; they made little sense initially, but they were there, and becoming more persistent. She continued to send out thoughts of encouragement to the entity, trying to determine who was attempting to reach her. Intuitively she felt it could be Emma or Josh, but that feeling arose from hope, rather than any logical deduction.

While she waited, Gwen continued to send out her request for the entity to keep trying. She reflected over how Jamie had said; 'use the resources of your spiritual guides'. She muttered a short prayer and waited; fighting off feelings intruding her mind that fuelled growing doubts. If it was only one word, she thought— something she could tell Jamie that would confirm her first success.

The soft, uttered word 'Gwen' drifted into her mind. Feelings of joy suddenly welled up in her as the word was repeated again.

"I can hear you!" exclaimed Gwen excitedly, "I can hear you! Take it in small steps; try to tell me who you are." She waited again; the thoughts were becoming stronger, but still a little confused. Gwen knew this could be possible, as the dormant facets of the remote mind were, undoubtedly, gradually awakening, trying to string sentences together. She was beyond herself, determined she would capitalise on this golden opportunity.

Quite by chance, her carer entered the room to administer her mid-morning medications. The intrusion distracted Gwen, and in that moment, she lost focus. After giving Gwen her medication, the carer left, oblivious of the event she had inadvertently stumbled in on. Gwen tried to re-establish the contact, but there was no response. She was furious. Unable to suppress her disappointment, she allowed malicious feelings to swamp her mind; directing irrational, vindictive thoughts toward her carer.

"What has happened, Gwen?" queried Jamie; suddenly sensing tense, disruptive thoughts emanating from her.

"Oh Jamie, I'm so disappointed. I was on the verge of a contact, when my wretched carer came in with my medications. Subsequently, I lost the focus, and now I can't get it back."

"Settle down, Gwen, it'll come again, and let's be honest, you need to take your medications. Your carer wouldn't be aware of what you were doing anyway. Perhaps it's something we must consider in future; develop our technique with them."

"I've already tried to do that without success, Jamie"

"Not, I think, Gwen, as intensively as you're applying yourself to your current project."

There was a pregnant pause, as Gwen considered his response. "Yes... I suppose you're right..., but then you always are."

"Whoo! That was bit below the belt, Gwen. My! We are feeling sorry for ourselves today," joked Jamie.

"Oh I'm sorry, Jamie, but I felt I was so close then. Whoever it was knew my name, and projected it."

"In that case, Gwen, I would think you *have* experienced the first indications of a successful contact. The fact they've made an effort to communicate with you, signifies to me they might be considering the solution that appears to have worked for you. I feel bound to place my bets on it being someone from the new group; I'm very encouraged over what you've achieved, Gwen."

Gwen settled down for the rest of the day, mentally listening for a repeat of the intrusive thoughts, but none came. After her chat with Jamie, she felt disappointed with herself over her irrational outburst, and the uncivilised attitude she had directed toward her carer. It focused her again on Jamie's constant reminder, that she should use, and trust, her new-found relationship with her guides beyond.

~2~

Gwen's disability, paradoxically, had given her an advantage over those in Jamie's group, who were free of any infirmity, as when she addressed anyone chronically afflicted like her, the disabled argument dropped out of the equation. The more she thought about the previous, brief contact, and the utterance of that single word, it did seem to support the idea that she *had* experienced a modicum of success.

The next meeting arrived, and Jamie's trance address was received with the usual enthusiasm. Gwen, however, kept her mind alert, hoping for a repeat of the thought-event two weeks previously. The fact that Emma's group had appeared at the meeting for the second time, signified to Gwen there had been some level of interest developing among them. It raised the optimistic feeling in her, that the next contact might be more positive. Meanwhile, Jamie had struck up a conversation with Jane Bayman, Emma's carer, chatting sociably about the letter she had sent, and his subsequent response to it.

***

In the dimension beyond, Sarah's and John's spiritual group were going from strength to strength. The evil minion had been slowly squeezed out of the picture, and so much so; the situation was attracting the scrutiny of its hierarchy in the dedicated realms of evil. John's band of spiritual guides were acutely aware of this, contemplating the six physical planes Vicky and Jamie still had to travel across.

John, on occasion, had cast a wary eye toward the next physical experience Jamie had chosen. Describing a world in the grip of an age of evil, he knew Vicky and Jamie would need all the power they were amassing to meet the challenges there. The dark legions were not without their own resources, possessing powers that allowed them to remotely perceive, and monitor, the most intimate hopes and plans of innocent young souls. Carefully developing their seditious strategies, they patiently waited for their opportunity; concealed in the shadows of their abysmal world.

John knew it was folly to deliberate on such depressing thoughts, but having endured similar experiences in their physical life-spans, Sarah and he were only too aware of the strength of evil, once it had a foot-hold on a world. With no means to estimate any time-scale in the spiritual dimension, Sarah and John could only prepare for the impending events by assessing the status of their charges' life-spans. Already showing on Vicky's and Jamie's celestial horizon, Jamie was pushing middle age, indicating how quickly his incarnate life was slipping away.

Over recent decades, he had dramatically increased his spiritual prospects by adding knowledge to what he had already learnt. His accumulating power was unprecedented— maturing into a formidable asset. However, happily applying himself to his task, he was oblivious of the gathering legions of evil preparing for Vicky and him to enter their next incarnation.

For the time being, Sarah and John knew the advantage temporarily rested with the minion. Monitoring Jamie's strengthening allegiance to the Infinite One; it lost no time sensing that information out to its masters in the realms of evil. Jamie, enjoying success on this first incarnation, was oblivious of the evil rendezvous that loomed in the next phase of his and Vicky's Voyage to Infinity. Sarah and John, however, were not. Watching the dark legions gathering to confront their charges, they were preparing their legions to meet that threat.

***

~3~

Gwen sensed Jamie's conversation with Jane Bayman, taking hope from the dialogue that appeared to indicate the new group's growing, sympathetic mood towards their movement's objectives. As she concentrated on their train of conversation, she sensed alien thought-intrusions penetrating her mind again, similar to those she had experienced on that occasion two weeks previously. She immediately focused her mind; determined she was not going to let anything interfere with this new opportunity. Her carer had already administered the final medications to her for the day, and had retired to her crocheting.

Gwen focused again, sending out encouraging thoughts. Would this be the day she had, for so long, hoped for? The sudden breathless utterance of her name drifted into her mind, with a clarity that was unmistakeably clearer than the previous time.

Suppressing her excitement she responded. "I am Gwen, There is nothing to fear; just tell me your name." There was no doubt in Gwen, that, somehow, she was going to secure the contact this time. A brief silence followed before she repeated her statement.

"Gwen, I'm so frightened and confused."

The words stopped Gwen abruptly, pondering over their meaning. "I don't understand. What's frightening or confusing about talking to one another, whether it's through the mind or by voice?" Gwen paused, intuitively sensing she was talking to Emma. "You're simply developing a method to share your most intimate fears; use it, and let us help you."

"You don't understand, Gwen."

"Don't I?" replied Gwen. "Think about that statement for a minute."

There was a brief pause. "... I'm sorry..., that wasn't what I really meant to say. More..., that I feel my life has no direction; each day is such a trial to just simply survive. There is no respite. The mundane, boring routines make everything such an effort, with nothing to look forward to in the future. Josh and I have learned to link mentally, but it hasn't helped; our lives, fruitless; continually focusing us on our physiological prisons."

The mention of Josh's name confirmed to Gwen that she was,

indeed, talking to Emma. The despairing dialogue, so far, depressed the atmosphere of their introduction, forcing Gwen to reflect back over the time before she had met Jamie and his group. As a result of that meeting, and contrary to Emma's present belief, Gwen fully understood the despair in her statement.

Gwen had followed Jamie's original, opening address to them; instinctively sensing, from Emma, that some of the values he had tried to get over, had stuck: was this then, a cry from within that was seeking more information? Gwen felt the presence of Jamie's thoughts in the background, but sensed he was deliberately holding back. The reason was obvious to Gwen; he was leaving her to counsel one on equal ground— stricken like her. This was the challenge she had committed herself to, and having accepted it, the reality now was staring her in the face.

"Emma, it isn't our purpose to dictate to you what you should do with your life, nor will we judge you, whatever choice you make. My future seemed as fruitless as yours, yet, Jamie has set me on a path that has given purpose to my life, irrespective of my infirmity." She paused, searching for words that would maintain Emma's attention. "Have you any idea of the extent the power of the mind can be developed? Linked to Jamie's spiritual solution, the opportunities are limitless, even to those suffering chronic illness like us." Gwen paused, wondering if she was directing her words towards a dormant mind.

"I know what you're trying to say, Gwen, but we're so tired. The misery of facing each day requires a supreme effort; we are constantly taking resources from the system, never able to give anything back.'

Gwen sensed Jamie's mood intensify, listening to Emma's last statement, but he remained resolved to leave it to her counselling.

~4~

Gwen knew she was not on her own, but also under no delusion that she was in the driving seat. She fully appreciated the feelings those like her suffered. For others around her to understand, one had to experience the isolation of being trapped inside one's body; how one never acclimatised to that situation. Watching the world, milling around them, focused a soul on the unfairness of their lot, seemingly cheated by life.

She had gained strength listening to Jamie's guide, John; speak through him at each meeting. His voice seemed to penetrate deep into her soul; the wisdom of his words; indelibly embedded in her memory. Jamie's spiritual solution had introduced her to a way of life that had given her purpose. Caged in her body, Jamie had taught her how the spiritual solution, linked to her mind, could release her. It had enabled her, to not only converse with those around her, but to sense the freedom of the dimension beyond into where her spirit would one day be liberated.

Gwen knew it had all been said. The practicality of the task, now, was to continue taking the message to others, as Jamie did. As an afflicted soul herself; how, coming from her, that fact increased the impact of her message, confirming the opportunities to those sensitive enough to realise; they did have a purpose in life. All the while Gwen related these thoughts to Emma, Emma had listened, moved by the sense of truth and wisdom in Gwen's thoughts.

Emma began to see that her and Josh's mental achievement had only realised half the solution; oblivious of its true potential. The missing link had seemed to be Jamie's spiritual solution, and that to learn more, they had to take life by the scruff of the neck.

"You paint a very different picture, Gwen when you tell us of your beliefs..., but they are... only beliefs."

Emma's statement sounded unconvinced. It was the old, old story; she wanted proof that Gwen knew she was unable to give. Essentially, the emphasis on Jamie's spiritual solution asked people to apply logic to their lives here, as well as faith. To carefully consider the real meaning behind the transience of their physical lives, and how to use the practical values that were available there.

Gwen's experience had taught her, that Jamie's solution could lead to a realistic understanding of how both dimensions' environments differed. If an incarnate soul could awaken the spiritual attributes lying dormant in the mind, by applying a combination of logic, and faith: from their subsequent deductions, they would be able to successfully map-out the path they should follow.

Gwen sensed this was her moment, letting brief pictures from her past-life flash across her mind. Back then, like Emma and Josh, she had given up on life; reflecting on her last attempt to end it all. It was on that dull, miserable day that the future had towered above her, like some gigantic ogre; creating unbearable fantasies of what the future held. Trapped in her body, she was powerless to stop the emotion welling up in her. Silently crying out for help, her mental cry landed on the dormant aspects of the minds who were administering to her. Unaware then, of how the decision to end her agony would change her life, she had gazed at the swirling torrent of the river facing her— her mind in turmoil, like some overpowering entity within her had taken control of her senses.

The small voice of reason had grown fainter: powerless to resist, she pushed the control-lever of her wheel-chair forward. Committed, and yet terrified, the cold water beckoned ominously as she gathered speed, racing toward obscurity. Before she realised it, she had passed the point of no return. In the midst of her confusion, a sudden rational moment took hold; a voice, crying out in her mind 'I don't want to die!' but it was too late— she was committed.

Strapped securely into her wheel-chair, the chilling water enveloped her as she slowly sank beneath the surface. She gazed up toward the light at the obscure shapes of the towering trees above, disfigured by the flowing water. As she came to rest on the river-bed, the current gently rocked her. The instinct to survive superseded her intent to end it, and she began to struggle as the embers of her life began to dim.

In that moment, the scene had begun to transform; Gwen, sensing as if she was floating on air rather than in water. Increasingly, she felt free of the disabled affects imposed on her by her illness. It was a freedom the like of which she had never experienced before— she did not want to turn back. In the midst of her euphoria, a thought kept niggling at her that this was not her time.

One particular soul in a strange, surreal foreground approached; she felt she knew him, but was unable to recall his name. He smiled at her. "It's alright, Gwen," he said softly. "Everything is going to plan." He kept repeating it over and over again, as he slowly with-drew. His words had strangely uplifted her, but she was sensing an irresistible pull that was gradually drawing her away from him. She instinctively cried out; begging to be allowed to stay. It was in that moment her spiritual mind took hold, revealing that this event had been part of a plan she had to complete.

In the event's next phase, she was slowly coming too, gazing up at a bright light shining down from above on her. A jumble of words penetrated her consciousness, wafting in and out of her hearing. The sense of freedom had gone; the reality of her physiological prison was encroaching upon her once again.

"We've got her back!" echoed a voice.

"We'll leave her sedated on the vent for the night," echoed another. The obscure dialogues faded as she finally succumbed to exhaustion, drifting off into a deep euphoric sleep.

During the night, she seemed to be floating in a state of ecstasy, confused; listening to the voice of that soul telling her 'It was all going to plan.' Had she dreamt it? The sincerity attached to that man's statement had raised her curiosity. She contemplated the various aspects of the event passing through her mind— what plan had that soul referred to?

Gwen finally resurfaced from her nostalgic venture; that question now having been emphatically answered. She hoped her story would help address many of Emma's and Josh's doubts

For a moment, there was no response from Emma, until; "Gwen! We had no idea," sensed Emma incredulously. "I can't begin to imagine how you survived with your chronic disability."

"Jamie explained to me after, that as I had approached the time when I was to take my place in his team; the near-death experience was used to trigger the knowledge I would need in my part of our plan; the resources to see it through, provided by those beyond."

Gwen sensed that Emma had followed her story with growing interest, but it would need time to confirm to what extent. What Jamie had done for her, she could offer to others. Gazing towards a future of misery had now suddenly been transformed into one of personal fulfilment and limitless potential.

CHAPTER EIGHTEEN
TRIAL BY MEDIA

IT WAS A FEW DAYS after the monthly meeting that an excited Richard invaded Jamie's office, waving an opened letter at him.

He abruptly drew up a chair, tossing the letter onto Jamie's desk. "What d'you think of that, then?"

Jamie picked up the letter, smiling at Richard's enthusiasm. "Bit excited aren't we?"

"Read it, Mate! and you'll see why," prompted Richard.

Jamie gazed at the television logo heading the letter; it raised no similar enthusiasm in him. He had never envisaged anything more than attracting local interest, feeling able to cope with anything at that level. This, however, was vastly different; the potential existing now that could canvass their work to an ever-increasing audience.

"Why so quiet, Jamie... think of what this could do for our cause, to say nothing of what it might mean for the company." Jamie flashed a quick look at Richard, in response to his company comment. "... Now! Before you chuck any mercenary accusations at me...," said Richard, anticipating a lecture on morality from Jamie. "...The Company's backing has been something that has provided a sound basis for our movement to develop on. In fact, there are those among the hierarchy who have become quite intrigued with our spiritual solution."

Jamie gazed at Richard through narrowing eyes, sensing that now the media were becoming involved, the corporate aspect seemed to be taking over in him.

"You surprise me, Jamie," said Richard at length. "I thought you would've been over the moon about this, like me."

Jamie nodded thoughtfully. "Forgive me, Richard..., but it isn't fame I'm after. I simply want to offer help to those like Vicky."

"But that's what we all want, Jamie. Everything we've done, since that first meeting, has been leading us to this moment." Richard paused, gazing hard at Jamie. "You can't be so naive as to have believed that the success we've had, during the past, would remain exclusive to the few around us?" Richard rose from his seat, and paused by the door. "I'll see you for lunch. We can discuss it more rationally then. After you've had time to think on it. I believe you'll see the real potential of this opportunity clearer."

Jamie feigned a smile, as Richard disappeared behind the closing door. He had not admitted it to Richard, but he was afraid. All the while their events were localised, any conflicting opinions were bearable, but exposure by the media was a whole new ball-game. He gazed down at the letter asking for an interview with the team leader— there were no prizes offered to guess who that was going to be.

He thought of his grandmother, but it did not help much, feeling this was much bigger than anything she had been involved with. How would she have dealt with this, he wondered? A nagging feeling had persisted within him since she first introduced him into spiritualism; telling him it was going to be his task to take the spiritual solution to the world. Over the years, he had tried to manipulate his inner thoughts to support his doubts. However, no matter what excuses he tried to generate, his conscience would not allow him any respite. Faced by the media event now, it had focused him on the truth of his grandmother's prophecy.

Historical transcripts made no secret of how those, who worked for the Infinite One, would always be on the front line. Jamie had years of experience behind him now, and supported by doting followers and helpers. Had Richard been justified in commenting on Jamie's naivety: Jamie, assuming that the future success of their spiritual solution would comfortably occupy him in his little corner of the world? They had Gwen as living proof of its power. Gwen betrayed no hint that she would duck out of any confrontations with the media— she was ready to shout her success from the roof-tops.

During the early years, Jamie had been lulled into thinking that this was all that was needed; to simply be there for people. To some extent, to be there for people was true, but only met part of a wider need. Now as Jamie slipped beyond middle age, the Infinite One was calling in the pledge Jamie had made to Him; it was as if the real task had only just begun.

~2~

For days after, Richard discreetly went about his business, supporting Jamie, as Jamie accepted the idea it was his destiny to demonstrate the power of the spiritual solution. Jamie could not help but wonder where Richard got his strength from; so steadfast in his resolve in wanting to reveal all they had achieved to everyone, regardless of how surreal it appeared.

Gwen had moved on with Emma and Josh, breaking new ground, persuading them to join in and spread the word. Running thought-transference classes: this small team were leading the way into what was developing into a mind-educating revolution, and not only among the chronically disabled. It was their efforts that were finally proving the value of Jamie's spiritual solution— revealing clever intellects caged within crippled bodies.

He could see there was no justification for doubts, as to query one's strategy now, could waste precious resources that might be generated by future achievements of these disabled souls. It was his to simply show them the way by becoming their link with the world beyond: their own success, then, would prove their faith, ability and determination to the physical world.

Thinking back to that time in his office, when Richard had dropped the media bombshell, now only embarrassed him. It was with a clear idea, of how he was going to present their spiritual solution, he set a date for the interview. This media development in the plan, was gradually leading them all to its climax.

The transformation in Emma and Josh, had added weight to their cause. For Emma and Josh to have challenged the law on an aspect they considered limited their human rights, then suddenly, turn one hundred and eighty degrees on their quest, was more evidence that demonstrated the power of the spiritual solution.

***

Viewing it from the dimension beyond, the importance of the

potential offered by the media event had been carefully assessed. There were special souls in the employ of that media group that had been spiritually placed and prepped. Sarah and John would direct this source from beyond, using these resources at their disposal to overcome the influence of the dark entities, as undoubtedly, interference could be expected.

There would be those focused more on viewer-ratings, rather than the subject under discussion. Carers, emotionally affected, watching their loved-ones struggling against their disability, and finally, the disabled souls suffering the agony of their illness. It was hard for those on the physical plane to sense the thoughts of others, but the souls, representative of the spiritual guides, were able to penetrate the minds of all.

As the event approached the climax on Orburn, Jamie was set to enter the final phase of his plan. John had scanned Jamie's celestial horizon, and was aware that, though Jamie had prepared himself to meet this new challenge, doubts from the thought of facing the scrutiny of the world, still lingered in him.

The reserves at Jamie's disposal were powerful indeed: Richard and Gwen, intuitively aware of their roles in the plan now would complete their part. The Infinite One's pledge that no soul would be left alone had been met. Sarah and John now fielded a formidable force for good; confident, that whatever the dark legions threw at their band, on the physical plane, they would be protected.

***

~3~

Sitting quietly in his study, the evening before the television interview, Jamie gazed at Vicky's picture on his desk. She had told him on numerous occasions that their reunion was close at hand, but with the media interview looming, that re-union appeared surreal— as if an eternity away.

He clasped his hands together; the niggling disquiet within him refusing to abate. Focusing again on Vicky's picture, it displayed her as a young, smiling girl. He found himself instinctively drawn to her eyes that seemed locked onto his, and in the soft, eerie glow of his desk-light he sensed they were speaking to him.

Her softly spoken voice drifted into his mind. "Be at peace with yourself, Dear One," she whispered. "The plan approaches completion.

Our celestial guides have everything in place, and we have sensed the Divine Spirit of the Infinite One descend upon us all. Tomorrow's interview will set a precedent that will change the future for everyone on Orburn. The dark influence will lose their grip on this world, as the Infinite One's legions set in motion the final stage that will move Orburn up to a higher plane. On this, our first incarnation, we have been privileged to be part of the divine reclamation of this world. I have seen what awaits us on our continuing voyage to infinity, but what we have achieved here increases the determination in me to meet any future challenges. Rejoice in the knowledge now, that after tomorrow's interview, the plan is complete. The dark legions will make one last concerted effort against the Infinite One, but it is too late; this world, Orburn, is lost to them. As your life here draws to a close, you will witness a change that will sweep across Orburn, and from the subsequent devastation a world of beauty will emerge. Under a united people, Orburn will blossom, and then in the closing years of your life, you will be able to walk freely in the forests and sense the true ecological balance of the Infinite One's creation around you. You will be aware of my presence walking by your side; sense the spiritual exhilaration I feel. The promise of all this will arise from the spiritual solution you will bring to the world tomorrow. Those who choose not to listen to the Infinite One will be lost; destined to take up the challenge again in another life-time somewhere out in the cosmos. Until we meet on that day in the celebration of our reunion, Dear One, may the blessings of the Infinite One be with you."

As Vicky's voice faded from his mind, so did any doubts. Still focused on her eyes, the warmth of her smile crossed the years to comfort him. Once again, her counsel had propped up his flagging courage. The true extent of their faith, and loyalty toward each other, confirming the link they had setup between the spiritual and physical dimensions.

In the wake of that brief audience with Vicky, Jamie persisted in gazing at her picture, savouring the memory of those fleeting moments spent with her. She had helped to dispel any doubts he had in what he needed to do, but the thought of addressing thousands of viewers, and a possible studio audience, continued to produce the traditional butterfly feelings in him. He gazed up at the clock, amazed at how quickly the time had flown. As usual, he would be travelling up with Richard, who was bringing Gwen, Emma and Josh in their unit's disability transit van.

He rose from his chair, suddenly feeling more relaxed and pleasantly tired. The events of the evening faded from his mind; it was a good night's rest he needed now, and his guides beyond were going to see that he got it.

~4~

The following morning he awoke completely refreshed, but still unable to ignore the gentle butterfly feeling turning over in his stomach. He gazed across at his bedside clock; there was no hurry. Another five minutes, he thought, shower, breakfast, and then after dressing, prepare for the media interview.

He wondered about how he would introduce his spiritual solution during his opening address. In the past he had never had to do it, it had always been dealt with by Richard. But after previous discussions with the others; for today, a strange feeling within had made him decide, he should do it.

Clearing away after breakfast, he got down to creating a transcript for his address. Half an hour later, the page was still blank. Nothing seemed to come; it worried him, suddenly feeling so isolated. Surely Vicky would not abandon him, not now they were approaching such an important climax. His thought made no sense. After all they had been through together, it was unrealistic; even an insult to her memory to even contemplate she would desert him: there had to be some other underlying reason why she had not been more forth-coming.

Opening his mind to her, he waited for a contact, but nothing came. He sat there in silence, confused, unable to generate any sort of theme of what he was going to say at the interview. Suddenly, he sensed an alien thought probing the periphery of his mind— he became excited, anticipating it to be Vicky returning to add something to her previous address.

"Jamie," whispered Gwen's voice. "Let things happen; just you being there is all that is required." Her voice sounded different; strong and resolute, like some strange manifestation in her had taken place. "Today, the inhabitants of this world are going to receive a message that will chill the hearts of those who have challenged the patience of the Infinite One— the day of reckoning on Orburn has come."

Jamie's concerns flooded back. "But, Gwen!" he uttered. "I can think of nothing to tell them; my mind has never been this blank—what am I to say?"

"Peace! Jamie. Everything will be revealed as the Infinite One has planned it— trust in Him."

With those few words, her presence faded from his mind, leaving him still more confused. Her message had aired a sinister meaning, but what was even more curious, was the confident manner in which she had said it; there seemed to be a strange remoteness about her. There was no hint of her past dependency on him. It was as if she had suddenly received an insight into the future; that despite the limitations her body placed on her, it was imperative she got that message across to those she loved.

Was this then, to be the essence of his message, to prophesy an imminent catastrophic event? If it was the case, he needed more information. It was not that he doubted any of his friends or what was being asked of him; after all, it had been him that had brought spiritual freedom to them all. As the source of that information, to show doubts was unthinkable, but the thought of standing in front of interviewers and cameras unprepared, unsettled him.

Undoubtedly he would be up there on his own; the others placed remotely away from him. Jamie thought of his grandmother; would she have faltered? The question, he felt, was redundant before it was asked, as the times she had faced cynical attitudes, brought on nostalgic reminisces in him of her erupting into fire and brimstone dialogues with them.

He smiled to himself, as the sound of the chiming doorbell brought him back to reality. He swung the door open, finding Richard and Sylvie standing on the doorstep, gazing solemnly at him.

"It's nice to be greeted by cheerful faces first thing in the morning," he commented humorously. His statement passed without response.

"Can we come in for a minute, Jamie?" Sylvie asked softly.

"Of course," replied Jamie. "But time is marching on, and we have a long journey ahead of..."

Sylvie reached out, placing her hand on his arm. "Only for a minute."

Jamie sensed something had happened, and gazing through the windows of the parked transit van, noted Gwen's absence. In that moment, he intuitively guessed the reason why she had approached him earlier.

"It's Gwen, isn't it? ..." he whispered. "She's gone, hasn't she?"

Sylvie nodded slowly. "It had been expected as her condition deteriorated, but she made us promise not to say anything. When the time was right, she said she would tell you herself."

Jamie turned away; another friend had departed the arena, but instinctively, he knew that from the world beyond, Gwen would continue on with her part of their plan.

"She chose the right time," he whispered, nodding slowly. He turned back to them, a faint smile on his face at the curious looks on theirs'. "She came to me earlier. I sensed there was something different about her, but preoccupied with the coming interview I gave it little thought. She's joined the team beyond. From what she said, I feel now, some apocalyptic message is going to arise from this event."

Ushering Sylvie and Richard out, he reached up for his coat. Closing the door behind him, he followed them to the van. Immersed in silence, they set off on the journey to the studio. Jamie knew it would be impossible to lift the sombre mood; they would all miss Gwen, but it was her presence, not her, that had gone— both she and Vicky were free of their fleshy prisons now.

Immersed in thoughts of Gwen's memory, they felt the power of the Infinite One descend over them all; drawing them together to focus on this task. Jamie sensed the presence of his guide John, and perceived that something wonderful was about to take place. There was no doubt in him now, that what was going to happen at that interview would effectively over-ride everyone's free will.

The Infinite One's patience had been tried, and through His actions now, Jamie wondered if the reality of the spiritual dimension would be revealed. He intuitively felt that if it was the case, any subsequent revelation of the spiritual existence could only mean one thing— that the day of this world's apocalypse was at hand.

CHAPTER NINETEEN
A STATEMENT FROM BEYOND

~1~

AS THEY JOURNEYED ON, CONVERSATION was sparse, artificial and meaningless. The mood contradicted all that Jamie believed in, and what he had taught others about the spiritual existence. His previous dialogues, with Vicky, then Gwen the night before, had hinted at a sinister future that seemed incredulous. But this past decade on Orburn had witnessed a steady deterioration of many societies' infrastructure, and which then, had gone on to fail, displaying heart-rending scenes of despair.

The wealth of the world was proving inadequate, trying to cope with the rising tide of human tragedy and the plight of wildlife, which was sweeping across the globe. Jamie gazed at Emma and Josh dozing quietly with their carers. Souls like them were especially vulnerable on the physical plane; how would they manage in an apocalyptic event? The morbid scenarios drifted through his mind with the realisation— they would simply be unable too. The thought raised the determination in him that he would try to help any life-form— while he had the strength, he would care for them all to the last.

Reflecting back over the current year, there had been many catastrophic upheavals affecting poorer communities around the world. The predicament those people found themselves in, had touched the hearts of the wealthier nations who had donated generously, but had it come too late? Past conflicts within humanity were witness to hatred among nations that had led to inhumane atrocities, but now the conflict was between mankind and his world. With their backs against the wall, the inhabitants of Orburn were finally showing signs of uniting— was this, understanding, then, what Vicky's and Gwen's message was leading everyone towards?

An incredible scenario was beginning to intrude his thoughts; it appeared too incredulous, even for him to accept, and yet the thought persisted. It seemed to ask the question; did a world have to approach annihilation before its inhabitants united, would that be the trigger that could finally release Orburn from the clutches of the dark entities? That any civilisation on a world should have to teeter on the edge of the precipice, before its people realised the futility of conflict, was a dramatic conclusion for anyone to arrive at.

Jamie felt these few thoughts answered part of the question, but deep within each incarnate soul, he had been taught that the spiritual bond between them existed. In the physical life, this benevolent attribute was suppressed, overpowered by a soul's search for the material resources that ensured a comfortable life. He reflected back to Vicky's address to him. *'Tomorrow's interview will set a precedent that will change the future for everyone on Orburn'*, in that, at least, she had implied there was a future?

Jamie took heart from her words, but sensed from them, that the amenities, parts of the world like his had grown accustomed to, were destined to become scarcer. No one left on Orburn would be spared. Those faithful to the Infinite One would be saved to return to the world. He deliberated on the scriptures, and how in the aftermath of such an event, it would be the meek, then, that would inherit the world.

***

Sarah and John were sensing into Jamie a preview of what was going to take place during the approaching media event. Though shown on the local channels at first, the dramatic impact it was going to have would send the broadcasters of the world scurrying to screen it. This initial scramble would be to compete for viewer-ratings; questioning Jamie's source and how surreal it appeared, but as time passed, Orburn would confirm Jamie's message from beyond as reality.

Sarah and John knew this to be another opportunity for humanity on Orburn; another period approaching where the Infinite One reset life on a world. The simple choice offered then would remain the same for those on Orburn, as on all worlds; either return to decadence, or take their world up to the celestial realm.

***

~2~

As the afternoon wore on, they were approaching the outskirts of the capital. The traffic was steadily building up, with Richard delegating the task of map-reading to Jamie for directions.

"Give me the good old countryside anytime," sighed Richard, wistfully.

Jamie grinned. "That's a fact, Richard, but there's been many a frustrating period that I've spent in jams, around our neck of the woods." Jamie gazed out through the windscreen at the queues stretching away into the distance. "No one wants to walk anywhere now."

Jamie buried himself in the map, following the arrows he had pencilled in earlier. "We're looking for exit thirteen; that'll take us out onto the ring-road. Fortunately the studio's located in the outer suburbs of the city." Richard nodded, gazing despondently up at a motorway sign indicating their exit to be several further on.

It was another tedious hour before they were finally cruising down the ring-road en-route to the studio. As they sped on, a large complex, with an array of transmitters was beginning to loom in the distance— its appearance raised the butterfly feeling in Jamie again.

"Like a lamb being led to the slaughter," Jamie murmured thoughtfully.

"Then we'll all be slaughtered together," whispered Sylvie, reassuringly.

Jamie smiled at her statement in support. "After it's over, I would imagine Dave might not be too disappointed, then, that he couldn't join us, eh, Sylvie?"

"No one could be more so...," she replied, gazing out over the view as the carriageway began to descend towards the studio complex. "... The outlook over the city is quite breathtaking from up here, Jamie."

There was no response from Jamie, his mind, once again, immersed in the coming interview.

After another ten minutes or so, they were turning into the studio complex. Richard parked up, asking everyone to sit tight while he checked them in. Sylvie began liaising with the carers to organize Emma's and Josh's disembarkation. The minds of the two disabled souls were alive with excitement, bombarding their carers and Sylvie with torrents of mental questions about the coming interview. Though not actively taking part, they would be able to listen in on the dialogues of those involved; their developed mental ability allowing them intimate discussions within their group.

Richard was making his way out of the studio main entrance, and paused on the steps, beckoning them to come over and join him. The small group stood in the huge studio concourse, gazing at the bustle of activity going on around them. As Richard introduced Jamie to the studio manager, Jamie was suddenly aware he had become the focus of attention: curious eyes coming to rest on him over the topic he was going to present. The studio manager greeted him, but unable to hide the sceptical gaze reflected in his own eyes.

~3~

The presenter arrived, beckoning them toward a door, having directed Emma, Josh and their carers to a waiting area. He closed it thoughtfully, gesturing for everyone to take a seat. Jamie intuitively sensed the presenter was finding it difficult to approach the spiritual subject, appearing to air the feeling that he had drawn the short straw on this interview.

Richard had already been introduced to the presenter and smiled, gesturing toward him. "Jamie, this is Mr Alvin Styles: Alvin, Jamie Hoskins and Sylvie Webber."

Alvin stretched out his hand to Sylvie, and then to Jamie, gazing pensively at him. "I've heard a lot about you, Jamie." His statement lacked conviction, but was no less than Jamie had expected, and far from increasing Jamie's earlier emotions, it had served to settle them. A short pause followed, while Alvin vacantly sifted through some papers, appearing to stare through them, rather than at them.

At length, he looked up. "I'm bound to ask the question, Jamie, whether you've had any experience of broadcasting before."

Jamie shook his head. "Though, I'm not expecting there to be any problems."

Gradually the fragmented discussion mutated into a more relaxed dialogue, with Alvin explaining how he planned to conduct the interview. He fanned through a wad of papers in his hand again, offering a transcript of the interview to Jamie. Jamie gazed at it, instinctively feeling he would never get to read it, but felt obliged to go through the motions for Alvin's sake.

As the meeting progressed, the business aspect took over, with Alvin engrossed in the logistics of the interview procedure: a visit to the make-up room first, to fine-tune appearances, and then the timing of the cue that would lead Jamie out onto the studio area. By the end of the pre-interview session, Alvin's appraisal had given Jamie some idea of the type of questions he would be asking about their group's spiritual solution.

Folding up his wad of papers, Alvin gazed hesitantly up at Jamie. "I'm sorry if I appeared a little distant earlier, I've not had any experience of the psychic subject."

Jamie understood his feeling, but remained unaffected by it. "This is an opportunity we have long waited for, Alvin, but during the coming evening, the spiritual solution will speak for itself. Simply by giving us this opportunity, you have made yourself part of our plan." Alvin seemed at a loss of what to make of Jamie's statement, and politely grinned in response.

Alvin rose from his chair, and shook hands with them, momentarily gazing intently at Jamie again. Extracting himself from his thoughts, he directed them to where they could join the others in the studio canteen. Jamie smiled as Alvin disappeared, and then gazed nonchalantly down at the transcript he had been given. Displaying the time-schedule, leading up to the interview, they had a little over three hours before the preparation period began— his interview slot, set to begin at eight later that evening.

Richard sauntered thoughtfully alongside Jamie as they made their way to the canteen. "You could have cut the air in there with a knife, Jamie when I introduced you. Alvin seemed relaxed enough with me, but obviously embarrassed over how to approach the psychic subject he'll need to discuss with you later."

"Seemed that way. My gut feeling is; it's going to be the other way around during the actual interview this evening. Alvin's appraisal described a panel of guests joining us out there; their names are listed here on the transcript." The thought should have brought on all his old fears, but strangely enough, Jamie was almost looking forward to the interview now.

Richard gazed hesitantly up at him. "Alvin said he would like

Sylvie and me to join you on the interview this evening... if that's OK with you?"

"I don't see why not; you're both as much involved as I am, I don't know how I've become so much the focal point."

Sylvie shuddered at the thought. "I'll just simply freeze. The thought of all those people staring at me, wondering how I manage the resources for disabled people with a head full of fantas..." She paused mid-sentence. "... I mean... What I meant to..."

Jamie rested his hand on her arm. "I know exactly what you mean. I too, have realised how our solution must appear, especially to those unfamiliar with it." He paused, gazing thoughtfully ahead. "I don't think we're going to have much to say in the interview anyway..." Sylvie and Richard stared curiously at him. "...It was something Gwen said last night when she came to me... *'Let things happen; just by you being there is all that is required.'* What does that signify to you, Richard?"

"I can't begin to betray what my intuition is telling me; it's too fantastic for words."

Following the signs, they entered the canteen, spotting their group tucking into an early tea. Emma and Josh mentally inundated Jamie with copious questions, bursting to know what had been discussed, and the subsequent interview plan that had arisen from the meeting.

~4~

Time ticked on through the remainder of the afternoon, arriving at the point when Jamie, Richard and Sylvie were to begin the preparation sequence. With a final update from the producer, they were left in the care of the program cue manager to await their call.

The distant sound of applause from the studio audience announced the beginning of the show; both Sylvie and Richard visibly affected by nerves. Jamie, however, had sensed a powerful presence he had not felt before, during past trance events. His guide, John's approach, was familiar to him, but markedly different from what he was experiencing now.

The definitive impression he was getting from this entity, aired an authoritative, superior knowledge, sensing him with a presence he felt reflected the age of the universe itself. In the presence of this master spirit, a strange, unworldly feeling humbled Jamie— aware of thoughts fleeting through his mind that unsettled, and yet, intrigued him.

As the time drew nearer to the interview; the presence of that master entity increased, and began to take hold of Jamie's consciousness. The physical environment around Jamie was taking on a surreal feeling; like he was slowly being transported into another dimension. It was a weird sensation; that despite the fact he felt he was slowly losing control of his physical being, he intuitively trusted that entity.

Throughout his life, he had learned that the power possessed by the dark influence on the physical plane was constant. Using the physical attributes available to them, they manipulated young souls into disobeying the Infinite One's laws, but comparing it with the presence of the power he was experiencing now, it eclipsed anything he had felt before. It seemed as if to harness the power of the universe itself, possessing the ability to crush a world, like an insect, under foot.

Jamie, sensing he was beyond the point of no return, sent out a plea to the Infinite One for His protection, and that he was ready to play his role in His divine plan. Jamie's soul erupted in a celebration of feelings, as the Infinite One responded, diminishing the unsettling emotions in Jamie.

Jamie now found himself in his usual trance environment, gazing across at the familiar faces of relatives that had completed their transition. His guides John and Sarah with Vicky, were joined now by Emily, Gwen and their partners: it warmed his soul to see them all smiling back at him. Instinctively, he sensed the time had come for the strange being to play out their role, and gazed down through the celestial window, watching, as his physical self moved out onto the studio set.

The iridescent light around his body glowed radiantly, with an intensity he had not been aware of before. The master spirit began to speak through him. Using past apocalyptic events as his witness, he illustrated the risk to humanity, if the present civilisation continued to ignore the doctrine of the Infinite One. The entity allowed no opportunity for the interviewer to offer any questions; continually commanding the attention of all those present.

The studio audience sat inanimate, displaying expressions that ranged from the incredulous to acceptance. The entity held nothing back, narrating the emphatic warning from beyond. The event had not turned out as Jamie had imagined it would, expecting a supernatural revelation that clearly revealed some idea of the existence beyond. Instead, the message used historical events that had seen countless, past civilisations founder.

The entity, related a lot of what ecclesiastics and his grandmother had taught him, Jamie, having accepted that on faith. The presentation of this event, though focused on his spiritual solution, had seized the opportunity to warn the inhabitants of Orburn that they were close to a reckoning with the Infinite One; everyone having to accept this on faith, similarly.

From the theme of the being's message, Jamie realised that nothing had changed. The onus, still rested upon the ability of an individual to accept existing doctrines, passed down through the ages. What Jamie felt added to their authenticity this time, was that they were being brought to the world by an angelic ambassador.

In that moment, it dawned on Jamie to whom the response from this interview would be directed: this address would appear to have come from him. It fell to his ability, to cope with recriminations from doubters or clarification of his beliefs to those searching for the truth. Being privy to this event in the spiritual dimension, made one thing graphically clear to Jamie. The fact the powers-that-be had chosen one of their divine entities to deliver their message, confirmed to Jamie that some level of global upheaval approached.

Paused in the spiritual environment, Jamie sensed his time was short on Orburn. Though beyond middle age now, it seemed unlikely he could avoid any, global, catastrophic event before his transition. He gazed across at Vicky, sensing from her thoughts, she would stay by his side. So many people, during this prophesied event, would come to depend on the strength of his faith; he, feeling obliged to accept this responsibility that the Infinite One had asked of him.

The spiritual entity completed its address, and Jamie sensed the familiar sensation of being drawn back in to his physical body. As usual he was aware of what had taken place, and that the presenter had seized the opportunity to take control of his show.

Alvin gazed at Jamie through narrowing eyes, a faint grin spreading over his face. "Well that was quite a revelation, Jamie," he murmured, gazing around the rest of the guests— waiting to expound their views. "I'm bound to say that what you've said doesn't really reveal anything one way or the other...," he continued. "...In fact, it feels to have produced a bit of an anti-climax for me personally." Alvin fidgeted in his chair, rubbing his chin thoughtfully as he searched for words to make his point. "Ecclesiastics have expounded the folly of mankind for centuries, and predicted approaching apocalypses, and yet, we're still here."

Jamie smiled. "That is a provocative statement to make indeed, Alvin. My objective has been to ask people to look at life here logically. Two irrefutable facts should cause us to question our existence more realistically. First is the transience of it, second, our inevitable exit when it ends. These two facts, alone should lead us to the conclusion that while here, none of the material attributes on the physical plane belong to any one of us..." Alvin made to cut in, but Jamie raised his hand, gesturing he wanted to finish. "... Thinking about what I have just said leaves us with a simple choice. We can either use the physical attributes to indulge our lives here, or we can share the use of those attributes, and manifest them into spiritual values we can take with us."

Alvin gazed across at one of his guests, renowned for their religious opinions. "Well, George; manifest physical values into spiritual ones?" inviting him to comment.

George clasped his hands resolutely together, gazing thoughtfully at Jamie. "I've listened to you carefully, Jamie, and much of what you've said in your address, confirms a large part of the doctrine I personally adhere to. But I must take issue with you on a certain point. To encourage people to dabble in matters of the occult can expose the soul to undesirable influences."

"That is precisely why we need to achieve an understanding of the spiritual existence here, so that we can make the right choices." Jamie became engrossed in his point. "Your comment implies a distrust of our Maker's ability to protect us. If we accept the revelations of ancient doctrines, that the spiritual life is the real existence, then, it follows, as children of that dimension, it is natural for us all to apply for guidance from our origin."

Jamie knew he was treading on precarious ground, as to encourage people to believe in what he deemed was the true life, first required them to accept the spiritual existence. He felt the two facts he had high-lighted, relating to the duration and eventual exit from the physical life, appeared to have had a vague impact on some. The way his grandmother had first mentioned them, he had considered she was trying to create facts from fantasy, but after, found himself intrigued by the logic theme she had used to present them.

Jamie had become committed to her logical theory, comparing his modern-day thinking with ancient scriptures. It was not that he felt those witnesses of old were confused, more how episcopal institutions, then, recorded and communicated divine events, using symbolism in their descriptions. Intuitively, he felt it more sensible to take it in small steps when presenting new ideas on subjects that appeared surreal. Like his spiritual solution; to try and reveal everything in one sweep, made it too incredulous for people to accept.

Describing how the uniting of a world's inhabitants could take them up to a higher plane, shared an affinity with everyone's hope for world peace. The sinister event that had been prophesied for the inhabitants of Orburn, Jamie hoped might be the incentive that could halt them on the edge of the precipice. The angelic entity had submitted just enough information, and combined with the focus on decisions, like Emma's and Josh's to abort their voluntary euthanasia issue, it could increase the authenticity of Jamie's spiritual solution.

The media aspect had offered Jamie the opportunity to disclose his logical theory to a greater audience; asking people to view their lives more realistically. The interview, however, had involved an element of risk by not providing outright proof of the life beyond. The belief in it still required faith, but the transcript of that evening's interview was gradually circulating around the world, and subtly focused on the increasingly persuasive power of Jamie's spiritual solution, was adding credibility to it.

CHAPTER TWENTY
THE EVALUATION

~1~

IT WAS DURING THE WEEK, following the inaugural media interview, that more prominent networks began taking an interest. Jamie's intent to help the chronically disabled, like Vicky, now threatened to immerse him deeper into age-old, conflicting opinions, debating issues arising from people's beliefs in the spiritual and physical dimensions.

Describing how he used logic to demonstrate the relationship between the two dimensions, revealed that if certain criteria were met, it would lead to opportunities that could link incarnate souls to their spiritual companions. Now that Jamie was exposed to a wider audience, opinions, which criticised his submissions, had set a precedent for more heated debates in the future.

The media were keen to exploit the discussions, arising from Jamie's story, but the negative themes they concentrated on, were inadvertently leading people away from the objective he was trying to achieve. The general public naturally focused on these reports, and in particular, those that centred on the on-going debate of voluntary euthanasia— Jamie viewed this turn of events despairingly. He thought he had already dealt with that challenge, feeling it a bitter revelation to see it come to the fore-front again; particularly, now, to an expanding world audience.

As a result of that inaugural media interview, the future, now, had become a volatile one for Jamie— two classic aspects governing its direction. The physical aspect was dominated by the usual misunderstanding and distrust that had plagued humanity throughout history. In Jamie's spiritual subject, he was seeking to persuade people to look at fundamental aspects of their lives logically, claiming it had succeeded in uplifting the lives of many disabled people.

The logic idea required a train of thought that looked at certain, irrefutable facts in the physical life: facts that applied definitive, limitations on the physical existence. What complicated this idea for Jamie, were the dialogues he continually found himself engaged in; demanding proof he was unable to offer to support his idea.

Possessing no stable argument, on which to address the queries constantly directed at him, his case appeared groundless. The only strategy he felt safe in pursuing was his developing logical theory: while it seemed to have made some people pause to think, the singular demand for the physical proof prevented the curiosity in the majority to explore it.

Over the weeks ahead, there was never to be any respite for Jamie: an increase in opinions that labelled him as unfeeling— one who supported help for the suffering, but used ideas based on fantasy. What was even more frustrating: he knew that Emma and Josh were living proof of the power of his solution, but their disabled appearance, refuted it.

The principles that governed life on all physical planes, remained the same— there were no short cuts. Each incarnate soul faced their chosen, physical challenges on spiritually equal terms. As a result of the new media development, Jamie felt he was losing what little credibility he had gained. As his plan took him further out into the world, he continually found himself challenged by intransigent attitudes: People who simply would not accept his spiritual solution on faith. The sanctity of life everywhere, seemed to be losing its value; the physical aspects, masking opportunities that revealed clues that could lead to a better understanding of life's purpose.

~2~

Relaxed in the sanctuary of his home, Jamie increasingly chose those moments to meditate on how humanity would cope with a progressively, insecure future. He felt so helpless, even after dedicating himself to the Infinite One. By applying faith to do what the Master Spirit had asked of him, the symbolic pathways, described in ancient scriptures he chose in life, had proved rock-solid— but how was he to get this over? Jamie felt as if his back was pinned against the wall, but to abort his plan, now, by suddenly yielding to the opinions arising in the wake of the media events, would be tantamount to admitting he doubted his own faith.

During these intimate moments, the presence of Vicky was unmistakeable; a powerful sensation welling up in him, like lava spewing out from a volcanic vent. He sensed a mood of urgency in her presence, impressing on him what lay in the future; his civilisation, destined to approach perilously close to the edge of that symbolic precipice.

Turning into work the following day, he found Richard waiting in his office.

Jamie hung up his coat, and then made his way to his desk. "It's the early bird that catches the worm, eh, Richard?" he muttered cheerfully. "To what do I owe this sudden honour then— more work?"

Richard smiled thoughtfully at Jamie. "Something a little more disconcerting. The board are getting a little concerned about the company's image, especially now that the media events are exposing us to a wider audience."

"But it has no reflection on the company." Jamie settled himself behind his desk and gazed studiously back at him. "I don't understand their concerns Richard, partly, as with any company; publicity is acceptable in whatever form it presents, but primarily, you know as well as I do, any serious repercussions will be directed at us..."

"And which they already have," interrupted Richard.

Jamie looked curiously at him. "How?"

"You must concede, Jamie, the policy of our society is based on what the majority of the populous consider as fantasy." Richard reached into his briefcase, drawing out a wad of letters. "I'll not bore you with the details. These are just a few responses from viewers who've been following the interviews— read them yourself." He closed up his case and gazed at Jamie. "I'm not particularly enchanted by the company's attitude, since, if you remember, it was the board who initiated the idea of the meeting concept through me. But they're having second thoughts, now that criticisms are being levelled at us. It is up in the air at the moment, but with the ball firmly placed in our court." Richard rose to his feet and paused by the open door; feigning a thoughtful smile, he disappeared behind it.

Jamie stared at the pile of opened letters on his desk, guessing at the theme of opinions in them from the reserved mood he had sensed in Richard. He gazed hesitantly at the phone, wondering if Sylvie's and Dave's departments had been targeted similarly. If it had affected Richard; one of his stalwarts, how would it have affected those two? Jamie suddenly felt isolated, but instinctively sensed something more lay behind Richard's mood. Richard had usually thrived on challenge during the past, meeting any problems head-on. Jamie, though looked upon as the leader, had often found himself dependant on Richard's counsel when metering out advice and encouragement to others in the team.

There was nothing he could do about it now; his thoughts, drifting back toward the stack of files waiting in his in-tray. By lunchtime, Jamie was feeling more settled as he made his way to the canteen. He curiously watched Richard spontaneously bury himself behind a newspaper, having clearly noticed him approaching. Jamie made his way across and seated himself at the table, gazing, intrigued by the opened newspaper hovering in front of Richard.

Jamie slowly began to smile. "What can cause someone to read the newspaper upside down?"

The paper slowly descended, revealing a rye grin breaking over Richard's face.

"Well I must confess; the grin is more preferable to the scowl I received back in the office earlier. Your present behaviour convinces me that you're either in love, or afraid of something."

Richard folded the newspaper up, staring resolutely at him. "You know me well enough now, Jamie to know I'm afraid of nothing..."

"Then what's up? This moody behaviour is not typical of you," grinned Jamie.

"True! So what's the other option?" replied Richard enigmatically.

"Jamie gazed at him confused, until the 'love' aspect, in his earlier comment, teased an incredible idea into him.

Jamie's jaw bounced off the floor, as a thought drifted into his mind that Richard's statement implied that he was, indeed, in love. "It can't be that you... No! No...! Surely not... I've always had you down as a confirmed bachelor." Jamie sniggered incredibly, watching the grin on Richard's face broaden; complemented by his soft, breathless chuckles. "Who is it?" insisted Jamie— surely not you and Sylvie...?

Come on, Richard, else I'll not get any sleep tonight— wondering about it."

A silent nod from Richard confirmed Jamie's suspicion.

Jamie was gob-smacked. So engrossed with the media project, it had blinded him to what was happening between two of his most intimate friends.

"Richard, old friend, I'm so delighted for you both... How long has this been going on for?"

"Since that conversation in the office when I made certain suggestions to you, and where you said you weren't interested."

It was almost with a sense of relief that Jamie declared how happy he was for them. "And I thought I was losing the support of one of my team stalwarts."

Richard shook his head. "After all we've achieved, Jamie it would be sacrilege to let anything divert us from our objectives now. However, from subsequent discussions I've had with the board, they plan to monitor the response from the next interview."

Jamie smiled thoughtfully, but lost in the joy of the moment, ignored Richard's statement. "You sly ole fox: this news really has cheered me up— we must go out to celebrate. I concede that two's company etc, but in this case..." Jamie paused, gazing at Richard incredulously. "You wait till I see Sylvie..."

"No! No!" interrupted Richard. "I'll break it to her that I've told you... she's a little shy. Anyway, you've enough on your plate preparing for the next interview. Sylvie tells me the network has focused on another chronically disabled young woman, and one who remains unmoved on what she considers to be our alleged success. Apparently she represents a significant challenge to our movement, and seems unlikely to be as understanding as Gwen was, or Emma and Josh are now toward our group."

Jamie gazed down at his empty plate. "We can't convince everyone, Richard, but that shouldn't deter us from trying. Leave it in Sylvie's hands. From past conversations I've had with her, she's as strong in spirit as we are.

~**3**~

Jamie got up, grinning down at Richard provocatively. "I won't see you later, as I've to work on this evening; got a particularly complicated schematic to workout." At first glances, it may help to uncomplicate lives a little."

Richard grinned coyly. "I couldn't see you this evening, anyway; I'm meeting Sylvie."

"Ho! Ho! Do I sense a precedent has been set here, making it necessary to approach your secretary for appointments to see you in future?"

Richard laughed, dusting Jamie's shoulder sportingly with his folded newspaper.

Making his way back to his office, Jamie contemplated the thought of how well the names Sylvie and Richard sounded together; they had certainly been discreet about their developing relationship. Their news had brought an uplifting moment to the current events in their lives, revealing how so many good things were coming from their spiritual solution. As he turned into his office, he sensed the presence of the spiritual team beyond; feeling they were also celebrating the news.

Moments, like Sylvie's and Richard's joining, Jamie considered were one of the true highlights in life. He compared it with his time with Vicky. Though their period together had been brief, the bond that grew between them was lasting— it would allow nothing to separate them now.

Sitting behind his desk, an intriguing thought drifted through Jamie's mind. It prompted the question; could Sylvie be Richard's spiritual partner? Could Richard's decision to dedicate his life to helping him execute his plan have revealed a mutual, spiritual affinity that already existed between him and Sylvie; the strength of which had drawn them together? A definitive notion in Jamie convinced him he was right.

Thinking over what Richard had said earlier, about the challenge from the young woman, Jamie's conscience was clear in accepting a person's right to think what they wished. As far as he was concerned, the guidance he received from beyond was emphatically the truth. Whenever he put questions to them, the link to the spiritual world appeared as open as that existing between those close to him in the material life.

After all his experiences over the years, Jamie recognised the purpose in his life now, and how much he owed others who had helped him develop his faith. Continually meditating on the future filled him with confidence, speculating on what awaited them all in the life beyond. The truth gained with each experience in the physical life, added to the promise of greater achievement in their spiritual future. It had taught him how the main objective, of the physical existence was to provide the learning curve that prepared a soul for the next phase in the life beyond— each experience, either adding to or detracting from the end result

In this, he felt compelled to share what he had learnt with others, perhaps triggering some aspect that would help that young woman to pause and reflect.

***

Sarah and John deliberated on the approaching global event on Orburn, and felt no concerns over Jamie's ability to cope with it. Constantly sensing into him, their satisfaction over his continuing success, they shared his moods of meditation, advising him during his moments of contemplation. As he approached, what promised to be an unprecedented event, he sensed the gravity of this last phase of his plan. The prospect of failure, now, was not a factor in the equation; only success, figuring in his and Vicky's spiritual future.

John monitored Jamie's celestial horizon, focusing on a point when the Infinite One's divine messenger would approach him again. He sensed the theme of the sinister message that divine entity was destined to deliver, and the demands it would place on Jamie's mental and physical resources.

Prior to the onset of Orburn's cataclysmic decent, Jamie's parent hosts would leave the physical plane; spared the misery of human disruption that was consequent of catastrophic upheaval. The Infinite One had already initiated His plan to save those loyal to Him. The divine civilisation, which had seeded Orburn eons of years before, had, once again, embarked on the voyage across the universe.

The gigantic motherships, their origin lost in the arcane past of the universe, were streaking across the infinity of space toward their rendezvous. Sarah and John reflected back over the experience of similar events, during their voyage to infinity. These magnificent vessels were the tools of the higher physical planes; created from a divine blue-print only the Infinite One administered from.

The presence of the souls from the higher physical plane, Jamie's guides, and the chosen ones present with Jamie in the material life, once again, confirmed the Infinite One's promise that he would leave no one alone who remained faithful to Him.

***

CHAPTER TWENTY ONE
DIVINE EMISSARY

~1~

*

EMERGING FROM THE NOSTALGIC REFLECTION of his life, Jamie continued to gaze at the gently swaying curtain that had closed behind his mother's coffin. In a morbid sort of way, if there was going to be any form of global disruption to life in the future world, he was glad both his beloved parents would be out of it. Over the past two decades, Orburn's environment had been steadily threatening change; the elements, unleashing chaotic events across the world that was reaching catastrophic proportions.

Each day, news bulletins reported on countless scenes of tragedy, but what Jamie found more worrying was the destruction of crops and their areas. So concerned was Jamie, he embarked upon an intense horticultural scheme in his own back garden. During the planning stage, the idea had seemed ridiculously unrealistic and inadequate, but should the unthinkable happen, there seemed no alternative.

Using every available scrap of ground, he planted high-yielding crops, placing tubs on the paths and patio areas. The idea would not seem so ludicrous, if the populous in general could be persuaded to do likewise. Complacent onlookers, however, deemed him as a wild eccentric living in a world of fantasy; over dramatising what they considered to be natural, evolutionary changes taking place over Orburn.

Jamie conceded to their opinion outwardly, but they had missed the point; evolutionary change needed to be prepared for. Those who chose to ignore the warnings, their world was offering them, were following humanity's traditions of the past. As inevitable as those past evolutionary changes appeared in the annals of history now, the ancient inhabitants of Orburn had continued on unaware: their civilisations, finally swept away due to their ignorance of the mechanisms controlling their world.

Now in these uncertain times, it served no purpose to recriminate over who was responsible today; to simply point the accusing finger at those displaying short-sighted, complacent attitudes. However derisory Jamie's solutions appeared to others, it was essential that he stuck to his strategy; try to persuade others to consider his logical understanding of where he believed everyone was heading. Now well beyond middle age, time was of essence. Jamie's twilight years were approaching rapidly, confirmed in him by the changes his body was undergoing, as he neared the end of his incarnate period.

The sinister nature of the daily, human tragedies, going on around Jamie, were changing, seeming to confirm the uneasy feeling of how close the major event could be. Daily evidence of the threat, posed by Orburn, was reflected in the intensity of the impact on lifestyles. The scale of the disruption had reached the stage now where it was not only measured in the death-toll, but more from the millions that had been displaced— their habitats and amenities, wiped out by the increasing magnitude of weather events.

The destruction of crops was placing ever increasing demands on the world's food resources, bringing into question the poorer societies' ability to survive. The help, currently offered by the more advanced nations of the world, encouraged Jamie, reflecting back over one of his earlier thoughts. Did a world's inhabitants have to approach the threat of annihilation before they united?

As the weeks passed, no amount of knowledge, spiritual or otherwise, could completely suppress the feeling of uncertainty that constantly haunted Jamie over what the future held. The spiritual knowledge and psychic ability he drew on, helped to settle the growing fear in those who had followed his interviews, while the media focused their concern on what was having an affect on world monetary systems.

Orburn's increasingly hostile mood was causing thousands

across the world to reconsider Jamie's spiritual revelations. In a world environment that was clearly approaching a crisis point in evolution, people were viewing the threat it placed on their lives from a different perspective. To hoard personal fortunes in a declining, market atmosphere, seemed pointless, but to Jamie, however, his new-found wealth allowed him the opportunity to plan ahead for his invalided souls.

As time moved on, others placed their trust in his group; stretching its resources, but still the means to provide for everyone came. During past audiences with Vicky, she had told him he would be contacted and directed to a safe haven: the resources, to achieve the mass migration of his dependent souls, released to him before the financial systems failed. Following his groups' resettlement, there would be a short period before relief arrived. Then, like everyone else, they would find themselves at the mercy of the elements.

Over the subsequent months ahead, those he had to care for, dramatically increased in numbers the more widely known he became. Fear, and the lack of spiritual understanding, were the two main reasons that sent people flocking to him. As time passed, the insurmountable odds that faced him pushed his faith to the limit. The various societies' amenities continued to fail; his beliefs criticised, with panic leading to a general condemnation of ecclesiastical doctrines.

Curiously, one of the last messages Jamie had received from Vicky, had referred to the safe area as, 'easily accessible'. The definition of what this phrase implied, he had considered was a forgone conclusion; it had to be, especially in view of the condition of some of those they were caring for. At the time, he had accepted it unconsciously, but a strange notion in him, now, sensed that there might be some underlying meaning behind what it implied.

Listening to the daily reports, the level of destruction, occurring around the world, continued to break records. Jamie felt it would inevitably reach the point where it could threaten human survival— what would happen to them all then? The question was unnerving, even with his spiritual knowledge. Jamie, however, implicitly trusted his sources; they had never once let him down, but it was the constant, uncertainty that frightened him. The information he received from those in the spiritual dimension, helped to offset his anxieties, but the physical aspect continued to test the faith in them all on the material plane.

~2~

It was on one dark winter's evening that Jamie made his way home from the office. The sky was unusually threatening and surreal in appearance. The strange hues it cast over the landscape sensed him with the feeling; Orburn was no longer the familiar home he knew— seeming to be holding its breath. The past decade had been the worst on record, save one particular summer: the summer Sylvie and Richard had arranged their wedding and short honeymoon.

Those few weeks had been breathtakingly beautiful. Amidst the blossoming flowers, it had given everyone a brief respite from the increasing violence of the elements. That short period helped to raise morale a little: seeming to offer another chance to pause and reflect over what was happening to the world. Jamie had deliberated on the false sense of security that had arisen: it felt as if some divine hand had stayed the fury of Orburn, offering one last chance for Orburn's inhabitants to put things right.

Jamie garaged his car, and made his way through the garden toward the house. He paused to gaze up into the sky, focusing again on the strange, unworldly glow from it. The terrain stretched away across the valley; the mist settled in it, drenched in that alien, unfamiliar shade of colour that added to its surreal appearance. As he stood there, he sensed he was not alone. It was a weird sensation that suddenly engulfed him, unlike anything he had felt before; powerful, commanding, sensing him with a definitive presence.

After a few minutes, Jamie made to turn toward the house; catching sight of a fleeting movement in the periphery of his vision— he froze abruptly. Jamie gazed intently at what looked to be an iridescent shape of a figure, paused behind some shrubs. Sudden fear welled up in him; his feet, seeming as if they were transfixed to the ground.

The silent figure appeared to shimmer through the gently swaying movement of the shrub's limbs in the breeze. In that moment, time stood still for Jamie, nervously waiting there: feeling the sanctuary of the house to be an eternity away. Paused, statue-like, Jamie gazed on, when suddenly the figure moved out from behind the bush, revealing it to be gowned in a robe with a hood drawn over its head. It paused again, before turning toward him. Jamie felt his heart miss a beat; simultaneously, a breathless voice drifted through his mind telling him not to fear.

Appearing to glide across the lawn, the strange spectre came to rest a pace or so in front of Jamie, towering at least a head above him. Jamie gazed up at the open hooded space, making out the hint of a bearded countenance. An atmosphere of majesty emanated from the strange entity, as they stood facing each other in silence.

Looking down at Jamie, the being's eyes searched deep into his. "Jamie, you were warned of my coming, and must listen carefully to what I have to tell you."

While the being spoke, Jamie was powerless to prevent himself from wondering over the origin of this strange entity. Calling on his spiritual ability, he sensed an aura of perfection emanate from the mysterious presence. He knew, intuitively he had never experienced its like before on Orburn, but as he listened, what intrigued him most was what the being was telling him. It seemed almost word perfect to the historic prophecies, written down in the sacred almanacs cherished in Orburn's ecclesiastical institutions.

As the being continued, he used no symbolism in his disclosure. What Jamie understood from him, was that Jamie's group was not alone; there were many others like them around the world— similar communities of people who had prepared for this event. The divine emissary continued, describing a location where Jamie's group was to rendezvous, and wait for the Infinite One to act. It all sounded so fantastic, sharing an affinity with other arcane events that had befallen their world during the past. As the strange being completed his message, he faded into the air, leaving Jamie deliberating over what he had been told. The task seemed insurmountable; the sustainable gathering of the resources needed, to see it through, even more remote.

Jamie pondered the logistics of transporting all their dependants to obscure locations, it made no sense: why take all their disabled souls to desolate areas that required resources to support them while they waited? He scolded himself when realising from where, and whom this instruction had originated. It was not for him to question or reason over divine directives; what had seemed impossible in the past, and then had manifested, settled his doubts. He scolded himself again for his lack of faith. Human frailty, on the physical plane, was one of the dark influence's greatest tools; without it, they could not hope to manipulate an incarnate soul's will.

~3~

Far into the night, Jamie tossed and turned as his mind took him on surreal voyages into Orburn's obscure future. Fleeting figures flashed before him, engulfing him in terrifying conditions as the relentless elements raged on. In brief moments of respite, he found himself gazing up at the heavens, watching, on a back-drop of fury, strange crafts descending from the sky.

He focused on those images, but they were constantly interrupted; Jamie, continuingly finding himself facing that strange, angelic figure who had approached him in the garden. Drifting in and out of these dreams through the night, left Jamie exhausted, but intrigued by them. Since the rendezvous with the strange entity, though it had confirmed the reality of their plight, he felt his fear receding, as if his soul had tapped into some celestial reservoir of courage.

Jamie gazed sleepily at his bedside clock; reality suddenly taking over, as its alarm announced the ritual rising for work: it was going to be another scramble through the rush-hour, made increasingly difficult by the elements. He thoughtfully sat on the side of his bed, reflecting on a brief discussion he'd had with Richard and Sylvie. Jamie no longer needed to convince those two of the task that faced them in the future, they, suggesting camping expeditions for their group to test out the environment.

During his meeting with the emissary, Jamie had learned that he would be told when he was to begin moving his group away. It was Jamie's intention, in the meantime, to occupy them with short trips to prepare for the mass exodus. He hoped this plan would help to divert the group's attention from the devastation going on around them.

For the more severely stricken souls, though possibly intrigued by the exercise, the practicality of it would seem daunting. The location for the first venture would need to be fairly localised, enabling them to research methods to manage in weather extremes. What Jamie hoped would encourage his groups to join him, was the deteriorating, moral atmosphere within the cities.

In the office that morning, Jamie briefed Richard on his dialogue with the strange visitor the night before.

Richard grimaced, as he pulled a wad of papers from out of his brief-case. "This is a new list of people asking to join our group-activities; I've no idea where we'll put them, Jamie if we take them on."

Jamie rubbed his chin thoughtfully. "The means will manifest somehow, Old friend."

"Jamie! I think we need to come up with something more concrete than that. The media will have a field-day taking us apart with a response like that..." Jamie made to comment. "...And before you chastise me for my lack of faith again..." interrupted Richard. "...I feel our team beyond will expect us to deal with the practical aspect down here more definitively."

Jamie smiled at Richard, sensing the resolute meaning in his statement. "It's the old story, Richard. Despite what you say, it still boils down to faith." Jamie gazed thoughtfully at him. "We're getting most of the resources in place now, but we've not had the sign to move yet..." Richard nodded; a frustrated expression on his face. "I still don't understand the purpose for waiting, Jamie. I worry for our souls, especially for those who are unable to do anything for themselves."

Jamie rested his hand on Richard's shoulder. "Don't you think the Infinite One is aware of that? We are the tools of his endeavours; He'll give us the resources when they are needed, and the sign when to make our move." Jamie gazed up at the ceiling, reflecting over his dreams that described fleets of alien crafts descending from the heavens. "I believe He has already initiated it."

Richard gazed at the thoughtful look on Jamie's face. "I get the feeling you've not told me everything?"

Jamie gazed down at the open folder on his desk; poised in silence. "We'll know when the time's right, Richard. Meanwhile, you need to look at the future from the spiritual perspective more, and not the material one."

Richard paused by the open door, a defeated look on his face. "OK! I'm putty in your hands from now on."

Jamie smiled, impishly. "That's the best offer I've had today— see you for lunch."

Richard huffed a smile, as he disappeared behind the door.

CHAPTER TWENTY TWO
RENDEZVOUS ORBURN

~1~

OVER THE SUCCEEDING MONTHS, JAMIE could have forgiven Richard for the lack of faith he had expressed in the office earlier. Richard, however, had rallied, providing the positive backup without which Jamie imagined their plans would have been difficult to implement. As more of the world succumbed to the evolutionary changes affecting Orburn's environment, evidence was increasingly pointing to the devastating footprint of humanity as a contributing factor: but there was little anyone could do about it now— it seemed to have gone beyond the point of no return.

Jamie's group was expanding dramatically, joined by other splinter-groups from around the world. The gradual process of colonising these people into larger groups dictated that the move to selected safe areas would begin soon. It was generally understood, by all those loyal to the Infinite One, that a mass exodus from Orburn was under preparation— how it would manifest or when, still remained unanswered.

Jamie, and his supporters, increasingly found it difficult to liaise with other contemporary groups; due to the rate at which the onset of the breakdown of the civilisation was taking place. As the infrastructure of the various societies began to fail, the richer ones were beginning to experience standards of living the third-world had endured for centuries. This rude awakening brought on many outcries from communities, protesting at the lack of life's essentials available in the shops. Outrageous prices for food were being asked by retailers, as they searched for dwindling supplies to fill their shelves.

The deteriorating climate, across Orburn, was the sole cause for the declining production of food. Reports were coming in of rationing, with conflicts breaking out across borders, as people competed for meagre provisions. Increasingly, Jamie was becoming aware of the anxiety rising in his group. Though trusting to his judgement, he could see the fear in their eyes as the threat to life became more real. Daily, he counselled them, as they listened to the escalating reports on lost societies, wiped out by devastating events: the fury of storms and tectonic disruption, outstripping records that reached back to when they were first begun.

Over the subsequent months, Jamie encouraged them out on excursions, but the mounting strength of the elements was proving too much of a challenge. The environment was descending to a level of intensity where all the groups, around the world, were being forced to delve into their stock-piles of resources. Jamie was one of the few who still had connections with his job; his salary arriving more by luck than judgement; it was the least of his concerns, as the currencies of the world were rapidly losing their value.

Sitting behind his desk one evening, Jamie gazed around his study; there was a remote feel about it— like all this was no longer home to him. He was reflecting over what Vicky had said before life on Orburn had fallen into decline: 'that from the ashes of the world, a beautiful one would arise.' It was a prophecy he had related constantly, when addressing his followers and their groups. But looking out through the window at the raging storm in progress, the reality of her prediction seemed so unlikely.

He focused thoughtfully on a table in the corner of the study, contemplating the sceptical atmosphere for the future, which was developing among his followers. It was growing harder to explain to all his groups why they had to wait, especially now, as he was fighting off the temptation to ask that same question. Instinctively, he thought the answer could be due to them on the material plane, relating to the time it was taking all the groups to get everything in place.

He thoughtfully gazed out the window. As far as he was concerned, the safe areas were ready, but a limiting factor existed, dictated by the level of resources stock-piled in them. Every aspect involving the success of this plan, leant toward timing; to make the move too early would rapidly deplete those resources. He fanned through the journal he was keeping; wondering— when *would* the sign to move come?

Suddenly disrupting him from his thoughts, a familiar glow materialised before him. His mind became a blank, as Vicky appeared, standing between his two spiritual guides Sarah and John. A sudden feeling welled up in him, hoping this visitation would give him the instruction to begin the groups' evacuation to the rendezvous points.

John's familiar voice drifted into his mind. "You anticipate correctly, Jamie. This event will bring to a close the present era of destruction on this world, and begin a peaceful one that will see the development of a new, higher civilisation. The event will bring to fruition prophecies mankind has wondered over for centuries, and confirm the presence of other civilisations out in the universe."

Jamie listened with mounting excitement, as John related the day, the location of where Jamie's groups needed to be gathered, and a brief description of what would take place after. The procedure, revealed how the Infinite One carried out His plan to colonise and maintain His physical planes out in the universe. The audience was short, and to the point, with Vicky sensing Jamie with her usual exuberance, as the three spirits dematerialised.

~2~

Jamie thoughtfully gazed down at his journal, and then began to write; his mind totally blown by what he had been told. The decision for him now was whether to relate all he had heard, or apply a simple strategy to eke out that information. Effectively, all the groups had consented to the reason for the move by completing their preparations for it.

This last directive, however, had been mind-boggling, describing an event one had only experienced in science-fiction films. It shared an affinity with an ancient story, centuries before, where a cataclysmic event had threatened all life. The logistics of the solution, then defied logic, but having been under the direction of the Infinite One; Jamie had accepted it on faith.

Now that he had something positive to tell his groups, the gravity of it required him to think carefully on how best to present it credibly. The news from beyond, in effect, had been timely. By giving them the green light and setting the plan's execution in motion, it would divert them all from the increasing violence going on around them.

Jamie paused to contemplate the gravity this event had on some of Orburn's inhabitants. Those, who had chosen to ignore the Infinite One, faced an uncertain, spiritual future. Saddened by this, Jamie's nature interceded for them, instinctively aware of what that choice would mean to them. When realising the physical values, they had clung onto no longer applied, the inability to rectify their misdemeanours would be devastating. Those, who had joined groups like Jamie's in the Infinite One's service, would be the ones that would inherit Orburn, experiencing the joy of taking their world into a celestial era, as it recovered.

Jamie reflected back on the strange spectre who had accosted him in his garden: was he a member of the divine civilisation, charged by the Infinite One to carry out the mass exodus of the wildlife and faithful from Orburn? If so, it confirmed all he had told his groups to believe in; the subsequent picture, destined to emerge now, illustrating the relationship existing between the physical and spiritual dimensions.

The following day found Richard listening, enthralled, as Jamie related the directive given to him by his guides. There was no time to waste; they would plan the final move under cover of a new adventure for all their charges; it would appear to doubters looking on, as another therapeutic vacation for their chronically disabled.

Over the succeeding weeks, Jamie, and his groups, got down to organising the trek. By far the most challenging aspect would have been the transporting of the in-ambulant souls, but the wisdom of venturing out on previous journeys had lessened the scale of that problem. Crucial to the whole exercise, now, would be the waiting period at the final location. Though provided with temporary shelters, the level of provisions governed that period. Now the directive to begin the move had been given, they had to place their trust in the Infinite One; there was no doubt in Jamie He would bring them all through this event, especially the vulnerable ones.

~3~

During subsequent liaisons with other groups around the world, one particular soul's name had become a prominence among those following the Infinite One. Through Jamie's ability to rendezvous with the spiritual dimension, he had learned of the task that faced this leader. A proven soul of immense age, the Infinite One had given him the assignment to lead the new inhabitants, and take Orburn up into the celestial realm.

Throughout the preparation period, the opportunity for Jamie to meet this man had arisen on several occasions. His first meeting with Samuel Bernard had been a memorable one; impressed by his dedication to the Infinite One. So strong was Samuel's commitment, the future of Orburn, as a celestial, higher physical plane, seemed never to come into question. Under Samuel's guidance, there was no doubt in Jamie's mind, that Vicky's prediction for a celestial Orburn was assured.

Following their return to Orburn after the event, all that remained of Vicky's prophecy, was their amble together on a cleansed world—intuitively sensing this as the prelude to their spiritual reunion. Firmly established now, as partners on their voyage to infinity; with one in the spiritual dimension, the other on the physical plane, they were destined to join together, safe in the embrace of celestial Orburn.

In the weeks ahead, the mass migration of all the groups was completed. As planned, due to the strategy behind their previous treks, no interest was attracted to their expanding ranks as more souls joined them. The majority of the populace were occupied with their riotous lifestyles, continuing to ignore Orburn's warnings. Less sincere in their attitudes, they pitied those incapable of exploiting what they considered were the true values to search for in life.

Thinking back over their media reports, Jamie's group had persistently tried to get their message over: the majority of those ignoring them, convinced, that the attributes available, in the physical life, were there for the taking. That Nature's intrinsic law, 'survival of the fittest' was instinctive in everyone, and therefore, legitimised their indulgence for them. Saddened by this misguided view, Jamie's conscience was clear, but offered him little consolation.

The deterioration of Orburn's environment continued relentlessly. Jamie counselled his groups daily, gradually filtering in vital aspects of the divine plan he had with-held previously. Standing alongside him were Sylvie, Richard and Dave, as they gazed out over the sea of faces stretching away before them. Some were settled in wheel-chairs attended by their carers, while others huddled together; their expressions displaying a blend of intrigue and trepidation.

As the first night approached, the sky darkened, heralding an approaching storm.

Jamie gazed at the ominous, dark clouds gathering on the horizon. "Better get everyone prepared," he muttered. "We may need to go through this routine for several days yet."

Sylvie gazed hesitantly at Richard, and then Jamie. "How long do you think it will be before...?" The question froze on her lips; made redundant by the unprecedented circumstance of their situation.

Jamie rubbed his hands together thoughtfully. "All I can say is, that throughout the history of our world, this is not the first time events like this have happened. Two millennia have passed on Orburn, since that divine soul offered its inhabitants the template of the Infinite One's truth. When considering our world as a finite body, the real question that dominates me, is, how much time should we have expected before the Infinite One's patience was tested?"

Richard gazed out over the sea of faces again. "So the writing's on the wall, then: it *will* be the meek who'll inherit this world."

Jamie shrugged his shoulders. "We're all in the hands of the Infinite One, Richard. It's not ours to reason over his strategy for us, or question his motives; just simply place our trust in him." Jamie returned his gaze to the masses. "These will be the ones who'll initiate the process to oversee Orburn into the celestial realm; given the means, and the ability to do that by the Infinite One."

Jamie's statement induced a penetrating gaze from Richard, he, aware of the vast spectrum of physical disability across the groups.

"I know what you're thinking, Richard. Like I've said to you many times, it all boils down to faith."

Richard gazed back out over the masses again, thoughtfully nodding his head.

CHAPTER TWENTY THREE
CELESTIAL VISITORS

~1~

FOLLOWING JAMIE'S DESCRIPTION OF HOW Orburn would be evacuated, all eyes were constantly trained on the heavens. Each uneventful day that followed increased the doubts among his groups; all of them impatient for the expected event to begin. The governing powers, however, were not going to be rushed: the Infinite One's munificence and mercy, intent on offering a last opportunity so that even one lost soul may reconsider their erring ways.

For whatever the reasons that had brought their civilisation to this demise, Jamie's main concern now was to bring all the faithful groups through this final phase. After only a few days into their move, the environment had taken on a more sinister feel to it; how life in the cities was coping, Jamie could only hazard a guess. If past traditions were any indication, he felt the souls there were most probably engaged on having a last fling.

Jamie spotted Richard approaching to make his usual report on the settlement's status. "Come on, then, let's hear the morbid news."

"A little bit pessimistic today, aren't we?" replied Richard. "People are, of course, poised on the question of why they have to wait, especially now, as the elements are deteriorating daily."

"Everyone must have this last chance, Richard. Seizing the opportunities that offer the truth in the material life is so important; no entity knows that better than the Infinite One. We, who have learned to accept truth, must converge on the side of patience. During our lives, we've tried to help those who were never able to develop their faith; this moment, now, offered by the Infinite One, perhaps, will allow those to learn for future incarnations."

Jamie gazed out over the masses. "I feel we are near to the time when we'll leave Orburn. It saddens me to think of those who'll be left behind. Not simply because they'll face certain death, but more for the disappointment they'll experience when realising the opportunities they neglected to seize during their lives."

"It was their choice, though, Jamie. We can't live out people's lives for them." Jamie made to comment on what appeared to be an unfeeling observation. "I know that sounds hard, Jamie...," anticipated Richard, "...but we've turned no one away, so far as I'm aware. We've been ridiculed for our beliefs, and even now, as Orburn heads into this cataclysmic change, the general consensus of opinion, held by the majority, believe it'll never happen."

Jamie knew Richard was right. They had done all they could to help people focus on the Infinite One, knowing that once that belief in Him was achieved, everything would fall into place. It remained that one, unrelenting requirement in life: it had to be through an individual's own ability the final solution was realised.

Jamie rested his hand on Richard's shoulder, and smiled at him. "I know I've said this many times, and I offer no excuses in saying it again now. I cannot imagine how I would have managed without you by my side."

Richard grinned. "We do our best," he whispered modestly. "But don't let's over-dramatise the situation, Jamie."

"Well then! I'll tell you something, which you seem to have missed by not mentioning it." Jamie smiled teasingly.

"Oh! And what's that?" replied Richard.

"I'll say only this. During the evening, before you and Sylvie settle down for the night, do a little star-gazing and tell me what you both observe tomorrow."

Richard's face screwed up in confusion. "You're talking in riddles again Jamie."

The conversation was brought to an abrupt close, as a bolt of lightning split the heavens, followed by a clap of thunder that shook the ground beneath them. A deluge descended upon the settlement, sending its inhabitants scurrying for cover.

"It looks like we won't be carrying out any star-gazing tonight; seems we're in for a real dousing," shouted Richard.

"Now don't let's be pessimistic," yelled Jamie, as they ran for their shelters.

~2~

Richard burst in through the door, water cascading off his clothes.

Sylvie gazed up at him. "Raining a little out there is it?" she uttered sarcastically.

"Oh! Very droll," replied Richard. "Just a bit." He shed his saturated jacket, and made his way across to her. "How are your groups coping with all this?"

"They're frightened about the future, as you would imagine. She patted the seat next to her. "Come, sit by the fire and dry off."

The shelters were of simple construction; equipped with basic essentials to sustain humanity for limited periods. The future continually worried Sylvie, as Jamie had not made any accurate prediction on when all their groups' evacuation would begin. The seasons were irregular, spontaneously changing from one extreme to the other. With winter approaching fast, the extreme, then, in terms of lower temperatures, could threaten the more chronic souls under her care.

Richard settled down beside her, offering his hands toward the blaze. "I don't know how long our stores will last when the weather gets worse, as it's quite likely to."

Sylvie thoughtfully stared down at the fire. "You must have read my mind." She picked up the poker and rattled it in the grate, sending a shower of sparks up the make-shift chimney. Picking up two logs she tossed them onto the fire. "I can't help feeling we might have been better off where we were; at least we would have been near to the remnants of our civilisation, able to share what is left of it."

Richard placed his hand on hers. "Jamie is following instructions from beyond, but we are in this situation because people did not want to share. Now our civilisation is under threat, do you honestly think anything will change their attitudes?"

"I remember you and Jamie saying, that once humanity teetered on the edge of annihilation, it could draw them together."

Richard nodded. "I believe that's right, and if you sense the mood of the people that have joined us, you'll be conscious of the benevolent attitude toward others that *has* united them...; there's not much evidence of that in those who have elected to remain revelling in the cities."

Sylvie returned her gaze to the fire. "I'm so weary of it all; everyday is such a struggle, especially for the ones who depend so much upon us."

Richard squeezed her hand, gazing at the hopeless expression on her face. "If ones like you are beginning to doubt; what chance d'you think those in your care stand then," he whispered.

She nodded slowly; poking the fire again, tossing another log on. "I know you're right, Richard, but it all seems so pointless. I ask myself constantly; why do I continue to follow a doctrine that appears to have no practical function? Enjoying my health and strength, I allow myself to be swayed by a belief, which dictates to disabled souls— life is preferable to death."

Richard cupped his hands around hers. "We need to look at life more intimately to see what those souls have done for us, Sylvie? You reproach yourself for generating a caring attitude, which arose from your desire to make life bearable for them. It's as Jamie described. If we accept the life beyond as the real world, these people become the unsung heroes of humanity on the physical plane: it's their sacrifice that gives us the opportunity to achieve the true values in the material life..." He paused. "Having said that, I do understand; as I too had my doubts in the beginning."

"What changed things for you, then?" She asked.

"Faith! Simple faith."

She nodded her head, giving him an old-fashioned look. "Well there's nothing else, so we've no choice but to stick with it."

They sat chatting together well into the evening; the topic of Jamie edging into the conversation over supper.

"Jamie seems confident we'll be away from here before the winter sets in proper," spluttered Richard, choking on his supper.

Sylvie slapped him on the back. "Don't speak with your mouth full, Dear," she grinned.

He offered an indignant smile. "Glad to see you're getting over your depressive mood..." The grin promptly disappeared from her face, Richard, sensing his humorous offering, redundant "...Anyway, Jamie said something strange to me earlier this evening. Though he constantly appraises us all of the approaching event, which'll lead to the evacuation of Orburn, no one, as yet, has seen any evidence of it. Employing his usual arcane method to divert our attention from the drama going on around us, he suggested we do some star-gazing this evening." Richard gazed up at the ceiling and shrugged; "fat chance of that tonight, with what's going on out there."

Sylvie perked up, a 'eureka' expression spreading over her face. "Strange you should mention that, as recently, there has been the occasional window in the weather." She stared at the fire; the dancing flames reflected in her eyes. "I was gazing up at the sky a few nights back, fascinated by the satellites tracking their way across it; there seemed far more than usual." She paused, looking up at him curiously. "I focused on one of the brightest ones, when suddenly, it changed direction. I continued to follow it until it disappeared behind a cloud."

"How curious," he muttered... Did you mention it to Jamie?" Sylvie shook her head.

Richard stared thoughtfully at her. "I wonder if what you've seen, implies, that the time to move is much closer than we think." Richard rubbed his hands together, offering them toward the fire. "You know! I think you may just have witnessed something significant, Sylvie. It ties in with the information Jamie has received from his sources, implying that our deliverance will come from above. Everyone has assumed it to be in the form of some sort of spiritual event, but more intriguingly, as Jamie feels, it could by a morally advanced civilisation up there."

Sylvie considered his assumption, rising from her chair. Pausing by the door she teased it ajar, gazing out at the storm raging outside. "Well! We won't see much tonight," she concluded.

"I'm convinced, anyway Sylvie— confirmed by what you've seen I feel there's no other explanation... It's going to happen, Sylvie! It's really going to happen, Dear One."

She smiled, noticeably uplifted by his supposition. "Oh! I do so hope you're right, Richard," she said— her hands emotionally clasped in her lap.

~3~

The following morning, they rose to a damp, gloomy scene; the heavier rain having passed over. From the settlements elevated position, one could just make out the valleys below, partially submerged in hazy mist. Sylvie, and Richard, made their way out into the settlement to begin their daily rounds.

He paused, giving Sylvie's hand a gentle squeeze. "I'll see you later, My Dear," he muttered softly. She nodded, as they walked off in opposite directions.

Spotting Jamie surveying the scene from his usual vantage point, Richard made his way up to him.

"Morning, Richard," greeted Jamie. "And before you say anything, My Friend, I realise last night was a dead loss for any star-gazing, but the advice still stands."

Richard nodded as he drew alongside him. "The evening, however, wasn't a complete washout, Jamie, despite what you're comment implies."

"Oh?" replied Jamie. "I'm intrigued— you have my complete attention."

Richard settled himself on a small outcrop of boulders, as he spoke. "Sylvie and I were chatting about the day's events last night, and I happened to mention the star-gazing topic you raised with me..." He paused, looking up at Jamie. "... It seems her powers of perception are far greater than mine, describing how she followed the path of a bright star that changed direction. She also commented on how there seemed to be more satellites trailing across the heavens than she'd been aware of before."

Jamie grinned pointedly. "And what do you make of Sylvie's observations?"

Richard gazed thoughtfully out across the settlement again. "Well, I've no reason to doubt the description of what she saw. Right throughout her increasing knowledge of our scheme, she's held an open mind, but she made no more of it: constantly possessed by concerns for those in her care. Our brief discussion, on the subject did, I believe, divert her, lifting her morale a little."

Jamie nodded thoughtfully. "Worrying over the same questions others are, I expect, Richard... is she alright now?"

Richard stood up from his perch, and wandered up to him. "Who knows? We chaps can only wonder at the depths a woman's emotions can reach. Sylvie's concerns will always be for the souls in her care, never for herself."

He reflected back over how he and Jamie had initially planned out their strategies. "Can't we be more informative about how we deal with spiritually, prophesied catastrophe, Jamie; be more specific about when these events will occur?"

"Don't you think, if it were possible, I would have done just that? It's not in my nature to dawdle on the boundaries of uncertainty, especially in dire situations like ours." Jamie gazed at some dark looking clouds, gathering ominously on the horizon again. Turning back to Richard, he offered a smile. "I can only repeat; the Infinite One will make His move when He's ready."

Richard nodded. "Then, I suppose we must be satisfied with that."

"If it's any consolation, Richard," muttered Jamie. "When I stepped out of my shelter this morning, it felt as if I was standing on alien soil— it came upon me like some sort of omen."

For a moment they stood gazing silently at each other, when Richard made to speak. "Possibly like a premonition, perhaps?" the question searching for confirmation. Jamie remained silent; a vague expression on his face.

~4~

Several days on, the inclement weather had still prevented any further observation to confirm Sylvie's strange, multi-directional stars. Her original disclosure of them had filtered out around the groups, raising opinions that were associating the stars' presence with the expected exodus from Orburn.

Jamie recognised the benefit the discovery was having on general morale, and questioned the wisdom of not revealing all he knew, sooner. However, in defence of that decision, having learned much during his trance events, the nature of each piece of information, required him to disclose it when people were able to accept it credibly.

As a young soul in the closing stages of his first incarnation, Jamie was becoming more *au fait* with the mechanisms governing life out in the universe. Each trance experience, revealed a little more of the relationship that existed between the physical and spiritual dimensions. Remaining loyal to that belief had submitted him to ridicule, but he intuitively felt he had offered his information in a way, which could benefit his followers in the life after.

Standing outside his shelter's door, Jamie gazed up at the clouds rolling across the sky. Intrigued by the thought, he imagined the entities above, preparing to play out their part in the Infinite One's plan. He felt Vicky's presence, and the celebration of congratulations showered on him by his spiritual guides, John and Sarah. It could so easily have ended differently; but for his grandmother, setting him on the road to success, his mother and father, teaching him how to use the material values, and finally, the sacrifice his beloved Vicky had made so that he could apply all he had learnt.

Now the truth of his faith was at hand, and hoped it would confirm similar beliefs in others, of what he felt awaited those obedient to the Infinite One. It all seemed to be coming together now, as they approached the climax, and which highlighted the importance each life-span was playing irrespective of ability. Jamie sensed the embrace of the Infinite One for playing out his part in this unprecedented, historical event, which had placed Orburn in the Infinite One's celestial realm: only proven souls, then, destined to grace its surface as another contingent in the legions of the Infinite One.

***

Jamie, settled toward the approaching event in his physical life, could never have imagined the impact on him of what he was about to witness. Sarah and John would share his euphoria, when he stepped upon the Infinite One's Universal Technology; gazed out upon the wonders of the universe that awaited Vicky and him, and sensed, on his return to Orburn, the embrace of a celestial world's environment he had helped to preserve.

The grief of the loss of all this, felt by those who had chosen to allow the material attributes to govern their lives, would touch his soul. But the wealth of beauty, he, and all his groups were destined to witness, would suppress their sadness; embedding it forever in their spiritual minds, to remain as a resource that would lead them to success on their voyage to infinity.

Sarah and John, though delighted over their young soul's success, knew the task for Vicky and Jamie was only just beginning. Having gained this unprecedented start to their voyage to infinity, the remaining six physical planes, for them, would place heavy demands on their resources. Destined to incarnate on a world in the grip of the dark forces, they would need all the power they had at their disposal now.

***

CHAPTER TWENTY FOUR
DIVINE EXODUS

~1~

OVER THE NEXT FEW DAYS, Jamie's faith was pushed to its limits; Richard, Sylvie and Dave, sensing the question, when would their deliverance begin, tracking through his mind. It was one they all wanted the answer to, but not wishing to impose on him, refrained from disclosing everyone's growing doubts for their future. What complicated the issue still more; reservations, among a few, were undermining the relative calm Jamie had established in the majority: gripped by uncertainty, the fears of this minority were rapidly becoming endemic throughout the groups.

One thing, Jamie had never thought of before, was to open a dialogue with the Infinite One. It was not that he felt embarrassed about talking to an invisible entity, but that there had seemed to be no need during the past— able to sense His presence constantly. Jamie realised the ungraciousness of this presumption, and how, though innocently applied, he had inadvertently taken the universal, Supreme Being for granted.

Early one morning, Jamie stood gazing out across the settlement from his vantage point; the clouds, seeming scant and wispy. The sun was peering over the horizon, casting strange, surreal shadows over the landscape. Jamie sensed his guide, John, draw close, impressing upon him the true gravity of his earlier thought. Overpowered by a feeling of humility, Jamie bowed his head in prayer, and asked for the Infinite One's guidance.

In his prayer, he recognised that success was not realised by mortal ability alone; the need, always present to be aware of the true power source. Trance events offered a brief window into the life beyond: a tool; not simply there to replace the supreme entity, but to work with Him. To have achieved trance ability arose from complete faith, and it was this development of faith that provided souls with another method, and the means, to open a dialogue with their Maker and His legions beyond.

Jamie poured his heart out, conscious of the Master's presence. It raised the definitive feeling in him: that in offering his prayer, it sealed a link between his Maker and him. By using that link, to help address the material issues facing them all, he had positively recognised his origin. After completing his prayer he perceived his guide's approval, and sensed, from his act of humility, he had helped to ensure the safe execution of another part of his plan.

Jamie gazed back up into the sky, aware of a translucent appearance spreading over it. A sudden feeling impressed him to summon his leaders together, and tell them to prepare the groups to leave Orburn. A blend of excitement and sadness welled up in him; he, unable to suppress yet another emotional confrontation within that interceded for their world's predicament— inwardly, relieved his companions would be spared the physical effects of the approaching onslaught.

Jamie's news was met with suppressed enthusiasm by his co-leaders Sylvie, Richard and Dave; they, appearing to carry out the group's preparations cautiously— due to the persistent uncertainty that had dogged them during the past. There was no such apprehension in Jamie's mind now, revealing all, after offering his prayer to the Infinite One.

Though having been more informed, Jamie shared in everyone's curiosity over how the exodus would be carried out. These were extraordinary times, with strange happenings taking place that had previously been considered inconceivable. He reflected back over historic annals, and how it was alleged events like this had taken place during the past; the evidence, obscured by symbolism, and time. If it had been the case then, one thing was certain: there was no future for anyone left on Orburn while the apocalyptic event took its course.

As the evening approached, the clearing sky began heralding the beginning of everything Jamie had been told. The heavens displayed a myriad of stars peering through a crystal clear atmosphere, but what grabbed the attention of them all, were the countless moving stars that appeared to have grown in size. Glowing in increasing magnitude, some were beginning to take up geostationary orbits above their settlement. Jamie, Sylvie, Richard and Dave could hardly contain themselves, and gazed up at them, anticipating the spectacular scenes that awaited them.

~2~

It was far into the night, before Jamie noticed some form of vague activity occurring around the stationary stars above. As he stared up at them, they appeared to be fragmenting into hundreds of points of light; the crystal clear atmosphere, making it easier for the naked eye to determine. The points of light began drifting further away, revealing the stars to be still intact; as if they were shedding some of their matter.

Jamie was soon joined by Richard, who had wandered up, he also having noticed the new activity.

He paused alongside Jamie, gazing curiously at the strange phenomena. "What do you make of it, Jamie?"

Jamie made no answer, continuing to follow the strange lights, which now appeared to be tracking their way down through the atmosphere.

"Not sure," he mumbled thoughtfully. "Though from the predictions I've received, I know it's from up there our relief will come, but in what shape or form remains a mystery to me as yet... Where's Sylvie...? She'd like to see this."

"She's liaising with her carers, preparing their groups for the night," replied Richard.

"I think sleep will be way down the list of priorities this evening when things get going." Jamie fleeted a quick look at Richard, and then back up at the stars. "I believe tonight will be the night."

Richard looked a little pensive; Jamie, sensing the immediate change in him.

"It's something we've all been expecting, Jamie, but now it's here... it's hard to suppress feelings of apprehension" Richard paused to gaze out over the settlement. "The mind boggles at the magnitude of the task to lift all these people..."

"I think to speculate on such matters will only confuse us more." Jamie smiled at Richard. "We are in the hands of a power that has, no doubt, carried out events like this before. This event, now, will confirm our belief we shared with humanity, and justify those who possessed the faith to believe in ancient prophecies."

Richard nodded. "It's incredible to think how we've all become involved in such an unprecedented event, though— especially a celestial one."

Richard looked out across the settlement again. "I think I should join Sylvie, Jamie; she might be unaware of this new development."

"I doubt it, as Emma and Josh will have sensed it; their minds are alive with what's taking place now."

"All the same, Jamie; I don't want to be parted from Sylvie, once things start to happen I want to share it with her."

"You will," grinned Jamie, as Richard walked off.

Jamie returned his gaze to the heavens; the points of light, now having grown in size. His assumption that others throughout the settlement had noticed proved to be right, sensing Emma's and Josh's excited dialogue drifting into his mind.

Over the past decade, there had rarely been any respite from the weather; sweeping-devastation increasing around the world. This evening, however, had seen a tranquil change in the environment, and one that could easily raise false security in unwitting souls. A feeling of excitement welled up in Jamie again, as the first of the points of light revealed it to be an alien craft; the magnificence of it, casting a spell of silence over the settlement.

He gazed, captivated at the glittering ship, as it slowly descended, pausing fifty or so metres above the ground. For a while it remained in a silent hover until slowly rotating, as if assessing the area. Other crafts, now, were joining it, creating a dreamlike setting that surpassed anything they had witnessed in the movies. Unlike those films, the absence of conflict here did not suppress the sense of power that emanated from these magnificent crafts. Instinctively, Jamie knew this amazing scene was just the beginning; much more awaited them above.

~3~

During his trance events, he had gradually become more aware of the role the higher physical planes played in the service of the

Infinite One. Piecing together each fragment of information had revealed a picture of, and what the future offered souls, obedient to the Master Being— the proof, now, was materialising before them. This great adventure was what a soul sacrificed for material values on the physical plane; an opportunity lost, to gain spiritual freedom of the universe in the service of the Infinite One.

While he had deliberated on these thoughts, one of the crafts had descended over a group, and had begun taking up the first of the souls. Gazing from his vantage point, the scene took Jamie's breath away. He watched, as more crafts moved into place, creating a picture of fantasy that not even he could conjure up the words to describe. After a while, his emotions settled; his curiosity focused on the fleet of crafts, wondering over the scene that awaited them above. He returned his gaze to the orbiting stars; his mind rambling from one scenario to the next— it was impossible for him to even imagine the complex up there.

Intuitively, he felt he would be the last to be lifted; he would have wanted it no other way. Throughout the night, the divine exodus continued, until, alone, he stood and looked into the distance, panning his gaze across the ghostly landscape of empty habitats. The atmosphere was uncanny; just the hint of a breeze gently embracing him. Through the eerie silence, he listened to the soft, whisper-like, unworldly sounds created by the wind blowing through the old shelters: the occasional door, banging loosely on faintly whining hinges, adding to the haunting atmosphere.

Orburn's mood was changing. The mighty hand that had stayed her fury was gradually ascending away, allowing destiny to resume its course on this world. Jamie instinctively knew history was repeating itself here: that somewhere else out in the cosmological complex, similar events like this were constantly evolving. He thrilled to the knowledge that his first incarnation now offered him so much, setting him on-course for his voyage to infinity.

His heart quickened, as a solitary craft came to a hover above him. Gazing up, he perceived an image of himself reflected in the deep lustre of the craft's underside. Awed by the magnitude of the moment, he stood, alone, gazing up at that amazing ship. Amidst the decaying artefacts of his civilisation, his mind, now, was on higher things. It was pointless rationalising where his civilisation had gone wrong— they had paid the price.

It was a sublime feeling; Jamie, totally awed by how infinitesimal they all were: no more than grains of sand drifting through the heavens, stretching away to infinity. Yet, the Infinite One cared enough to create a plan that rewarded their faith in Him. The craft, above, seemed to sense his thoughts, allowing him a moment to bow his head in thanks to the Infinite One for their deliverance.

Jamie took one final look over the landscape, suddenly sensing his body become weightless. He gazed down at the ground as it gradually began to drop away, feeling himself floating up toward the ship. Following a brief, dream-like moment, he found himself in what appeared to be an embarkation area. The first person he met was Richard, smiling, and babbling uncontrollably over what had taken place.

The words just would not come, as Jamie followed Richard in through a door. Milling around before him were his people; some in wheelchairs with their carers, others, just gazing at gigantic viewers displaying Orburn retreating below them.

What happens now? he wondered, when suddenly a voice spoke in his mind. "Take leave of your world, Jamie, then we shall talk." The voice sounded strong and resourceful, emanating the timeless intellect he had come to expect of his spiritual contacts.

Richard gazed at him; a humble expression on his face. "Jamie... Not in my wildest dreams could I have imagined this... If... If anyone had told me this was all part of a divine plan..." He gazed down at the deck of the ship, overcome by emotion.

Jamie reached out and rested his hand on his arm. "Just enjoy, Richard and know the choices we made on Orburn, earned us this moment."

Richard looked at Jamie. "If only I'd had the trance ability like you... The chance to peer into..."

Jamie shook his head abruptly. "That has nothing to do with it, Richard, and if it did, your achievement would have been the greater, as you offered yourself on faith alone."

Jamie watched a euphoric Richard join Sylvie. He turned and smiled at Emma and Josh, sensing their elation burst into his mind— this was their moment. He was unable to suppress the feeling that there was much more awaiting them in the Infinite One's plan. Though his time on Orburn would be limited, following their return, it was clear he was going to leave it an altered world to the one he had entered. The world, now, destined to rest in the hands of the meek, would be governed by a very different sort of power— the thought settled him.

CHAPTER TWENTY FIVE
THE CELESTIAL FLEET

~1~

GAZING INTO THE VIEWER REVEALED an extraordinary scene, imposing a moment of silent meditation on the whole group. During the past, news reports had displayed pictures of Orburn's pioneering astronauts, floating within their capsules as they orbited their world. This new experience, however, was not even remotely comparable to theirs. The simulated gravity in these ships, impressed one that the masters of these crafts had not only achieved a compatible, planetary environment in them, but that their achievement indicated the extent of the trust the Infinite One had in them to use that power.

Paused by Sylvie and Richard, the chance to engage them in any sort of dialogue was impossible. Instead, Jamie found his mind wondering about the origin of this strange civilisation and their ships— were they really part of the Infinite One's divine plan? There was nothing aggressive about their intention, despite possessing a power that could easily have wiped out the population on Orburn.

He had so many questions buzzing around in his mind; intrigued by these thoughts, he closed his eyes and focused on his guides, Sarah and John.

***

Jamie's guides in the spiritual dimension, perceived the level of understanding, in his incarnation, where Jamie accepted the reason why the spiritual dimension appeared remote from the physical life.

The scene manifesting before him now, represented an immense power; necessitating the need for a mandatory form of assessment while incarnated on the lower physical planes. Following success, as proven souls, such a power could then be released into their trust, when incarnated on the higher physical planes.

John knew, from experience, no time-scale existed that defined when a young civilisation would achieve this. While the inhabitants of a world refused to recognise the Infinite One, it wasted the period a world was able to support life. Since new worlds were future celestial planes, time became an issue, especially for those adhering to the Infinite One's laws. With no apparent connection between the two dimensions, the need for proven souls on the higher physical planes, was vital. This could only be implemented by a belief in the Infinite One; failing this, it was by His judgement alone the decision to reset a world was made.

Having learned to follow the Infinite One, Jamie's life was nearing its completion. On his return to the spiritual dimension, Jamie and Vicky could enjoy a brief respite, and then set off on the next phase of their voyage to infinity. For the remainder of his incarnation, Jamie would witness the settling of celestial Orburn, and the beginning of the development of the Universal Technology. It was an exciting time for the loyal souls of Orburn, now resting on the threshold of an event that would give them the freedom of the universe.

***

Jamie opened his eyes onto a scene of unimaginable beauty. Their ship had ascended beyond Orburn's atmosphere; the sun's rays icing the outer contours of the planet, as they moved away. Rising from the shadow, cast by Orburn, he gazed awe-struck on a technology that, up until then, had been a figment of fiction writers' imagination.

At first his mind would not accept it, raising wild, irrational scenarios that seemed to contradict its existence. He stared at a massive object approaching; it shone like a star; gradually exposed by the sunlight that revealed it to be a gigantic mothership. Milling around it were hundreds of small crafts, like theirs, some tracking down pale blue beams to disappear within it. The silence in the video chamber told the story; Emma and Josh, spell-bound, their eyes transfixed on the screen.

As their craft made toward the huge mothership, Jamie spotted several others beyond, rising in perspective out of Orburn's shadow. He sensed the thrill in the whole group, their excitement reaching unprecedented levels. The confirmation of other forms of life, now, had been realised— this was really happening. As they watched the picture unfolding before them, all that the lower physical existence had offered, paled into insignificance. Suddenly, they were all witnessing what had required faith before. This glorious scene, facing them now, was what an incarnate soul inherited by keeping faith with the Infinite One, and distancing themselves from tempting aspects on the material plane.

Jamie's life flashed before him, reflecting on moments when he had faltered. Now the Infinite One's plan had been set in motion, confirming His promise that a soul's obedience to Him would be rewarded ten-fold. The process was so simple. Proven souls like his gran helped others make the first move, and then, like a giant jigsaw puzzle, the pieces making up life, fell into place. He gazed on, enthralled by the expressions adorning the faces of his companions, experiencing this sublime moment together.

Amidst this torrent of euphoria their craft, by then, had reached the tractor beam, and was beginning its descent into the huge mothership. The excitement rose to a crescendo, as they passed out into a huge docking bay, towering above, and dropping away, below them. Conversation was sparse; one, unable to remove a gaze from the screen; for fear of missing an instant of this fascinating event.

~2~

Jamie found himself meditating again on the origin of this strange technology. Throughout history, the desire to follow the Infinite One had become fragmented into many, different disciplines. It dawned on him, that by executing this event, the alien civilisation seemed to have a vested interest in Orburn. While continuing to serve the Infinite One; were past sightings of unidentified flying objects, them, on missions to assess the current status of life here? To help them achieve this; had their technology originated from a divine source to ensure it remained invisible to unproven civilisations?

Jamie intuitively felt the answers to his questions would come now; not simply because they were experiencing the reality of this technology, but more from having obeyed the Infinite One's doctrines by uniting and caring for one another. Jamie considered the logistics of this huge fleet; how its technology appeared to blend in with, and naturally adopt the physics of the universal environment.

He contemplated the task ahead for those remaining on Orburn as a higher physical plane, and the process of how the constant stream of proven souls, required, would be seeded on it. Instinctively, he knew the answer to this question differed from the lower physical planes, and therefore, remained at the Infinite One's discretion.

It intrigued him to think of future voyages through the universe aboard similar, divine technology, leading them into an adventure the lower physical planes could never begin to approach. But what was more fascinating, they were going to achieve this in partnership with the spiritual dimension. As proven souls, the barrier between the higher physical planes and spiritual dimension did not exist— the Infinite One's truth running common in both.

As Jamie surfaced from his thoughts, their craft had settled upon a docking bay. The viewer disappeared, as robed figures peered in through exits, gesturing for Jamie and his companions to follow them. Walking along a brightly lit tunnel, they broke out onto a shelf-like platform that looked out over a gigantic shaft. Saturated in a strange blue-green light, the scene confronting them left them breathless.

Jamie gazed up, mesmerised by people stepping off the higher platforms; levitating momentarily, before gradually beginning the descent. It was then he noticed the absence of wheelchairs; those, who had been afflicted, standing erect by their carers. He instinctively knew this was the work of the Infinite One: tied into Orburn's ascension to the celestial realm. The Infinite One was preparing His new legion for the part they were to play on it.

There was no need for sacrifices on the higher physical planes; the Master Spirit had cleansed their bodies to match the purity of their souls. Now, as incarnate, proven spirits, they were charged with the task to complete the initialisation of Orburn as a celestial plane. For the remainder of their lives there, they would enjoy freedom from the vices of the dark influence that had plagued it for centuries. Their faith and obedience rewarding them as one of those among the legions of the Infinite One. Now poised on the threshold of the universe— only joy awaited them.

A robed figure approached, gesturing them to move out into the shaft. Jamie, though briefly hesitant, stepped forward; instantly feeling his body become weightless. He succumbed to elated feelings, watching the radiant expressions on Emma's and Josh's faces, as they glided across, pausing by his side.

Emma gazed up at him. "Oh, Jamie, thank you for all you've done for us— you helped us find the truth."

Jamie smiled down at them. "It is I who should thank you, and those like you, for giving me the opportunity to do that." She turned, smiling happily at Josh; from their expressions, Jamie felt that they had become kindred souls like Vicky and him; deprived of the physical relationship, the spiritual one would now become even richer.

~3~

The shaft terminated in a gigantic hall, with an elevated section to one side. Hundreds of people crowded toward it; the buzz of conversation hanging in the air above them. Jamie picked out Samuel Bernard standing near the front, their gazes, meeting by chance. Samuel smiled at Jamie; his eyes appearing to speak to him, as Vicky's had. Jamie sensed words were unnecessary, instinctively feeling again that Orburn's future would be secure under his guidance.

Suddenly, the lights began to dim, as a figure materialised on the upper section. Silence swept back over the gathering, as all eyes focused toward it. A bearded man, dressed in a robe similar to the prophets of old, spread his arms in a gesture of welcome; his soft voice, speaking in the minds of the masses reaching away before him.

Announcing himself as Tristram, from an ancient, celestial world called Earth; he described what was happening to Orburn, and the task that faced them all in the service of the Infinite One. His Earthenian fleet had monitored Orburn, since seeding it aeons ago. Governed by universal protocols, he, and his people, had then been forbidden from interfering with the growth of the new, unproven civilisation. Now that the majority of this last civilisation, on Orburn, had reached a stage of unity, the Infinite One had reset life there.

The spread of evil across the world had been the governing factor. Life on Orburn had descended to a level, where newly incarnated souls were being subjected to an environment that was too biased toward the darker influence. Relative to its age; life on this world had reached its allotted time to unite. Those, showing allegiance to the dark entities, would find they had frittered their opportunity away, leaving them to postulate over what might have been. Those who had followed the Infinite One would join His legions, and then continue on with their voyage to infinity.

Following the end of Tristram's address, they were given the freedom of the ship, and where, they would be able to view the scenery during the stand-off voyage while Orburn resettled.

Jamie joined Sylvie, Richard and Dave, gazing out a through the viewer at Orburn, far below. As he sat, reminiscing over all that had taken place, he became aware of another presence close to him. Having learned about the higher physical planes, it came as no surprise that passed friends, and loved ones now in spirit, could appear to them.

For Jamie, Vicky materialised first. Displayed in all her spiritual glory, it was as if in that instant his companions had faded into the air, leaving just Vicky and him to enjoy a moment alone together.

She smiled. "Hello, Dear One," she whispered. "Your incarnate period is nearly over. Now under the Infinite One's direction, the task starts on Orburn. The development begins of the fleet that will take Orburn's future, proven civilisation out into the universe to search out, and seed new worlds." Her elation intoxicated him, feeling the excitement emanating from her. "Oh, Jamie. We have learnt so much on our first incarnation, thanks to those who mentored us; their wisdom— our legacy."

Jamie gazed speechless at Vicky; stunned by the flawless beauty of her spiritual appearance. In the depths of his despair, when she had been struck down in her early years on Orburn, his grandmother had told him to look into her soul— her radiance now, had exceeded his imagination then. His physical being wanted to hold her, but she was reaching into his mind, sensing into him, a different form of love that now bonded them together.

~4~

The sun had risen over Orburn five times, since boarding the mothership, and on each occasion, the extent of the thrill was as great as the first. Tristram, the fleet's master, had begun to mingle among the inhabitants of Orburn, liaising particularly with Samuel Bernard. It was just prior to the sixth day that Tristram approached Jamie. Vicky, now Jamie's constant companion, fell silent as Tristram looked down at him.

While Jamie gazed into Tristram's eyes; there seemed an uncanny resemblance to the strange angel he had encountered in his garden, during that evening on Orburn.

Tristram nodded slowly. "It was I, Jamie. A necessary requirement for us to prepare you all for an event of this scale."

Jamie found himself at a loss for words, conscious of the sophisticated intellect confronting him. "What... What happens to us now, Master," asked Jamie spontaneously.

Tristram smiled at his humility. "I think you know, Jamie. Your task here is finished. The Infinite One is well pleased with you and your chosen partner. Enjoy a period together now, and take in some of the wonders of the Infinite One's universe, while we wait for Orburn to resettle. What you will witness, during this short voyage, is only a small part of what shall be yours, and Vicky's, when you have completed your voyage to infinity."

There was so much more Jamie wanted to know, but sensed that the time was not right.

Tristram looked intently at him. "The answers will come, Jamie, as and when they are needed. You are no longer limited by the lower physical plane. On this, your first incarnation, you have chosen to listen to your spiritual guides. In partnership with them, and others, now, Vicky and you will carry the light of the Infinite One's truth on each physical plane you journey through; you have become teachers. It does not fall to you both to force the truth on anyone, but simply to declare it. The choice to interpret it, then, rests upon those who hear it."

Jamie watched as Tristram dematerialised before them, confirming him to be in the spiritual incarnation. Jamie turned and looked at Vicky's radiant face, sensing the emotion bubbling up in her.

Gazing back at the viewer, he smiled. "Let us pause to preview what the universe has to offer, shall we, Vicky?"

CHAPTER TWENTY SIX
A DIVINE INSIGHT

~1~

THE MASSIVE MOTHERSHIPS HAD BEGUN to line up behind Tristram's craft, appearing, as if small worlds. They rotated gracefully, creating a breathtakingly, surreal picture superimposed on Orburn, and all graced by the back-drop of a myriad of stars. Once again, the viewing rooms were plunged into silence, as Orburn slowly began to recede. Jamie gazed at their world; the translucent continents masked in blue haze, rising up out of the shadowy terminator line. He nervously contemplated the chilling event that approached, praying for those who had chosen to remain ignorant of the truth.

At first, Orburn lingered in the centre of the viewer, progressively growing smaller, when suddenly it disappeared. Jamie gazed intently out into the infinity of space, unaware of the performance these motherships' were capable of— Vicky just smiled at his intrigue. None of the incarnate souls of Orburn had any idea of the voyage's duration, simply trusting their hosts; comforted in the knowledge, they were the agents of the Infinite One.

Jamie felt the warmth of Vicky's presence sharing his curiosity and wonder, as awe-inspiring celestial events drifted across the viewer. Each scene diminished the importance of the material values, available on the physical planes; confirming, to them, the unlimited bounty the Infinite One's universe offered. What they were feeling now was the sudden knowledge that greeted a returning spirit, and which either manifested in the sublime joy of success, or irrepressible disappointment in failure.

The loyal ones of Orburn had chosen wisely, enjoying a brief insight now into what awaited them. The physical planes, some still had before them, stretched toward infinity, but what they had achieved now, would help to diminish the potential threats on them. Orburn had played her part, offering an equal chance to all the incarnate souls who had passed through her. Now she had become a sanctuary for the legions of the Infinite One, and under His protection, provided another celestial outpost that would bear witness to, and endorse His truth.

The routines on the motherships fell into teaching cycles provided by Tristram's people. These counselling periods came as revelations, describing how everything evolved from the Infinite One. They learned that He embedded the spiritual seed of His truth in the physical mind; simply requiring faith to release it.

As they sped across the cosmos, the knowledge imparted to them was building up into a resource they could use on future celestial planes. Jamie learned that Tristram was the master of several worlds; to have reached that level of existence had not been achieved without its distressing moments. The grief of watching the worlds he had seeded, descend into the misery of war and greed, had tugged heavily on his benevolent nature.

Governed by the Infinite One's protocols, existing for all worlds under the auspices of His agents, the Infinite One forbade any intervention in a young civilisation's free-will on the lower physical planes. Following the conclusion of the event on Orburn, it would be through their trust and faith in the Infinite One that the meek and persecuted souls of Orburn inherited their world. The future rewards for their piety were the many wonders of the cosmos drifting past them, as the Earthenian fleet voyaged on.

~2~

Now, having risen above the lower physical planes, Orburn's people had access to their spiritual minds, unveiling the constancy present in that eternal life. It revealed an infinitive existence that was far removed from the physical planes. Governed by the Infinite One, it promised a free, unlimited world that imposed no restrictions on a soul; Jamie, sensing that remotely during his trance events.

To believe in the existence of this world, on the lower physical planes, asked a lot. A soul had to accept it on faith; suffer the indignation of ridicule from disbelieving persecutors. Able to see it, once established on the higher physical planes, it became the constant incentive. From that one submission of faith, on a lower physical plane, the voyage to infinity could begin.

Jamie and Vicky, instinctively knew they would join all their past relatives and friends, on completion of their voyage to infinity. The template of their plan had been set on Orburn; all that was required of them now was to apply it on each physical plane they journeyed through. Locked in their spiritual minds, that truth was the constant resource that would guide them.

Jamie had seen how attempts at world domination had been checked. Reflecting back over the history of Orburn revealed prominent souls, and who had then gone on to provide leadership through dark times. The infrastructure of the Infinite One's creation was complex, and yet could be resolved by logical deduction.

During the voyage, Jamie had many audiences with Tristram; some together with Samuel Bernard. Samuel's moment was near. Like Tristram and his people thousands of years before, Samuel and the people of Orburn faced a similar choice. Jamie had no doubts that from Tristram's teachings, and this experience, they would all remain loyal to the Infinite One.

Mother Earth had become the sanctuary for Tristram's people, which had then gone on to provide proven souls with the resource to go forward and seed new worlds. The first of these worlds, Avataria, had already ascended to the celestial realm— Orburn was now set to join it. The choice, Orburn's people had to make now, would be to develop another sanctuary for proven souls to work from. It confirmed that throughout the infinity of the universe, every soul had the opportunity to be part of the Infinite One's divine plan; make themselves a special case by developing and using their chosen gift to serve the Infinite One.

Vicky had followed Jamie's thoughts, and gently chastised him with her own. "So deep in thought, Jamie; you're missing the wonders of the universe."

He grinned, vaguely conceding the point. "But I've missed nothing, Vicky; merely contemplating everything we've learnt, by applying it to what has become visible to us now."

She nodded, following his gaze to the viewer, as a celestial event began to fill it. There had been such a dramatic change to the incarnate lives on Orburn, now they had to focus on what lay ahead for them in its new role. The two dimensions had come together, enabling a liaison between them. This would be an enormous asset, during a soul's voyage to infinity.

Faced by any young soul learning, Vicky's and Jamie's future promised to be fraught with all the age-old problems; greed, hate, scepticism, requiring them to defend their principles against passionate, irrational persecutions of their faith. The voyage of deliverance, they were on now, would soon draw to a close, and then the real task for Samuel Bernard, would commence. On the future worlds he was destined to seed; it would fall to him to administer patience, compassion, and benevolence in the face of irrational human ignorance and blind stupidity: his seeded worlds, subject to the menacing dark legions.

Jamie gazed out through the viewer at the magnificence of the cosmos, meditating on the thought; would the eternal conflict ever be resolved?

Vicky sensed the implications attached to his question. "That makes no sense, Jamie, it implies there would have to be an end to all this."

Jamie nodded slowly. "Is that a bad thing?"

She gazed searchingly at him. "Then what would happen to those who have chosen to worship the dark influence? With no access to material worlds to regroup, new opportunities for them would be lost. That question has no relevance in the world of spirit. Realistically, how could those who have failed, perhaps due to no fault of their own, renew the search for their solution?"

He gazed thoughtfully at her. "You imply that the eternal conflict should continue *ad-infinitum*?"

She nodded "When thinking about the mechanisms existing throughout the universe, Jamie, I've learnt that the Infinite One is constantly recycling matter to create new systems. It signifies to me there are new chances for everyone, but that it remains a soul's choice on how long it takes them to learn His truth." Vicky felt he was viewing a soul's options too singularly. "In the short time I have been in spirit, I have learned not to judge the conduct of others; only the Infinite One can arbitrate on a soul's progress. Everything He stands for reflects forgiveness, compassion and benevolence. I don't believe, for an instant He has ever lost a soul from His fold, so why should the present procedure be any different in the future." She smiled. "You over-complicate the issue by applying material aspects of life, rather than spiritual ones."

He smiled, feeling a little squashed. "Well that's told me! Speaking now as a spiritual expert are we?"

"Everything comes into focus Jamie, when the spiritual mind dominates and we apply its values, but don't take my word for it. As a master of several worlds, ask Tristram."

He grinned. "I concede the point, Vicky, but it does appear somewhat confusing when viewed from the mortal perspective."

"I understand, Jamie, but that's when a soul can apply their faith, and ask us for help."

He grinned again at her astute response. "I'm not going to make any headway in this discussion... am I?"

She shook her head, smiling.

CHAPTER TWENTY SEVEN

CELESTIAL ORBURN

~1~

THE MOTHERSHIPS HAD BEEN VOYAGING on for some considerable time, and even after applying estimates to Tristram's sleep and waking periods, Jamie still had little idea of the distance they had travelled, and how long they had been absent from Orburn. Every waking moment, Jamie's mind was constantly filled with intrigue for Tristram and his people; the story of their beginning, similar to what was happening on Orburn now. What was Earth like, as a world long-since established in the celestial plane? Tristram had made no mention of a fleeting visit there, but the hope in them all was that the mothership fleet would make a pass close enough to give them a brief insight.

It was several days on into the voyage that Jamie and Vicky were gazing out into space. There was always something new, but this notable period was to prove in itself memorable among others. A particular star had attracted the attention of all those present with Vicky and Jamie in the viewing chamber. The velocity the mothership fleet travelled at, soon revealed the star to be a sun like Orburn's.

Sweeping past the massive star, the motherships checked their speed, making for the third body of the star's solar system. Circling around the planet, an awesome silence descended over the whole group, as they feasted their eyes upon a breathtakingly beautiful world contrasting greatly with Orburn. Here was a world that clearly reflected the presence of the Infinite One— lovingly cared for, its celestial appearance was overwhelming.

At once, Tristram's voice spoke in their minds. "Behold, our world, Earth. We have no time to spend here on this voyage, but let her image remain in your minds as an incentive to achieve a celestial Orburn. Once you have accomplished that, the freedom of all celestial worlds will be yours." After many discussions with their contemporaries, Vicky and Jamie constantly found their minds migrating back to relive the picture of that gorgeous world.

Ever mindful of their return to Orburn, they wondered how long it would be. and what would they find there? Could Orburn really be as Earth and support them similarly; their world, dramatically changed by scathing, evolutionary events?

It was soon after the departure from Earth's system, Tristram approached Jamie; Jamie, attributing Tristram's visit to the constant flow of questions turning over and over in his mind.

Tristram smiled. "I sense your curiosity, Jamie, and on one aspect you anticipate correctly. I won't bore you with the logistics of the return voyage, just tell you we shall be approaching Orburn's solar system shortly after three sleep periods.

Jamie wasted no time in questioning Tristram on the state of Orburn, especially now in the aftermath of its upheaval.

"Relative to voyaging through space-time, Jamie, the velocity we achieved, travelling away from Orburn, your world will have aged much quicker than you. This means that the scars from the evolutionary changes, on it, will largely have disappeared. As a future incarnate, on higher physical planes, it is one of many factors of the physical universe you will become familiar with. Until then, clear your mind and simply enjoy the remainder of the voyage; watch the approach to your world— it will be a thrilling sight."

Fascinated by Tristram's brief description, touching on the subject of astrophysics, Jamie was still concerned over what awaited them on Orburn. Undoubtedly, from what Tristram explained, the various infrastructures of their previous society would have succumbed to evolution. Though the task to set up the new civilisation fell to Samuel Bernard, they were all required to pitch in, but with what?

Tristram grinned at him. "You're still thinking 'lower physical plane', Jamie; that existence no longer applies to you— your people have become novices on the higher physical planes now."

Jamie gazed back at him, grappling with his confusion. "But we still need the resources to build in that type of environment..."

"They're already there, Jamie" assured Tristram. "From the moment Orburn became part of the celestial realm, the Infinite One implemented those resources. Do you think that Orburn is the only celestial plane?" Tristram smiled intently at him. "The raw materials and the method will be provided. Samuel Bernard will lead the new civilisation, and as a united world, like thousands before them, they will develop the Universal Technology. This last stage will be the final test of their allegiance to the Infinite One. Should they succeed, they will go forward out into the universe to seed new worlds; the celestial task to monitor those worlds from Orburn, then, will begin."

Over the following three periods, Jamie considered Tristram's explanation of how the master plan worked— the Infinite One, in His wisdom, leaving nothing to chance. With a soul's ability to gaze into the spiritual dimension, that alone, was sufficient to encourage newly proven spirits to maintain their focus on the spiritual plan. Coupled with a tiered flow of proven souls, ascending in varying levels of knowledge and experience, a new world entering the celestial realm, could be established relatively quickly.

Vicky had remotely monitored Tristram's and Jamie's discussion. Effectively, Vicky was proof of one aspect of it. Now in the spiritual incarnation, she, unlike Jamie, on the physical plane, rationalised events using spiritual values, and not physical ones.

It was after rising on the third sleep-period, Jamie and his people made straight for the viewers. The sight that greeted them, though none the less beautiful, appeared unremarkable, displaying the usual myriad of stars. Richard and Sylvie had remained in contact with Jamie, on and off throughout the voyage, having to mingle with their other groups. Their reports were nothing less than amazing, describing the complete rehabilitation of those who had totally depended on them before.

~2~

The unmitigated commitment to the Infinite One, in the people of Orburn, focused them on the task that loomed on their world. Richard, Sylvie, and Jamie felt they had played out their part in its regeneration, and in the closing stages of their lives, relished watching the new civilisation begin the development of the Infinite One's

Universal Technology. Intuitively they knew they would never witness its physical reality, but after their part in helping to bring it about, they would remain aware of it from their spiritual incarnation forever.

As the waking periods passed, the excitement grew among them all, searching the thousands of stars for Orburn's sun that would lead them toward its solar system. Emerging from his thoughts, Jamie's eyes focused on one particular star growing in magnitude near the centre of the viewer; it, also raising a little excitement in several others close by. Among his group were Sylvie and Richard, chatting about the concerns for the future Jamie had queried with Tristram earlier.

Jamie shook his head slowly. "It's all been dealt with, Richard. It only falls to us to apply what already exists. The complexities in life that arose from multi-national civilisations, no longer exist. To make the most of this new opportunity, we need to think as one people. The fact that the spiritual dimension has become visible to us now, on the higher physical plane, enhances that opportunity."

From the teaching periods given by Tristram's people, Samuel Bernard was mapping out a plan, by applying the system that had stood the test of time. Many, who had come through the initial stage on Orburn, would soon make their transition back to the spiritual dimension. In their place, legions of proven souls were ready to incarnate onto Orburn's celestial plane to begin processing the resource that would allow future chosen souls to seed new worlds.

Sylvie was still awed by the sudden healing of her stricken ones, finding her expertise required to care for them redundant now. What was even more amazing; her spiritual knowledge had revealed many of them to be proven souls in their own right. Their assignment complete, on the lower material plane, the Infinite One had released them from their physical bondage. They were destined now to become some of the ones who would begin the celestial task on Orburn.

"The star is growing bigger," whispered Sylvie, suddenly gripping Richard's hand in frenzied excitement.

Silence descended over the gathering, like the stillness that follows snow-flakes falling on a landscape. Jamie and Richard gazed at the wonder spreading across her face; thrilled at watching the mothership fleet close in on the star. The viewers began to dim, as the glow from the star grew into a blinding sun. The countless scenes they had witnessed out in the universe had taken their breath away, but now, could not suppress the momentous feeling— they were coming home. As Orburn began to fill the viewer, what was striking about her appearance was the clarity of her atmosphere.

"Stunning!" whispered Richard, as their mothership manoeuvred into orbit. Watching the other motherships follow into their orbits revealed another unimaginable scene. The picture, confronting them, was still more evidence that supported the beliefs loyal ones had adopted on pre-cataclysmic Orburn; that a threat to a world came from its inhabitants, and not from other civilisations out in the cosmos.

As the keepers of a world, it confirmed how the inhabitants had to manage their planet's resources sensibly. The Infinite One's strategy for humanity was to take only what was needed, not to bleed a world dry or starve its creatures into extinction that helped to maintain its ecology. Instead, find a balance that merged in with the Infinite One's plan, helping to maintain a steady flow of new physical planes as teaching environments.

~3~
***

Jamie's guides, Sarah and John, had relaxed their vigilance, as Jamie approached the end of his incarnation. They were well pleased with his and Vicky's achievement, and anticipated Jamie making his transition back to them soon. The plan for their young souls' next incarnation was beginning to show on Vicky's and Jamie's celestial horizon. Sarah and John, had few concerns, in light of their unprecedented success, despite considering again, how the next physical plane remained a formidable challenge for them all.

Orburn's inhabitants had strayed close to the edge of the precipice, but souls who had followed the example of groups, like Samuel's and Jamie's, had pulled back. It was unlikely that the dark legions would sway Vicky and Jamie from their quest in future incarnations, but focus more on attitudes that challenged their faith. More sinister still, the minions would seek to remove them from the physical plane; it was then a world approached a notable dark age, only then would the Infinite One act by sending in His agents

Vicky and Jamie were two such proven souls, now, and neared the time they were to enter the snake-pit. Immersed in an environment, where allegiance to the Infinite One had steadily waned, they were to become His messengers. Like thousands of worlds before, the inhabitants on Vicky's and Jamie's next material plane had tested the Infinite One's patience. Sarah and John recognised how the threatening nature, engulfing this world, had descended to a sinister level. Their two young souls would be two, among many other chosen ones; the odds stacked heavily against them. However, in possession of the truth now, that knowledge invoked the protection of the Infinite One. On entering that menacing incarnation, they were destined to offer another chance to the inhabitants of that world in His name.

***

CHAPTER TWENTY EIGHT
JAMIE'S TRANSITION

~1~

ONCE IN ORBIT, TRISTRAM PAUSED them on their disembarkation, allowing them time to study their world. On closer examination, it was obvious that continental shifts had taken place. One particular area intrigued Jamie and Richard, it having been submerged under one of the polar ice sheets. Somewhere under that ancient, risen land, they intuitively felt that secrets from the past had lain hidden for thousands of years: a Universal Technology, left by the seeding civilisation of old.

Tristram sensed the theme of what was tracking through Jamie's mind, and briefly described to him what he, and his people, had discovered on their return to Earth. Jamie and Richard listened intently, as Tristram related how the Infinite One prepped each world with those tools, able to destroy a civilisation or lead it into the celestial realm. Like Tristram had been on Earth then, Samuel Bernard was Orburn's chosen one now.

Tristram gazed penetratingly at Jamie. "Your life-span on this world has placed you in the sights of the Infinite One. On each physical plane, you travel through now, you and Vicky will increase. Your achievement on this world has set a precedent in your progression, only you can destroy your continuing, future success now. Deep down in my spirit I sense the strength of your will, and feel the trust the Infinite One has in you both: I feel you will not fail us. Now,

Jamie, along with the others of your world, prepare your group for disembarkation."

Tristram faded from view; the words he had spoken, dominating Jamie's thoughts. As he and Vicky stood on the threshold of their future together, the ability to liaise with the spiritual dimension had added security to his and Vicky's plan. It was time for them to prepare their strategy, and apply their knowledge, ready to meet the next phase of their voyage to infinity. Vicky and Jamie were under no illusion, now, that their next world would be a different proposition. The dark legions were strong there, and would give no quarter in the eternal conflict. Jamie closed his eyes and opened his spirit to the Infinite One; instantly sensing His presence.

Jamie had no idea what awaited them, but he remained determined. Even though out-numbered in a world dominated by evil, he was beginning to feel invincible. What added to his confidence was one, irrefutable fact he had learnt from his experiences in life: there was nothing to be gained when bargaining for immoral, physical advantages to maintain life in a material existence dominated by evil. So long as the truth was adhered too, the power of the Infinite One would always be there to draw on— it was His will that decided life or death in those situations.

Vicky had sensed Jamie's thoughts, and was ready to offer her support, and meet whatever the future had in store for them. As Jamie stood on the threshold of his return to Orburn, his task there was complete; his transition, close to hand as he entered into his old age.

Vicky smiled at him. "Come, Dear One, it's time to go."

He gazed at the viewer, fleets of small crafts, streaming out along the tractor beams. With the sun-light reflecting off their glistening hulls, they descended, as if a cascading waterfall of light that was disappearing into Orburn's atmosphere. One breathtaking sight after another flashed across the viewer, and always in their minds, they pondered the poignant words, 'but if'; that small phrase, focusing them on how different things could have turned out.

The right choice had been made; they were free from the clutches of the evil legions. The pull on their benevolent natures now would be for other souls, gazing on as the eternal conflict took its toll on new worlds. In the service of the Infinite One, they had inherited the beauty and freedom of His universe. With such an adventure facing them, the future offered a picture of companionships that were no longer complicated by free-wills. Now existing in sight of the Infinite One, the term, 'Thy will be done' had a real meaning.

~2~

Soon Jamie, Sylvie, Richard, and their group, were underway. Their eager eyes, scanned the viewer as they descended through the upper reaches of Orburn's atmosphere. The further they penetrated, the sky above took on the familiar hue of deep blue, with sun-drenched pasturelands drifting past below them. Wispy clouds wandered lazily across the sky, complimenting a scene of complete tranquillity.

Richard Gazed at the scene, reminiscing over the turmoil they had left previously. "It's hard to imagine how all this was here before; can humanity really turn such beauty into ugliness, simply by manipulating a world's ecology?"

Jamie looked cock-eyed at him. "I'm surprised you can even ask that question, Richard, having experienced the reality first-hand."

Sylvie shook her head in frustration. "You two exasperate me. Forget the past and look to the future. Accept now we've all learned valuable lessons, and realised a prospect full of promise, and which now offers us the joy of sharing experiences with others."

Jamie and Richard smiled at her, like scorned children— enticing a grin from her.

Sweeping down over lush pastureland, revealed that the setting up of the first settlement areas was underway, as Tristram had described. The fleet of small crafts, making up their contingent, were descending toward a clearing a few kilometres ahead. Already, Tristram's forward groups had begun erecting temporary habitats to initialise their settlement.

The weeks quickly turned to months. It was obvious that Orburn would depend upon the ongoing support of the Earthenian people; that the new civilisation, initially, would remain part of Tristram's higher physical plane. As the new civilisation's infrastructure became established, and the Universal Technology's development got underway, the Earthenian people gradually withdrew. Contact, however, was maintained between all celestial planes, each one, able to liaise with others and the spiritual dimension. In this atmosphere of benevolence and companionship, the higher planes continued their work for the Infinite One.

Celestial Orburn had become a cherished planet; its new civilisation, taking only what they needed. With the technology available now, the new civilisation was learning how to extract resources from the remote worlds that made up their solar system. Under the guidance of the Earthenian people, the development of the Infinite One's Universal Technology began, and the prospect of a new celestial Orburn, established.

~3~

Jamie was now in old age; enjoying many intimate moments with Vicky, strolling through pastoral landscapes that were worlds away from those of the old world. It was on one beautiful morning they were walking; breaking out onto a favourite vantage point that overlooked a spectacular view. The warmth of the breeze caressed Jamie, as he gazed out over the mosaic patterns of pasturelands reaching away below.

He sensed a mood of euphoria emanating from Vicky he had not been aware of before. "You are particularly vibrant today, Vicky."

She smiled at him. "I'm always vibrant, aren't I?"

He grinned, gazing out over the view again. "It must be me, then; probably feeling my age, and can't match your spiritual energy."

She looked at him with a teasing expression. "Yes, My Heart! We both know that to be the reason, don't we?"

A sudden silence broke over them; Vicky, sensing the question in his mind. She waited, as he wrestled with it.

He gazed at her, knowing his curiosity of when he would join her was the one query in life, no one really knew the answer too.

"I sense you already have the answer to that question, Jamie. Such a solution can only come from the Infinite One, Dear One."

He nodded. "I'm not afraid, Vicky, but is it wrong to ask one close to me— one who has experienced that event?"

"My transition was an event I found exhilarating, Jamie; not simply because it released me from my suffering, but more for the successful completion of my life-plan. The sudden knowledge of the vastness of the spiritual world, and the potential it offered, was overpowering." She paused, as her expression softened with emotion. "The climax for me was the unmistakeable presence of the Infinite One— it was so moving: that He should have bothered to welcome me— just one, insignificant soul among the host of his universal subjects."

220

"You've said enough, Vicky." whispered Jamie. "Your answer reveals that a soul's transition, from the physical life, is not to be deemed as a sinister event."

She nodded.

"I'm so tired, Vicky. Even now in this beautiful world, the past has taken its toll."

In the sanctuary of his shelter, that night, Jamie contemplated the future for Orburn. As he sat there, the story of his life began to dominate; nostalgic pictures of events panning through his mind. It was as if he could reach out and touch the people in them as they approached. His mother and father smiled down at him, pointing to someone else. His emotion increased, as he focused on his grandmother. She was nodding and smiling, with the figure of a man standing next to her. It all felt strangely surreal, yet he knew it was happening. All those, who had touched his life, were present. There was something different about this reunion; he could sense a floating sensation.

Suddenly, they all paused and bowed their heads, as he felt a definitive presence descend upon him. It was unmistakeable; bringing to mind the brief description Vicky had offered to him earlier. Instantly he knew what was taking place; the Infinite One was calling him home. The Divine Presence sensed His satisfaction over Jamie's achievement; it was a sublime moment that would stay with Vicky and Jamie throughout their voyage to infinity.

On completion of his transition, Vicky embraced him, filling his spirit with her affection and pleasure at having him back with her— they would never be parted again. Inundated by a welcoming celebration of good wishes, he joined his guides Sarah and John, showering upon him their congratulations. There was no mention of Vicky's and Jamie's next incarnation. This was their moment; allowed to revel in the wake of their unprecedented success. Together, they all bowed their heads, and offered their thanks to the Infinite One, pledging their continued allegiance to him.

※※※

The Spiritual Inception

About the Author

***

Since writing the first of his books, the author's main objective continues to be his plan to try and help the creatures and people of our planet. Gazing over the world, the trend on Earth descends deeper into violent change, and insurgency, impacting most on the lives of stricken people who do not possess the resources to defend themselves. Catastrophic events, across the globe, not only destroy food harvests, but desecrate their crop areas. The theme of this sixth book; the first in the series 'A Voyage to Infinity', delves deeper into the theme offered by the Cyannian Trilogy. In the introductions of this series, the author seeks to suggest that we view life logically; imagine how the spirit might develop while travelling across several physical planes, similar to Earth. He persists in his belief;  the demise facing humanity can only be addressed by a united world. Remaining dedicated to our Maker's doctrines, the author continues to guide his life by Him.

***

Published Works by Chris J Berry
***

Cataclysm Earth - DJ - ISBN: 9781425946784
*

Cataclysm Earth - SC - ISBN: 9781425946791
***

Heritage from Cyan - DJ - ISBN: 9781434315076
*

Heritage from Cyan - SC - ISBN: 9781434315069
***

Avataria - DJ - ISBN: 9781434377494
*

Avataria - SC - ISBN: 9781434377487
***

Poems of Petals, Poodles and Prayers
by Ivy Berry
ISBN - 9781438938356
Compiled and Illustrated
by Chris J Berry
***

Sixty Psychic Years - DJ - ISBN: 9781452010397
*

Sixty Psychic Years - SC - ISBN: 9781452010380
***

All titles available in
ebook and Kindle formats
***

Chris J Berry
*

http://www.chrisjberry.co.uk
*